Baker's Dozen

A Novel

M. Will Smith

Published by Red Frog Publishing a division of Red Frog Media

Visit our website at www.redfrogpublishing.com

First published in 2013

ISBN 9781949877427

Printed in the United States of America

This is dedicated to my loving wife Carrie whose insistence that I publish the book was the inspiration for digging it out of deep storage where it had been hidden for a decade. It is also dedicated to my brilliant daughter Becca who did the hard work of getting it into a publishable form.

Chapter 1

"It's a very old affiliation," said Judd as he sipped his martini from deep within the brown leather over-stuffed chair. Outside through the tall multi-pane window that was guarded on either side by sheer curtains, large snowflakes fell in such numbers that they darkened the sky in the late afternoon. Judd stared up at the flakes as the gray gobs came down, a few wandering aimlessly out of the darkened background into the pale light from the lamp beside him.

"That's what I understand," said Rose, standing across from him near a wall of books that filled two walls of the darkly finished study.

"It's not a conspiracy as you suggest," Judd muttered calmly, not in a defensive tone, but one with the confidence and security of someone who is quite sure of himself.

"Not in the classic sense to be sure," said Rose, following Judd's gaze out the window to the quiet transformation of the landscape into a soft wonderland of white.

"Not in any sense," Judd nodded as he took another sip and glanced at her over his glasses.

"The results are the same," Rose smiled sarcastically, anger beginning to seethe to the surface.

"We only repeat our message of truth and patriotism," said Judd smiling back through the corner of his mouth as he continued to watch her over his glasses.

"But it's a network...a group of idealogues passing on your message in terms and methods that lead to action...... said to people who are prone to take action.... action that has been deadly...."

"What others do is not our concern," said Judd, breaking off his eye contact with her and resuming his peaceful monitoring of the snowflakes.

"Not your concern?" asked Rose, almost laughing, then shaking her head, her voice wavering somewhat now as she was no longer able to hide the anger inside.

"Any of those events could have happened without us saying anything," he said without looking at her but feeling her rising displeasure.

"A president. A candidate for president. A civil rights leader. A senator. Plus how many other liberal leaning people? And you admit to having championed their demise as the only solution...."

"It was.... it IS the only solution," Judd nodded curtly, almost sarcastically, suddenly having the urge to confront her challenge. "And besides, you weren't supposed to be snooping in my study!"

"I wasn't snooping....the emails were on your desk in plain sight. Your friends must be getting sloppy."

2

"Maybe they are, we're getting older....but sloppy or not you had no right to pry."

"You're my brother!"

"I have a private life."

"Some private life!"

"We have a right to our beliefs...."

"Beliefs, yes, but you and your little club carry it much farther. You know how to goad potentially unstable people into believing in your twisted ends and convincing them that they are doing something that must be done..... you're using half-insane dupes to achieve your ridiculous ideological ends."

"They're not ridiculous..... we're the true patriots not you liberal bleeding hearts.... and besides we paid them nothing. We provided them with nothing. We had no connection with them. We simply repeated our message. They did what they did on their own volition. We didn't hire them. They weren't our friends. They were alone. Ultimately they did what was right."

"The perfect alibi. Leaving you and your cronies not only blameless, but untraceable, unconnected and respectable members of the community to boot."

"We can't be responsible for the acts of crazy people," he laughed as he looked at her standing angrily against the bookcase, her face now flushed.

"But your plans were carried out," she said, now in a firm but clearly unnerved voice. "You deliberately set about to talk people into doing your dirty work for you without them really even realizing that they were merely pawns.... whipped into a frenzy by your encouragement...."

"Amazing, isn't it?" he laughed again, rolling his head back in the chair and shutting his eyes.

"For over fifty years," she said, her voice now becoming somewhat shrill as she began to lose her composure.

"Even before us," he corrected, his head still back in the chair.

"Before?.....Oh my gg....It has to stop!" she almost shouted, her hands stiff at her sides as she moved slowly toward him.

"It can't stop," he said in a lilting voice, sitting forward and meeting her gaze with one now suddenly firm. "It's too deep, too important."

"It must stop!" she now shouted as she continued toward him. "It's heinous!"

"Heinous? Can you even begin to imagine what this country would be like if that wild-eyed liberal Kennedy or his bleeding heart brother would have lived? That would have been heinous."

"And King?"

"That black letch had no right to live!"

"They were human beings," she said unbelievingly, stopping a few feet away, trembling in rage.

"They were the idealogues, not us," he shot back. "Dangerous idealogues."

"But why Hal Stohr? He's so harmless."

"He champions too many dangerous ideas," he countered.

"The environment is a dangerous idea?"

"It undermines the very lifeblood of our economy....one of those elitist liberal myths that are foisted onto the public."

"How could doing something to address global warming undermine the economy?"

"Oh paalleeeezz!" he shouted. "The answer to that is so obvious that I choose not to even begin to answer it..."

4

"You're delusional!" she screamed, waving her hands in front of him. "You people are all a bunch of pompous Nazi's!"

"Nazi's? Hah! Nazi's indeed...we're patriots! We are the ones who will save this country!" he said, now matching her shouting, and then standing up and taking a step toward her. "We're the true patriots! And you.....you're way out of line here!" he wagged his finger at her with a scowl.

"I'm your sister, and I'm a fool for not having found out about this years and years ago!" she screamed, taking the step that remained between them and smacking him across the face. He grimaced in pain, then quickly recovered to grasp her by the wrists as she attempted to hit him again. Judd in his eighties and Rose her seventies were clearly not as nimble as they were when they were younger and they stumbled into a lamp table and sprawled out onto the carpet, with the lamp, a blue decanter of gin and a glass crashing to the floor in a jumble of broken parts and liquid. They wrestled awkwardly on the floor. Rose used her superior quickness to smack him repeatedly on the head and face as they struggled. Judd finally got to his knees and crawled free, grabbing the arm of a chair to help him to his feet.

"You're mad!" he shouted as he staggered toward the door. Rose was upon him by now flogging him with an umbrella that she had retrieved from the canister next to his desk. Hands over his head to shield the blows, Judd swerved past the fireplace, catching his toe on the brick landing and tripping, falling headlong onto the fireplace tools with a terrible racket and an anguished cry of pain. Draped over the tools above the floor, he tried to move but could not. He was impaled on the sharp decorative spear on top of the tool holder. He feebly attempted

5

to move as he looked down at the black metal holder that was propping him up, a sickening moan emitting from his tortured lips as blood gushed to the floor. Rose stood over him, wide-eyed, in momentary disbelief.   Trembling in anger, her teeth still bared and the umbrella still gripped tightly in her hand, she held it out as if to continue to pummel him.   Now realizing that Judd was badly hurt with blood spewing from his chest onto the bricks and across the floor into the adjacent rug, she hesitated. But continued to stand motionless, the umbrella still poised to strike, as Judd let out a long muffled groan and slowly slumped onto his side in a heap, the fancy tool holder shedding its tools with a clatter. Her hand dropped as she released her grip on the umbrella and it flopped noiselessly onto the soft Persian rug. Judd lay still, his blood covering a four foot arc across the floor and onto the already reddish rug. From beneath his body, the red pool shown up at her from the wood floor that edged the rug in front of the fireplace. She just stood there resisting the impulse to kneel down to assist him or even to check to see if he was alive. She just turned and walked the few steps to a little sitting area with a small table that fronted the fireplace and sat down in one of the comfortable chairs. She stared at the flickering flames and could see the ghostly fluttering of the snowflakes in the window behind Judd's desk reflected in the glass doors of the fireplace. A tiny smile formed on the corner of her lips and she nodded slightly. A pang of guilt was quickly extinguished by the fury inside for what she had just found out about him.

I feel no remorse she thought as she sat there in the complete silence of the moment. The only justice that could have been wrought has been wrought she nodded. And the others. Her thoughts flashed on the smug faces of the dozen other 'members' of Judd's elite group. Twelve of them. Thirteen including Judd. Thirteen. A baker's dozen. Yes, Baker's Dozen she nodded. Judd Baker and his dozen murderous conspirators. Her fists tightened on the arm of the chair. Any guilt or sadness that she should feel with the death of her brother right in front of her was replaced by anger once again. Anger at what had gone on for so long. Anger that she was too naive to recognize the true nature of their political hatred. The whispers. The dark whispers. The snide comments that she simply dismissed as political prejudice and ignorance. Her mind wandered. These men would live out their comfortable lives in complete safety. Free of all blame or implication. Yet guilty. Yes, guilty. Horribly guilty.

It was two in the morning. Rose had been sitting in the study contemplating what she would do next for nearly four hours. The maid would be in at eight the next morning, she thought. Rose would have to call the police before then. Perhaps now, to get it over with. But what to tell them. They had a struggle over....over family issues....and he fell onto the fireplace tools. Actually, that was what happened. It was an accident. She went over to the desk and pushed the speaker button. She dialed 911, reported what had happened to the operator, then walked out into the vestibule and sat on the steps to the grand staircase to wait for the authorities to arrive. The others must also be brought to justice she thought as she waited. Even though they were her age or older, they must all be punished. Somehow.... and, yes, the ultimate punishment. And she would see to it... somehow... that they were punished.

7

Chapter 2

It had been her home for many years. The art studio on the top floor of the old Bigelow building, with its arching skylight, high ceiling, brick walls and beautifully finished hardwood floors. It was inspiring for her. She had a bunk on a loft at the far side of the massive room. As the turmoil surrounding Judd's death swirled around her, it was her sanctuary. Now, almost a week since that fateful evening the day after Thanksgiving she sat in the middle of the floor with a small green blackboard in front of her. Twelve names were scrawled on it in her almost undecipherable handwriting. After studying the list for a while, she put a one in front of a name and circled it. Then a two in front of another, until she had all twelve numbered and circled.

Brewster Dunfrey was first and the name with the largest circle. She shuffled through a stack of folders that she had compiled from Judd's file cabinet, pulled one out and opened it. Seattle. The Highlands. A gated community just north of the city. Eighty four years old. A wife who lives with him. One child who lives in Tacoma, the other in Vancouver, British Columbia. She sorted through some papers that were part of their correspondence. Studying a few pages, she then put them back into the file and turned to stare pensively at the blackboard, finally nodding as a plan came into her head. Brewster loved to sail. He had a nice sailboat moored on Lake Union in Seattle and he never missed being in the Christmas Boat Parade around the lake. That was sometime in early December she recalled. He would decorate his boat and invite friends along, then parade around for all to see. She would ask him to invite her along this year saying that with Judd's passing, she would be alone this Christmas. Rose's only daughter would be spending the holidays in Saint Louis. Rose had also been invited there, but now would make other plans. Plans that would put her near Brewster Dunfrey. He would be the next to pay the price.

She went back to the blackboard, going through each name and writing the city where they lived next to the name. One other name had Seattle beside it. A city across the lake from Seattle. Bellevue. Wes Freidhopf, also a boater she noted as she glanced through his file. She wondered if Wes ever went on the Christmas Boat Parade with Brewster. She nodded to herself. Perhaps this year he would. He was number six on the list. He would now be number two. Two for one she thought. It was now a matter of imagining how she might complete the execution of these two and make it look like an accident. Or at least not point a finger at her as the perpetrator since she would have others to take care of after them. She had sailed on boats. In fact, she had sailed boats herself and once made the passage across the Atlantic from the Azores to the Bahamas with some friends and stood watch and pulled her weight. So she knew her way around boats and was comfortable on them. Of course that was nearly thirty years ago. But she would still know her way around a boat. This should make it easier. It would be dark on the boat but with bright lights glaring all around. She just needed a plan and an invitation for both her and Wes Freidhopf. And then try to figure out how she would kill them. A gun of course. Something she loathed. She had been a staunch gun control advocate almost her entire life. But now it would be necessary. For them it would be: live by the sword, die by the sword. But she needed an invitation from the Dunfreys. That would be the first order of business.

The next day Rose drafted an e-mail to Brewster Dunfrey and his wife Estelle, asking if she could visit them and go on the Christmas Boat Parade with them. She then suggested that it might be nice to invite Wes Freidhopf and his wife since she hadn't seen them in years. It had been twelve years, in fact, at a political convention in Phoenix where Judd and his dreaded conservative cronies would lather each other up over the riff raff that was supposedly ruining the country. Why she had gone with him to that convention in the first place was beyond reason. But Judd had begged her to come. She despised Wes, but was always polite and kind to him. She did like Wes's wife, Judy. So the pleasantries would be a good cover.

In a drawer, she kept a large map of North America rolled up. She had circled the places where Judd's twelve disciples lived. They were as far north as the San Juan Islands in Washington State, as far south as Puerto Vallarta, Mexico and from Maine to Florida to California. The four corners, literally. From her home in Cleveland on the lakefront she would plot her route of retribution. Seattle first. Two down there. Number three was on Lopez Island in the San Juan islands north of Seattle. That visit would be arranged as part of the same trip to Seattle. Three on that trip and then back to Cleveland. Maine was number four. Number five was in Pittsburgh. Number six in New York. No, she would switch those to make it an easier sweep. Maine, New York, Pittsburgh. Then seven was in Los Angeles, eight in Altanta, nine in Denver. Ten in Orlando, eleven in Palm Springs and finally, twelve in Puerto Vallarta, Mexico. That sequence would not work. From Pittsburgh she would do Atlanta next. Then Orlando. After that the long haul across to Denver, Palm Springs and Los Angeles before traveling down to Puerto Vallarta. It had to be done in a relatively short period of time before they had time to begin putting it together. All within a week or two, or it wouldn't work. One big continuous sweep. No dawdling. Constantly on the move.

As she stared at the map she reflected on their ages. They must have been in their twenties when this all started. And there must have been others. Older men, now passed on. How far back it went, she could not guess. Apparently before them, according to Judd's confession that fateful night. But she recalled a funeral a dozen or so years earlier that was attended by almost everyone. A big event, someone important, and much older. And it seemed that after that Judd had apparently assumed more of a leadership role. Perhaps he had taken over the group at that point. She didn't know. What she did know is that this was likely the last of them. And she had to make sure that they paid for what they had done.

She had no idea how she would do it. But her frail, sophisticated elderly-lady appearance would certainly not attract suspicion from anyone looking for a killer. No, she was not a killer. She was an executioner. Someone doing a public service for crimes that could never be proven nor brought to justice. It would be a blow for fairness and right and against those who smugly pursued their deadly ideological ends under the cover of dignified, upstanding citizens. Perhaps, she would be caught along the way, but no one would suspect her motive. Only the dozen would even begin to suspect. And they would not dare reveal their true identities. Who else would know? By the time someone in authority began to put the pattern together, if at all, it would be too late.

She pondered her strategy that evening while staring out of the massive skylight at the stars. Ice crystals had formed on the edges and as the stars shown through they broke into a spectrum of rays, like a kaleidoscope. Of course it would have to be a gun, because the assassinations that they had facilitated were all done with guns. It would be a gun. Something small that she could hide easily in her handbag. And she didn't want to attract suspicion by shopping for guns. She would buy a magazine and read about them or go to the library. And then get one at a pawn shop where she would pretend to look at other things, then sneak a look at the guns. Maybe even ask to hold one. A pawn shop somewhere on Euclid where no one would recognize her or be able to check on her. But she had to register it if she bought one. That was the law. And that was a problem. Maybe Judd had a few hand guns around the house. He had guns at one time but wasn't sure if he still did. Yes, she would ask to go through his things more thoroughly. She hadn't done that yet even though his children and other relatives had already descended upon his home and were pawing over his possessions. Like vultures she thought. Perhaps the hoards hadn't rifled through everything yet and maybe there was a gun somewhere. But then again, an innocent old lady in a pawn shop on Euclid might get away with something that a young adult male wouldn't, and so what if she did have to get a background check. Nobody would suspect anything until it was too late. She'd give that a try first and then try Judd's house.

It was icy cold the next morning as she scraped frost from the window of her old Buick. It was just after rush hour…nine A.M. The drive to Euclid was over side streets packed with ice. She crept along slowly, delaying impatient motorists trying to go faster. Ahead, she could see the heavy traffic along the strip that was Euclid. She parked on a side street and then stood on the sidewalk not knowing which way to go. She should have driven along the route first to locate some of them she thought as she looked into the distance, first in one direction, then the other.

"Can I help you find somethin', mam?" came a deep voice from behind.

"Uh, well, maybe……," Rose hesitated as she turned to see a large black man in a black wool watch cap and a heavy brown coat that had lamb's wool around the collar. He wore sports pants and an oversized pair of brightly trimmed running shoes. She glanced down at the shoes for a moment, then into the clean shaven, smiling face.

"I'm looking for old things….," she said, trying to think of a good excuse for wanting to find a pawn shop without telling him she was looking for a gun.

"You mean like an antique shop or something like that?" the man nodded, still smiling and beginning to point down the street toward downtown.

"I thought maybe a pawn shop or whatever they call them these days," she quickly corrected.

"Oh, you want to buy a piece," the man nodded again, a broad toothy grin creeping over his face.

"A what? Oh no....." she began.

"I can get you a good rod.... no registration.... no numbers..... no nothin'," he laughed, opening his eyes wide in anticipation of her acceptance.

"Hmmmm," she mumbled, her brow furled for a moment as she searched the man's eyes.

"You go over to that little cafe right across the street over there," he pointed. "Get a table for two. I'll bring a couple of good ones for you to look over."

"Uhhhh," she hesitated. "Could I see something with a silencer?" she asked, surprised at her own question.

"A silencer," he said pulling his head back. Eyes looking up in thought. "I'll check around. Not sure..... wait...... give me about fifteen extra minutes and I'll come up with somethin'....."

"Do you know....well....how....." she sputtered.

"How much?" he completed. "Cheap," he laughed. "Real cheap."

"And exactly what is 'real cheap'?"

"Maybe five C notes," he said after scratching his chin and looking at her for a moment. "For you, four," he corrected.

14

"That would be four hundred?" she asked.

"That's less than what you'd pay in a pawn shop," he nodded, cocking his head sideways.

"No, I'm sure it is.....just clarifying in my own mind what a C note was."

"Go over to the café and have breakfast or lunch. I'll be there in less than half an hour with exactly what you're looking for," he said, again pointing to the cafe across the street.

"Will it have bullets and a holster or something to carry it in?" she asked.

He looked at her for a moment, the smile replaced with a more serious expression. He nodded slowly, seemingly in deep concentration.

"You're not a cop or something are you," she said finally as he continued to stare at her.

"A cop? Shoot lady you gotta be kiddin'..... you watch too many movies or somethin'...... I'm just wonderin' what a sweet little old lady like you would want with a gun with a silencer," he pondered, beginning to grin again.

"Protection, what else," she said, smiling at him for the first time.

He stared at her for another moment, then burst into laughter as he nodded vigorously, pointing at her. As he continued to laugh, he turned and ambled down the street. He looked back once with a cry of laughter, pointed his finger at her again, then finally disappeared around a corner a half-block away.

Rose had finishing her donut and coffee in the seedy little cafe when the rickety door opened and the man with the black watch cap entered. The waitress behind the counter pointed to

15

his hat. He took it off and came quickly to her table, taking off his huge coat and draping it over the chair before sitting down. Underneath, he wore a navy cable knit sweater that was stretched tightly over his rotund body.

"Did you bring it?" she asked, looking for a package or some bundle.

"Of course," he smiled, catching the eye of the waitress who grabbed the coffee pot and a cup and came over to the table. As she poured, he reached over and tugged gently on her apron.

"How you today, Clance?" she smiled, swatting his hand off.

"I'd be better if I could get suma dat," he giggled, starting to reach for her apron again.

"You must believe in miracles honey," she snuffed, again swatting his hand clear.

"Bring me one o dem," he said, pointing at the rotary tray full of donuts. "You know what kind I like," he smiled, rolling his head sideways at her. She shook her head and returned a moment later with a chocolate- covered donut with colorful sprinkles. "Mmmmm," he nodded with a smile. She again shook her head and left.

"Well?" Rose asked as he put half of the donut in his mouth, closed his eyes in ecstasy, then sat back in his chair, making it squeak and strain under his enormous weight.

"It's in my coat pocket," he said after a long moment of careful and sumptuous chewing.

"May I see it?" she asked impatiently.

"You wouldn't need help doing whatever it is you're going to do with this piece of firepower?" he asked after he chased the donut with a big swig of coffee.

"Help? No, of course not..... I told you, it's for protection...."

"Yeah, whatever," he said, fishing a cloth bag from his coat pocket and carefully laying it on the table beside her. "Don't be taking it out in here," he cautioned, leaning forward and speaking in a whisper. "Just lift the opening and look in. Feel it. There's maybe two dozen or so shells in there and the silencer screws on the barrel. It's a twenty-two caliber with an eight shot clip. You just slip the shells in the clip and slam it up into the handle. Small, but perfect for a lady like you. Very quiet even without the silencer. With it, it barely makes a sound. More like a hiccup. The ammo is real easy to get. Those are twenty two long rifles 'cause that's the size that fits in the clip. The ammo comes in three sizes. But you want long rifles. They have the biggest slug. It was a little harder to get it than I thought. So I'll have to have five for it in order to cover my expenses."

She nodded as she peeked in at the shiny gun. She put her hand inside the bag, feeling the gun and the loose shells, and what felt like a metal cylinder. Most likely the silencer. She took her hand out of the bag, pulled the strings to close the top, then reached to the floor for her purse and took out her wallet. After looking him in the eye for a moment she looked around to see if anyone was looking, then retrieved five one hundred dollar bills. She folded them in half placing them in a napkin and pushing it toward the center of the table.

"Nice touch," he said, jutting out his lower jaw. "But nobody in this dive really gives a rip what goes down in here. And lots of shh... stuff goes down here. If there were cops or stoolies, we'd have smelled 'em by now, but it never hurts to be extra cautious."

"This thing works, I assume," she said, nodding toward the

bag on the table. "You wouldn't try to cheat an old woman who just wants to protect herself, would you."

"I'm always fair and kind to the elderly, and especially to elderly women," he nodded in a serious tone. "This is a fine weapon. It'll do whatever you want it to do. And if there's anything I can do to help you out with your..... uh.... problem, well, just come by this neighborhood, usually mornings, and I'll be glad to hep. Just as for Clancy."

"Thank you... Clancy.... for the offer, but I think I can handle this on my own," she smiled. She took the cloth bag and stuffed it into the pocket of her overcoat. She then stood up, took her ticket and walked toward the cash register.

"He's OK, whatever it was you bought from him," said the waitress, taking her ticket and a ten dollar bill as she blew a wisp of hair from her mouth. Rose nodded at her and smiled, waving her hand to keep the change, and turned to leave.

"Thanks lady....why....thanks a lot," said the waitress as Rose walked out of the cafe and promptly jay walked across the busy arterial, getting a horn just as she reached the other curb. In her car, she pulled out the cloth bag and laid the pistol, the silencer, a clip and the pile of bullets on a wool blanket that she always kept in the front seat in the winter. She picked up the pistol and looked at it, finally managing to figure out how to put the bullets in the empty clip and how to fit the clip into the gun. Very small shells, she mused. Hope it's powerful enough. She held it in her hand, then reached down and screwed on the three inch long silencer. It was heavier with the silencer and she had to use both hands to steady it as she aimed at a mailbox on the nearby street. As she put the gun down on the blanket, she looked up to see two boys, maybe ten years old, standing on the sidewalk watching her. She quickly put the key in the ignition and pulled out of the space, looking into the rearview mirror as she drove away to see if the boys were still watching. They had gone back to what they were doing as if it were normal to see someone, especially an elderly lady, checking out a gun. Perhaps it is in today's world she mused.

She had a gun which was presumably untraceable and nobody she knew had seen her skulking around down on Euclid. So far so good. At least now she wouldn't have to rifle through Judd's things trying to find a gun and it probably would have been one without a silencer. The silencer would make a big difference and would make things a lot easier. She went back to the studio to lay out the sequence more carefully. There were many details she must anticipate ahead of time such as how she would travel and what routes to take. It was just two weeks to the Christmas boat parade in Seattle and just a little less than a week until she left. She had a great deal of planning to do in that short time… target practice with the gun for one thing. She had fired pistols with her father when she was in high school and had become a very good shot. But that was a long time ago and she would have to get used to it again. Her studio became a firing range with a stack of sandbags which she cleverly stole from a construction site nearby. She carried them home one by one in the fold-up shopping cart she used for groceries. The day before she left, Rose had fired off several boxes of shells which she bought at a local hardware store. There were fifty shells to a box. She was now comfortable shooting and was able to fill the bulls eye of the self-made targets she had drawn on typing paper. The gun was so quiet that she received not a single complaint from anyone in the building. Clancy was right. It was almost noiseless. Like a hiccup. Soon, she would have a chance to try it out on something other than sand bags.

Chapter 3

The next morning Rose would leave for Seattle. She would drive. It would be impossible to get a gun onto an airplane through security. Driving was really the only option and then possibly a private plane to Lopez Island after she took care of the two in Seattle. She had checked on that. Hopefully, there would be no in depth security checks on a private plane for a local flight. That plane would leave just two days after the parade, so she was going to have to act quickly during the parade, if possible. The visit with number three on Lopez Island would be unannounced. She would just show up and hope he was there. Based on the information she had collected on him from Judd's files, he was almost always there. As a backup plan, she would drive up there instead of fly after the first two hits, taking the ferry from Anacordes on the mainland. Besides, getting a rental car on Lopez had not been arranged since she had been unable to make contact with the only company that rented vehicles there. Opportunity was something she had to determine once there. Location was the big concern. Getting off the island immediately after the deed was done was the key issue. The only way on or off was by ferry or private plane. Plane schedules were irregular or nonexistent and driving presented the problem of sitting in a line of traffic waiting to get on a ferry. Plus she could be traced more easily if she left by airplane. Either way had high risks.

The entire string of twelve shootings would have to be done in less than a month if everything went exactly as planned. It would involve driving from one part of the continent to the other and never stopping except to sleep, eat and get gas. From the Northwest to the Northeast, then south to Atlanta and Florida, across to Denver and California and finally to Puerto Vallarta for the final assassination. When would the authorities begin to catch on and start looking for her? After Seattle? On the other hand, how likely was it that they would be able to make the connection with her at all. Twelve seemingly disconnected murders in totally different parts of the country. Why would they even suspect her in the first place? Or that the killings were connected. Who knew of Baker's Dozen's co-conspirators or what they had done over the years? They wouldn't tell anyone. Perhaps their wives, if in fact they really knew or if they did would share with anyone. It would be a string of murders… correction: executions…. that they may never even think to connect in any way and almost nothing to link her to them. She would say she's going on a month-long trip and just drive off. All cash, no credit cards. Seemed straightforward.

There would be three planned stops on the way to Seattle.

South Dakota, Montana and somewhere in Eastern Washington. Long, hard days of driving, but the old Buick was comfortable and well maintained. She would need a lot of cash. Everything in cash. She would take twenty five thousand in twenties, fifties and hundreds. That should be enough for just about any situation. She didn't want to use a cash machine or cash a check since it could lead to her whereabouts. She would take a selection of books-on-tape to keep her occupied on the long drive. She would stop at little motels and not at the big chains. The little fleabag places that she often found charming in their own way and usually clean and not as likely to have the 'no vacancy' sign out. Or be that fussy about identification. She would be less conspicuous.

Her friend Ester wanted to wish her farewell on her trip. She had mentioned it to her to lay out an alibi. She told her that this would be a pleasure trip to the South where it was warm just to get away for a while after her brother's untimely death. Rose had said she was tired, and rather than having Ester come over they met for coffee at a local Starbucks that afternoon. The trip was 'open' she told Ester. She wasn't really sure which places she would visit. She would just see the sights. Then probably be back in about a month or maybe a little longer. But Rose knew she may never come back. She wasn't really sure what she would do when it was over. Maybe come back to Cleveland for a while. Maybe not. It would depend upon whether anyone became suspicious of her as the assassin. Of course if she didn't come back, it may cast suspicion upon her if it wasn't already on her at that point. But then, if it was over, it really didn't matter. Even if she were caught in the end and in jail, it wouldn't matter.

But again, she tried to imagine how anyone could even begin to make the connection. The motive was invisible. And she was an entirely unlikely image of an assassin. So her focus now was getting herself invited to the Christmas boat parade. That would kick off the effort. Otherwise she would have to come up with another plan. All other 'visits' after Seattle were without invitation and unannounced. A possible flaw in the plan was that someone would know she was there. That might turn out to be a mistake. Maybe she should have just gone to Seattle and found them without them knowing what she was up to. But she had already done the invitation bit and would have to live with the consequences.

*****

Soap Lake was a sleepy little town in Eastern Washington at the edge of a lake so full of minerals that it foamed in the winter when the wind blew and the shoreline looked like soap suds. People came there believing in the therapeutic value of drinking the foul tasting water, smearing the black mud all over themselves and then lying in the intense semi-desert sun in the summer. The key was that they believed it was helping them to a cure from everything from arthritis to Parkinson's disease. Of course, there were plenty of testimonials that kept the true believers coming back even if it really was largely a placebo. Suds and Sun, Health and Fun was the motto on the sign.

Rose pulled into the dusty drive of the Suds and Fun Motel on the south shore adjacent to the main part of town. It was dusk, and as she got out of the car, a large locust with yellow wings flittered away into the dry bunch grass and sagebrush that skirted the drive. It seemed strange to see locust in December, but this had been a very mild winter in the West unlike the East where the snows had started in November. There were only two other cars at the semi-detached pale blue and green cabins that snuggled under a canopy of leafless elm trees. It was very quiet and unseasonably warm as she got out of the car and looked for the office sign. As she started for the buildings, a rotund man in his sixties with a ruddy complexion, and sporting a bright red sweater, waddled out of the door labeled 'manager' and started walking toward her.

"Need a room?" he wheezed as he lumbered toward her, his finger pointing to the row of cabins off to his left.

"Please," said Rose, nodding as he came to a halt in front of her.

"Great, number six is ready." He pointed to the cabin nearest his office. "Best cabin in the complex."

Complex, thought Rose, a smile forming on her lips. Collection of tired old structures that looked as if only that season's fresh coat of paint was holding them together. They did look tidy, she thought. Windows clean. Roofs appeared of recent vintage despite a bit of a sag to a few of their rooflines. The steps were slightly askew from settling but clean. Perfect.

"That would be fine," she nodded, pointing to the trunk of her car. The man quickly moved into position as she opened the trunk.

"Just this one suitcase?" he asked. She nodded.

"Two nights or just one?" he asked in anticipation.

"Just the one."

"Where you headed?" he asked as he wobbled along toward

the cabin.

"Everett, then Vancouver BC," she lied.

"Stevens Pass, then" he said.

"Right," she replied, knowing she would take Snoqualmie Pass since it was on the Interstate that led directly into Seattle.

"Not much snow this year so you won't need chains," He noted. She looked at him for a moment, then nodded.

Chains? A possibility she hadn't even thought about. That would have been a disaster. At least now she wouldn't have to worry about getting stuck in some little town trying to figure out how to put chains on her tires. Something she had never done before with all the salt they used on the roads in Cleveland to keep the snow and ice clear.

"Need to get something to eat?" he asked as he set her suitcase down and opened the door. Inside was a very clean, nicely decorated room with an open door into a bright and shiny bathroom. The room even smelled clean as she stepped inside. Not the musty odor she encountered at the motel in Missoula the night before.

"Is there a nice, inexpensive restaurant in town?" she asked.

"Several," he nodded. "I'd recommend the one on the other end of Main Street. Great prime rib and barbecued ribs to die for."

She smiled and nodded, reaching into her purse for a five dollar bill which she handed to him. He looked at it for a moment in surprise, then realized it was a tip and bowed.

"Thank you very much," he said, looking at the bill again before putting it in his pocket.

"What's the room?" she asked.

"You mean how much a night?" She nodded.

"Thirty-four plus tax." She pulled out two twenties and handed it to him.

"I'll bring you change and you'll need to register," he said, backing out of the door, scraping on both sides with his body and then finally turned sideways so he could fit through.

"Mary Worth, Cincinati, Ohio," she replied. "You register me and keep the change for your trouble."

"But I..... you should....." he began, then looked down at the two twenties, nodded, smiled and swung the door shut as he left.

A half hour later after a quick shower, Rose drove the short three blocks to Main Street. Red meat was not what she wanted to eat. At the end of the street she saw a neon sign with one letter blinking and pulled into the angled parking spot in front. Maybe they have something a little healthier than red meat she muttered as she wandered in the half open door and looked around. A few patrons looked her over carefully as she walked in, as if she were the new stranger in town.... which of course she was. In the corner was an empty table but she waited a minute to see if anyone would seat her.

"Go ahead, take whatever empty table there is honey," came the raspy voice of a woman with a dark complexion, coal black shoulder-length hair and a knubby, almost masculine face. Rose looked at her and nodded, then went to the corner table. As she sat down, she was a little startled to find the woman standing over her, not having heard nor seen her follow.

"Oh," said Rose, putting her hand over her mouth.

"Sorry, didn't mean to sneak up on ya," the lady apologized. "Got anything in particular in mind that you like?"

27

"Uh, well I was looking for something..... well, kind of...."

"Healthy?" asked the woman with a smile and a nod.

"Well, yes, actually."

"We're the first and only chance for a healthy meal in this town," said the lady.

"Do you have a menu?" asked Rose.

"Up here," she said, pointing to her head and tossing her black hair back with a broad smile that displayed a remarkable set of pearly white teeth. "Also on the blackboard." She pointed to a board near the entrance. "Or I can do just about anythin' you want if you jes ask."

"OK, first, do you have Bombay Sapphire straight up with a twist of lemon?"

"Like I say, jes about anythin'......but.....well, I got Beefeater....."

"Close enough," said Rose. "How about vegetable stir fry?"

"Oh sure, can do," said the lady. "You ain't from around here.... I'd say midwest somewhere.....Indiana?"

"Ohio."

"On your way to west of the mountains..... Seattle?"

"Everett."

"Long way to drive..... you don't like airplanes."

"Correct."

"By yourself?"

"I like traveling alone."

"I'll get started on your veggies. Dennis will bring you the gin. Welcome to Soap Lake, home of the miracle water." She turned and chuckled as she walked away.

"You a liberal?" asked a man at the next table who looked to

28

be over the century mark. His face was so thin that you could see his teeth through his cheeks. His eyes were sunken deeply into his head but a bright sparkle still resided in them. His hands shook as he tried to use his napkin and the lady next to him who appeared to be his daughter helped him wipe his mouth.

"Well...I....yes I am I suppose," said Rose, at first not sure whether to answer, but then deciding she would.

"See they popped another of 'em last month," he quipped.

"What do you mean?" she asked.

"Another bleeding heart liberal, spreading that liberal claptrap to every woman or sissy they can..... shot the son of a bitch," he rattled off quickly. His daughter looked at her in terror and tried to put her hand over his mouth which he fended off.

"It's all right," said Rose. "In the end, that kind of blind hatred will be corrected. In the final judgment."

"Final judgment my ass," said the old man.

"Would you like me to move him to another table?" the daughter asked with an apologetic look.

"How did he think I was a liberal?" she asked the daughter as if the old man could not speak for himself.

"Woman by herself, dressed like a faggot, ordered vegetables, no makeup..... easy to spot," said the old man.

"If you say another word, I'm taking you straight to the home," said the daughter. "I mean it!" she added firmly when he opened his mouth. Then he looked at her and thought better of saying any more, finally looking away. She looked back at Rose and shook her head in apology.

Rose smiled and nodded. How ironic to be on the mission she was on and stumble upon the very mindlessness that this whole thing was about.

Dennis, a young man who looked to be no more than sixteen, waited on her. He was thin, clean face, pointed features, and dark hair like the lady who had taken her order.

"Your mom?" Rose asked. He nodded.

A few minutes later, her dinner was brought to her. It was one of the best stir fries she ever had and she stayed and talked with the waitress after she had eaten. She offered to show her around town the next day but Rose told her that she was on a tight schedule and had to get to her destination on time.

At six the next morning, when it was still dark, Rose got up, showered and was on the road by six thirty. It was a six to seven hour drive to Seattle and she wanted to get there by early afternoon. She was to meet with the Dunfrey's for an early dinner that evening. Five o'clock at a restaurant on Lake Union called Dukes. They would have their boat at a nearby dock at the head of the lake. They would then go to the boat after dinner and begin the parade from there, forming up with other boats as they went around. She had suggested that Wes and his wife be invited too, but in the confirmation e-mail it wasn't clear that it would be certain. She hoped it would.

She arrived in Issaquah, just east of Seattle around noon. She had made good time going over the pass which was entirely clear of snow. She had decided early on that it was best to stay in a motel rather than with the Dunfreys. She spotted a little motel off the interstate which was very basic but modern. It was nothing like the cute little cabin in Soap Lake and it was well over fifty dollars with tax. It was definitely not worth it, but it was closer to the big city and on the Interstate and therefore able to command a higher rate. Again she used a false name and paid in cash.

After lunch at a local cafe, she went back to her room to prepare for that evening. She would wear a lined Gore-Tex jacket that she wore on winter hikes. It had several very large pockets. In one of them she would stash the pistol, loaded with the silencer on it and loose shells so she could reload the clip if necessary. Everything else would go into a small backpack she also used on hikes.

The Dunfreys had wanted her to come several days earlier and stay with them in their home to show her around Seattle. She had declined, saying that she would only be able to be in Seattle for the day and evening. She told them she had to catch a flight to Canada on important business the next day. She told them it was a business appointment she could not miss. They asked to pick her up at the airport when she arrived from Cleveland, but again she declined while leading them to believe that she indeed was flying and that a friend would pick her up from a late evening flight. She told them she would be staying with the friend and would meet them at the restaurant at five. Rose had carefully checked airline schedules to make sure that there was a late night flight carrying passengers from Cleveland just in case they checked.

What was missing from her plan was how and when she would carry out the executions. She knew it would be primarily a matter of opportunity. Several scenarios were possible and she went over them in her mind.   She knew she would just have to look for her chance preferably taking both of them out at the same time or, if necessary, one at a time. Something would present itself, she thought, sometime during the evening, either on the water or off. She would complete her mission one way or the other and would not fail..... of that she was sure. Just as importantly, she would have to get away because there would be ten more to go after these two.

Rose arrived early on Lake Union and saw the large restaurant sign. She drove past and parked three blocks away along the wide but lightly used arterial. She then crossed the street to the boardwalk and wandered through some of the shops to kill time until just before five. She then watched to make sure that no one was in front of the restaurant. She slowly made her way along the boardwalk under the cloak of some trees and stopped before she went into the bright lights of the entry drive of the restaurant where valets greeted incoming cars. She waited until several cars were backed up and then slipped down the walkway and into the lobby.

"I'm to meet the Dunfrey party," she announced to the hostess who greeted her.

"Yes, you must be Ms. Baker," said the hostess. Rose nodded and followed the young woman down past a large fish tank into the darkened interior, finally being led to a corner table overlooking the lighted marina. As they approached, a tall distinguished gentleman, with graying temples but a full head of short salt and pepper hair, rose and held out his hand, smiling broadly.

"Rose! good to see you again," he said politely.

"Hi Rose," said one of the women seated.

"Hi," Rose nodded as she shook Brewster's hand.

"Rose," said another gentleman at the end of the table.

"Wes, good to see you again," said Rose. "Judy," she nodded at the woman next to him. She smiled and nodded back.

The dinner was polite and enjoyable but lacked a real feeling of friendship. They had never been very close. Wes and Brewster, aside from their political affiliation and ideological zeal, were obviously not in frequent social contact with Judd or her. The whole thing seemed a bit strained but no matter, thought Rose, she had essentially staged it anyhow. It was not as if it were their idea.

After dinner, about six thirty, they walked along the boardwalk to the little complex of shops and restaurants that Rose had been past earlier. Along the way, boats were moored and people could be seen gathering around those that were clad in Christmas lights and decorations. Some had elaborate Snowmen, sleighs or other holiday symbols. Brewster's boat was moored in one of the prime locations, right in front of an elegant restaurant on the central pier. It was tastefully decorated with white lights and plastic head-high candy canes. The mast, boom and foresail formed a large Christmas tree with a bright star on top. It was quite impressive as was the perfectly maintained boat that had every piece of metal shined and a wax job on the hull that sparkled in the evening lights. Following the ooohs and ahhs, they settled in the main salon and Brewster and Wes went up to start the engine and cast off. At first Rose wanted to go up to help but realized that in this arrangement the women stayed below and the men did the sailing. This was an arrangement that Rose could never have lived with, but she politely went along with it and settled around the table with the two other women. Judy closed the hatch to the cockpit, shutting off the chat between the two men.

"So, you have a little business up in Canada tomorrow?" asked Judy as they could hear the engine start. Everyone got up and looked out the portholes for a moment as the boat began to move, the bright colorful lights gently drifting by. Momentarily they sat down again around the table.

"Yes, a business transaction that is still one of the loose ends following Judd's death," she nodded once they were settled again.

"May I ask what it is?" asked Judy.

"Real estate," said Rose, not having really thought through a detailed response to such a question and not wanting to elaborate. Judy nodded.

"Too bad you can't stay for a few days more," said Estelle, politely, but it was obvious that she really did not mean it.

"Yes," said Rose just as politely and just as insincere. "I like Seattle. It is a beautiful city, especially in the summer."

"You mean the month and a half of sunshine that we usually get but not always," quipped Judy sarcastically. They all laughed.

"At least it doesn't look like rain tonight," said Judy, knocking on the wood table.

"It's chilly, but it doesn't look like it will," Estelle agreed as they looked out the ports at the lights moving by.

"I prefer to sit inside pretty much the whole time," said Estelle, looking first at Judy, then at Rose.

"That's fine, so do I," said Judy. "We can drink. What do you have?"

"Just about anything," said Estelle.

"Vodka and tonic then," said Judy as Estelle got up and walked over to a specially designed bar and opened it up to reveal a wide selection of bottles.

34

"Rose?"

"Just a Coke or Pepsi if you have it," she replied, strongly resisting the urge for the blue bottle of Bombay Sapphire that was prominently displayed in the rack. She was even more tempted when Estelle poured herself a glass of it on the rocks and put a slice of lemon on the lip of the glass. But Rose knew she had to have a clear head all night. Coke had caffeine and so did Pepsi. That would be better than alcohol. Judy brought her a can of Coke with a glass of ice.

After hearing several long and boring stories from Estelle about their travels to India and Tibet, Rose stood up.

"Where is the bathroom?" she asked.

"You mean the 'head'," Estelle corrected, as if Rose did not know. "One up forward and one way in the back. You have to go through the master suite to get to the aft head if you want to use that one."

"I'll use the aft head," Rose nodded, starting down a short hall and through a door which she closed behind her. She found herself in a nicely appointed sleeping area with a queen sized bed in the center. As she moved past it, she noticed a skylight overhead that was open a crack toward the front of the boat. Rose sat up on the bed and peeked through the partially opened skylight. Through it she could see just the heads of Brewster and Wes. A cold chill ran down her spine. This was it, she thought. Before she could think about it further, she unsnapped the pocket to her jacket and pulled out the pistol, released the safety and steadied it by resting the silencer on the edge of the open skylight frame. She took aim at the base of Brewster's skull and pulled the trigger. She saw Wes turn his head toward him, his mouth agape and without thinking she aimed at the side of Wes's head just behind the ear and pulled the trigger again. Both heads were gone. She quickly put the pistol back in her pocket, slid off the bed, and started to open the door to the salon. She felt something under her foot and looked down. It was the two spent cartridges. She picked them up and put them in her pocket, then opened the door and walked calmly out into the salon.

"Did you hear something just now?" she asked as the two women looked up at her with puzzled looks on their faces.

"No, what did you hear?" asked Judy.

"Like two puff-like noises, then something sliding along the deck above the aft cabin, then a splash," she lied.

"Maybe one of the guys threw something overboard," said Estelle, with a little laugh. "Brewster!" she shouted. "Brewster!" she shouted louder a few seconds later when there was no answer. When no one answered the second time she got up and walked to the head of the gangway to the cockpit and opened the hatch door. "Brewster!" she shouted again with her hands on the ladder. When he still didn't answer she took a couple steps up the ladder so she could see the wheel. "Brewster!" she shouted once more, this time sounding a bit shrill. Now she went the final few steps up the ladder and let out a blood chilling scream that she continued until she was out of breath. She then started it over again as Judy sprang from her seat and scrambled up the steps beside her to try to see what was going on. Rose stood below as the two were jammed near the top of the gangway, both now screaming and clinging to one another.

"What's going on?" shouted Rose from below as the two continued to scream uncontrollably.

"What is it?" Rose repeated as Judy descended into the salon holding her hands over her ears and still screaming at the top of her lungs. Rose went up the stairs to find Estelle cradling Brewster's blood-spattered head in her lap. She began to moan his name as tears poured down her face taking mascara and eye liner with it.

Rose stepped past the bloody tangle in the cockpit and calmly took the wheel just as they were about to collide with another boat whose occupants were trying to see what the screaming was all about and at the same time avoid being hit. She backed the throttle and put the boat in neutral as the other boat did the same.

"Is everything all right?" a woman on the other boat shouted.

"No, something terrible has happened," shouted Rose. "Call the police and an ambulance immediately."

In ten minutes, sirens were blaring everywhere and two rubber dinghy's, one with 'harbor police' on its side and another with a 'vessel assist' were alongside. Soon the boat deck was filled with officers and medical personnel.

"Are you the one who heard the funny noises?" a patrol officer asked Rose after five minutes of attempting to talk with the other two women.

"I was in the aft head going to the bathroom and heard what I thought were two puff-like sounds, then what sounded like something sliding down the deck, and then a muffled splash as if someone or something had slid off the boat and into the water."

"Roger, get a patrol craft with lights and a helicopter and scan the lake for anyone out here in scuba or snorkeling gear," the man said after turning to one of his compatriots who was

standing in the rubber dinghy. "Fast, we don't have much time."
The man nodded and picked up the handset and began barking
instructions.

"Anything else?" the officer asked.

"No, I came out and told Estelle and Judy that I heard some
strange sounds and Estelle started calling for Brewster but he
didn't answer. Then she came up...... it was horrible." Rose was
able to garner real tears and began to shake, partially because
she was truly empathetic for Judy and partially because she was
getting cold in the chilly night air.

"I know, this must be traumatic for you," said the officer,
patting her on the shoulder. Too close to the big pocket with the
gun in it, thought Rose, as she hugged herself tightly pulling the
gun closely to her bosom.

It would be nearly three hours before Rose was finally able
to get away. She excused herself after giving statements to the
police and telling both Judy and Estelle that she would call them
in the morning to see if there was anything she could do for
them. They were so shaken and disconnected by the events that
they barely heard what she was saying and simply nodded and
said goodbye. Rose went with the police to their outpost in the
nearby Denny Regrade area. After giving them her statement
again, she took a cab back to her car, telling the officers that
she would be spending the night with some friends and that if
they needed to contact her they could reach her through Mrs.
Brewster. She would work out that excuse the next day from her
motel room in Issaquah. Maybe she would get a pay-as-you go
cell phone and give them that number so it wouldn't appear that
she was running away. She hadn't worked out that detail yet.

It was after midnight as she walked into the motel room and sat down on the bed. Two down, she thought coldly as she sat staring at the blank TV screen. And easy. Almost too easy. Especially the spent shells which she had never even thought about in advance. But she wasn't able to confront them beforehand as she had wanted to do so they would know why their time was up. For some reason that part bothered her. The shot to Wes's head was the same type of shot that took Bobby Kennedy's life. That much was retribution. But Wes never knew why. And they should have known why. From now on she must attempt to face them and tell them the reason they must die and that they didn't get away with it. They would now pay the price for their evil behind-the-scenes maneuvering, manipulating and orchestrating of ideological poison. And that they must know why before they died. Otherwise, it's just lights out and they'll never know. They have to know and they have to know why they're going to die for what they've done. They must even suffer some, if she could arrange that. But how? She didn't know but maybe she could figure out how to do that from now on. Another twist and essentially a modification to her plan. Confrontation, torture, then execution. She turned on the TV and tuned to an old black and white re-run sitcom and lay back on the bed with the sound turned up high enough to flood her senses with noise. She had never killed anyone before and it brought a kind of trauma unknown to her. She hadn't really thought about how she would feel afterward, seeing the faces of Judy and Estelle and understanding the gravity of extinguishing a human life. She knew her mission and knew she must steel her nerves and get used to what she had just done and was about to continue doing.

Just like on the farm when she was a child. Slaughter time. Chop off the chicken's head. Slam a butcher knife into a pig's throat even though it had been like a pet to her. A life snuffed out. After all, they were no more than animals for what they did. In fact, not innocent of wrongdoing as animals are before they are killed and eaten. Yes, they were worse than animals and there would be more to come. She fell asleep with Lucy's voice in the background talking to Ricky.

Chapter 4

It was six A.M. as Rose raced down the Interstate. She then went north on the bypass around Seattle toward the San Juan ferry at Anacortes, some eighty miles away. She didn't have a ferry schedule but would just show up and wait in line. She felt rested and fresh after a surprisingly sound sleep, having awakened only once to click off the TV at some unknown hour as the Beaver was trying to explain something to Wally. By eight, the Buick was sitting in a line for the San Juan Islands ferry. Change of plans. Or rather making plans up as she went. The airplane to Lopez was too complicated. She decided to just drive up and take care of this one, then return to Seattle so the police would not be suspicious. Then she could stick around for a few more days, answer any questions they might have, and then eventually beg off and leave. Maybe even attend the funerals to allay suspicion.

Since the ferries stopped at each of four islands, the cars had to be loaded in sequence so that the cars getting off at the first stop were in front. Lopez was the first stop, so Rose would load first. The scheduled departure at 8:45 was right on time. She got out of her car and went up into the main part of the ferry to find a buffet breakfast cafeteria and had pancakes, sausage and coffee. Not her usual breakfast, but somehow satisfying.

As she sat eating, Rose's mind was occupied with her next mission, Rex Beeler. He had an estate on the south end of the Island overlooking Alec Bay. The folder on Rex even had an aerial photo of the property showing its cliff side overlook of the bay and the Strait of Juan de Fuca. One of the letters described the road, the countryside, and gave driving directions for Judd, who once said he might travel out to visit him, although he never did. Rex had a wife, a housekeeper and gardener who came out twice a week on Wednesdays and Saturdays. It was Thursday and one reason Rose decided to change her plan. His wife would fly to Bellingham on Wednesday night and return on Friday. At least that was the routine she had mentioned in the last letter that was dated about six months earlier, so presumably she would not be at home. Rex would be alone. That would be very convenient. Now she wouldn't have to kill them both or a gardener or a housekeeper either. Minimize collateral damage as they called it in the military.

Lopez Island was lightly populated. There were small farms and only a few small settlements. There was no real town to speak of. There were apparently problems getting water, so permits to build were hard to get. And it was rather remote, even though not that far from the metropolitan Vancouver and Seattle areas. The central road went to the south part of the Island. Rose kept looking for the first turnoff. She then went down a hill and along an open beach area with a few houses inland. She took a left at the Bed and Breakfast onto a dirt road. Then about a half mile to a large wrought-iron gate on the right. Surprisingly, the gate was open. A potential complication she had not anticipated, but one that did not materialize. As she pulled in, a pickup truck was pulling out and she had to drive onto the grass on the one lane entry to miss it. The middle aged man behind the wheel waved and smiled as if he knew her. She waved back, looking carefully into his face, but did not recognize him. It wasn't Rex, she was sure of that. Rex could not be mistaken for anyone else. He was very distinctive looking and big. Six foot six and well over two hundred pounds. He had played football in college and was a lineman or a position that called for a very large person. She looked into her rearview mirror to see the pickup pull onto the road and disappear. Hopefully, that would not be a problem, she thought. People just appear at someone's house out in the country. They would just show up, but they can also be very observant of strangers. A potential issue.

The house was stunning. It was literally carved into the rock with the bay in the background. It was framed between two stands of Douglas fir and the house was standing alone. There were no other houses in sight in any direction. So, it was very private. The color of the house was gray stucco, matching the surrounding rock. It seemed to flow and blend in with the surrounding terrain. There was a black Mercedes convertible sitting in front of the three car garage. She pulled up under the grand entry port which was almost as large as that of a hotel. She had checked over her gun before she left the motel and had reloaded the two spent cartridges. She now unsnapped her

43

pocket and took out the gun, putting it into the unzipped front of her jacket. She then got out of the car, closed the door quietly and looked around. There was no one in sight. She walked slowly up to the door and hesitated for a moment, checking the layout and looking through the narrow window on the side of the large double door to see if she could see movement inside. Seeing nothing, she pushed the doorbell and waited. When no one answered she rang it again. There was still no answer. She reached for the knob and turned it. It opened. She swung the door open and looked inside. She could neither see nor hear anything. She very slowly and quietly stepped into a large vestibule with a very large skylight overhead. There were a number of carefully groomed plants around her and a fish pool with gold fish moving about just in front of her. Her eyes were on the archway ahead and to her right. A door was on her left which she assumed was a closet. Through the archway, she could see through the windows at a sweeping view of the Strait. She also saw the turquoise blue of a swimming pool in the foreground with the water moving. She thought he must be swimming. She stepped down the three steps into the living room area. Off to her left was a sliding glass door near a bar. As she moved forward, she could see movement at the end of the pool.

"Oh!" came a voice from across the living room. Rose spun around to see a middle aged woman in a bathrobe attempting to close it, her breasts flapping free momentarily. "Was that you at the door?"

"Yes, I apologize for just barging in like this....." she began.

"Uh....oh.... no problem, we on the Island do that all the time," she smiled as she approached.

"And you are?" the woman inquired.

"Rose. Rose Baker," she replied.

"Baker. Oh yes, Judd Baker's..... errr sister?"

"Yes," she nodded.

"Oh my, tragic, his death."

"Yes."

"I'll get Rex in here," she said, moving past Rose to the open sliding glass doors.

"Thank you," said Rose as she passed.

"Rex!" she shouted, repeating it as she slid the glass doors wider. "Rose Baker is here."

"Rose Baker?" she could hear his faint response. "Really.... OK...... let me get a robe....." He pulled his large frame out of the pool and disappeared into a small cabana. He then emerged a moment later with an oversized white robe with a red rose on the pocket. He half jogged the length of the pool and burst in through the glass doors.

"Rose, my God, how long has it been?" he asked, not sure whether to come forward to hug her or to extend his hand to shake hers.

"I'll get something decent on," said the woman, scurrying quickly back across the huge living area and disappearing into a doorway which she closed behind her. They both watched her until the door was shut then turned to each other. Rose thought about shaking his hand but the gun was in her right hand in her pocket. Perhaps now is the right time she thought, no reason to prolong this. With that she pulled out the gun and aimed it at his forehead. His eyes opened wide and his mouth fell open.

"Whaaaa..." he tried to say.

"The thirteen of you," said Rose. "Your clique of conservatives. Your secret dealings. Your orchestration of death. It will not go unpunished."

"Our group?" he said with a confused expression on his face. "You mean with Judd? Unpunished? We did nothing illegal."

"I know that, and that's why I have to exact justice because otherwise you will go free," she said, almost in a monotone.

"You can't be serious," he scoffed. A reaction that infuriated Rose who quickly pulled the trigger, hitting him squarely between the eyes. He lurched backward and sat down as if trying to right himself, then flopped over backward onto the floor. Rose turned and walked straight to the room that the woman had entered and waited. A moment later she saw the knob turn and the door opened. The woman didn't know what hit her. The bullet went into the same location as it had Rex and she quickly collapsed back into the room on her back. Rose turned, put the gun back in her pocket and went to the front door looking back momentarily to scan for the spent cartridges. She went back and picked them up and then headed back toward the front door. On the wall just inside the door was a panel which she opened. Inside was a row of keys and a little touch pad. She found the keys to the Mercedes and picked up the touchpad. She went outside, stood in front of the garage doors and pushed the pad. The door in front of the Mercedes opened as she got in the car and drove it into the garage. She wiped the steering wheel and door handle off with a tissue, then closed the garage door. After putting the touchpad back inside and wiping it clean, she locked the door, got into her car and sped down the drive. Back at the ferry terminal she parked her car in line and got out. Since she had picked up a schedule, she saw that a ferry would leave Lopez Island at 11:15. That was less than a half hour. Hopefully, no one would drop by Rex's place before then. If they did, it would take more time than that to figure out what had happened and then notify the police. At exactly 11:15 a ferry rounded the bend and pulled up to the dock. There were four cars ahead of her and by now five behind her. As the ferry pulled up, it looked as though it were full. The attendant came up the ramp and held up four fingers meaning four more cars. Rose knew she could not get out and protest since it would attract attention to herself. Ahead there was some kind of discussion. Her heart sank again with thoughts that they had found Rex and what she assumed was his wife. She hadn't even asked. Sweat began to form on her forehead now as the discussion ahead heated up. Then the second car in line backed up a little and pulled around the first car. The next car did the same as well as the third car. Rose just fell in behind the other three cars as they passed the first car with a very distraught woman inside madly cranking an engine that would not start. Rose breathed a sigh of relief as she slid into the very last space on the ferry. The chain went up and the ferry pulled away from the dock.

They could still stop traffic at the other end if they found Rex before the ferry docked in Anacortes, thought Rose. So she wasn't out of the woods yet. She forced herself to eat a very soggy tuna salad sandwich in the ferry cafeteria, washing it down with some very good Starbuck's coffee. She went down to her car early and just waited there. This time she was the very last one to exit the ferry. As they landed, she tried to look ahead to see if she could see any activity that was out of the ordinary. Anytime she saw someone come down the steps, she wondered if it were the police. Finally, she drove off the ferry as the very last car and into a string of traffic down the local road into Anacortes and eventually to the highway. She then drove back to Seattle.

Back in Seattle she called both Judy and Estelle to extend her condolences and asked when the funerals would be. Brewster would be cremated the next day and a funeral service was scheduled for the following week. Wes would be buried the next day. Rose decided to attend his funeral. She told Estelle that she could not stay for Brewster's funeral but would send flowers. Using cabs to conceal the fact that she had a car, she attended the funeral and afterward was asked to go to the police station to review with them her account of events. After only a half hour of questions, she told them she would be continuing her vacation along the coast but that they could get in touch with her via her Cleveland phone number and address. She then took a cab back to the motel and then headed north on the interstate, planning to cross the Cascade Mountains on Steven's Pass east of Everett.

It had snowed lightly on Stevens Pass and the going was slower than she expected. Fortunately, they were able to clear the road and chains or traction devices were not required. It was getting dark by the time she got over the pass. So, she decided to spend the night in Leavenworth, a little mountain town dressed up like an alpine village. As she stood waiting to be seated in one of the sparsely filled cafes not far from her motel, she noticed that the snow had not extended to the town and the conversations were about the lack of snow and consequently the lack of visitors since this was a ski destination in the Cascades.

"Where you headed?" asked the waiter as he seated her and

handed her a menu.

"Across the mountains," she lied.

"Seattle?"

"Yes," she lied again.

"Snow on the pass," he declared.

"Oh really?" she feigned surprise. "Hope they don't require chains."

"I think it's just a duster," he nodded. "There's nothing much at all this year, which is very unusual."

"Global warming."

"Yeah, could be right."

"It is right," she said definitively.

"You headed over for the big game maybe?" he said enthusiastically deciding to change the subject. She couldn't resist his exuberance and nodded.

"A Husky fan no doubt with a daughter or son at the U dub," he guessed.

"A cousin."

"You from Spokane then?" he asked.

"No, actually I'm from back east, just visiting my sister here east of the mountains."

"Oh," he answered, trying to piece things together.

"Where abouts?"

"Spokane," she nodded.

"Oh really, nice town."

"Yeah," she agreed with a smile.

"What would you like or would you like time to look over the menu?"

"Chef's salad," she replied, having scanned the menu while

they talked. "And do you serve drinks?"

"Beer and wine," he nodded.

"White wine.... just a house variety is fine."

"That's all we have really," he snickered. She nodded with a smile and handed him the menu.

Rose stared out the window. It was starting to snow in the falling darkness and the flakes could be seen in the street lights and in front of passing cars. Big flakes, coming down with increasing intensity as everyone sat transfixed. Even the waitresses and chef whose head was visible over the counter stared out the window. Big flakes, just like the night Judd died. Now, she was more than two thousand miles away from that scene. There were three down, four if you count Judd, and nine to go. Her mind flashed momentarily on the surprised look on Rex's face after she pulled the trigger. Utter disbelief. She wondered what he must have been thinking in that instant. He had started that arrogant, patronizing, belittling tone of voice that he and others of that group used when talking down to those who weren't of their enlightened view. She could never stand that tone. It infuriated her. It was an unforgivable tone. A laughing, taunting, ridiculing, sneering tone that sought to entirely destroy all opposing thought. A tone that made you feel unworthy of even being in the same room, the same house, the same town, the same planet as someone as superior and in touch with the truth as they. A tone he will never use on anyone else again. She flashed momentarily on the woman. Who was she? She seemed too young to be his wife. Yet, she had never met his wife and she was never mentioned by name in his correspondence to Judd, which in itself was strange. Perhaps this was his mistress since his wife was supposedly in Anacortes on Thursdays. It didn't matter. She was there. She was a witness. She was somehow affiliated with him. So, she had to die. Collateral damage. Rose never thought she would ever have cause to use the term for something she had done. It seemed right for now as well as appropriate and so unavoidable. Although, it was unfortunate that Rose had to experience it herself. That part was too bad. Hopefully, she won't have to involve others who may be innocent in the future. It's just the principals who will be taken out. There will be no more collateral damage she resolved, if it can in any way be avoided. Rose did not want to kill innocent people. The mission must stay on the group…the thirteen men. Baker's dozen.

Chapter 5

The snow was eight inches deep the next morning. A quick check of road conditions at the desk told her that she would have to wait for road crews to finish plowing the road between Leavenworth and Wenatchee before she could safely travel without chains or approved traction devices, whatever approved traction devices meant. It didn't matter what it meant, she had no such equipment on her car and decided to stay at least until noon.

She had wanted and needed to keep moving. The news report on TV that morning mentioned the murders on Lopez Island and that a man had seen a woman pass him coming out of the drive to the murdered couple's home. He said the car was dark blue and looked fairly new. He did not remember the type of car or what the woman looked like, except she looked middle-aged. Rose's car was ten years old and a medium green. So, the lead was not too damaging, but if they interviewed passengers on the ferry she was the only car there with just one woman inside. They might remember other details about her or her car, even a license number. It would be best if she got as far away as soon as possible.

By noon, the roads were clear and Rose was back on the highway, aiming for Spokane by that evening, choosing a route that avoided the interstate. By the time she had reached Wenatchee, the snow subsided to a light but continuous dusting. She managed the outskirts of Spokane as it turned dark and the light snow began to intensify. She had only stopped once, in Odessa, for a quick lunch at a Taco Bell which she saw from the highway as she sped along the open plain that was Eastern Washington.

The motel just outside of Spokane was another of the small, dull-looking, off-name varieties that was tucked in between the more glitzy chain motels that sported bright lights, manicured landscapes and fresh paint. The room was clean but previously used by smokers. This was something Rose disliked, but she had decided early on not to make waves. Again she signed in with yet another alias and paid in advance with cash. As she sat on the bed staring out the window at the gentle snowflakes beginning to pile up across the landscape, she decided that it might be wise to change cars at some point. It was possible that someone had made a connection. Upon further thought, she finally decided that buying another car right now involved a transaction that could be traced. Hopefully, tomorrow, she would be out of the state if the snow didn't slow her down or stop her. The storm that followed from Seattle was dumping snow all the way into Montana and beyond. Rose thought about the possibility of having to hole up somewhere until the roads were clear. She would just have to see what the weather was like in the morning and go from there. She had to try to keep moving, but at the same time not panic and make a mistake. So she needed rest and it was no time to be driving across country in a snowstorm in the dark.

The next morning Rose awakened at the first light of dawn and looked out the window into the motel parking lot. It was still snowing lightly and her car was covered with the white stuff. She did not know how much, but it looked to be at least six inches. She craned her head to see if she could see movement on the highway and had to wait a few minutes until a car finally drove by in a cloud of white dust. The snow was still clinging to its fenders and the top of the car. It was blowing off in whiffs as the car moved along. So, this was a big decision to either stay or go. She turned on the TV and changed channels until a local newscast came on. After watching the weather and discovering the bad news about the extent of the first snowstorm of the season, there was a short bit about the murders on Lopez Island. There were still no leads except for a middle-aged woman in a dark-blue car whom they were seeking to ask questions. "She may have seen something," the newscaster reported. Apparently, she was not even a real suspect. Nonetheless, it was time for Rose to get moving. Storm or no storm, she had to get back on the road. Besides, being from the Midwest, this type of snowfall was not that uncommon and driving on packed snow was almost second nature to her. So, after finding free donuts and coffee in the cozy little lobby, she borrowed the manager's broom and brushed the snow off her car. He was alarmed that she would even attempt to leave, but she assured him that she was experienced at driving in snow and ice.

There were surprisingly few vehicles on the road as she jumped onto the interstate and ghosted toward Idaho in the powdery snow along with a few odd truckers and other cars that braved the conditions. The road had been plowed and there was just packed snow to contend with. It was still snowing lightly, but visibility was impaired primarily by blowing snow kicked up by the few vehicles that were out on the road. Shortly after she entered Idaho, however, conditions began to deteriorate. The snow was now coming down harder and a strong north wind was blowing clouds of fine sand-like flakes across the roadway making visibility very poor. Rose began to think about staying someplace and sitting out the worst of the storm. She looked for road signs advertising lodging and, finally, as she reached Kellogg, Idaho, took an exit and found herself on a road so packed with snow that her car had to literally plow its way forward. She must keep the car moving forward and not stop, she thought. She knew the technique of driving with her foot lightly on the gas. Off to her right and up a slight incline was a fairly nice-looking motel and decided she must stop there. She kept her speed up as high as she could and just barged up the incline with enough momentum to keep the car going into the parking lot. She drove into an empty space between two mounds of snow that hid two other cars and barely had to put on the brakes in the foot-deep snow. When she tried to open the door, she had to grade snow with the bottom of the door to get it open. She retrieved her backpack from the back seat and removed her bag from the trunk. This was all the luggage she had with her. She waded almost knee deep in the white stuff toward the office as the snow suddenly began to come down so heavily that it filled her mouth and covered her eyelids. She stumbled into the warm office and dropped her bag on the floor. The elderly lady behind the counter was grinning ear to ear.

"Little bit of the white stuff," the lady drawled in what could have been what was left of a southern accent, undoubtedly diluted over many years of living in this part of the country.

"I'll have to stay here for a few days I'm afraid," Rose nodded. "I hope you have a room."

"Look for yourself," the lady gestured to a nearly empty parking lot. "I think most fokes stayed home. We got pleny o' rooms..... you can have yer pick o' the litter."

"What's the rate," asked Rose, expecting the worst.

"Usually forty plus tax, but since yer stranded, if you stay two nights, sixty..... thirty a night."

"That seems fair," said Rose, pulling out three twenties and a ten from her purse. "I'll just pay in advance."

"What's the monicker," asked the lady picking up the pen.

"Lane, Penny Lane," said Rose, having always wanted to use that name from the Beatles song.

"Oh, pretty name," said the lady, starting to write it in the register, but then remembered that the guest was supposed to sign. Rose quickly signed it using her left hand.

"It's number 124, three doors down," the lady pointed as she handed Rose the key. "Need any hep?"

"No, I'll be fine, thank you..... oh, is there a restaurant nearby?"

"Thru them trees there's a decent place, The Antler," she

56

gestured.

"Thanks," said Rose, opening the door and being hit immediately with a face full of flakes and again up to her knees in the snow. The room was cold inside and it was a half hour before the heater had warmed it up sufficiently for her to feel comfortable. She opened the curtains so she could see the snow falling and sat back in the large comfortable armchair that graced the oversized room. As she sat there, she noticed, to her great surprise, that the unit also had a fireplace with a stack of logs beside it. This was great for thirty dollars, she thought, shaking her head. It would have been two fifty in New York. However, this was off season and it was a snowstorm special. Even at twice the price it was a bargain. This was not bad if she had to be cooped up for a few days. Though it would affect her schedule. That was a concern.

After lighting the fire in the fireplace, Rose sat at the table and pulled out her day planner from the backpack. She went over the schedule. What if members of the group, after seeing three of their lot fall, decided to increase security around themselves. She took the laptop out of her bag, placed it on the table and then dialed the office from the phone next to it.

"Do you have internet?" asked Rose.

"There's high speed on the desk next to the phone."

"Oh, ok," she said, noticing the wire. "Thank you."

Rose set up the laptop and was soon on line. She typed in the common address of Judd's group, 'freedomrings', then the password, 'lazaruth'. The page came up and she scanned it for any new information about the killings. Seeing nothing about it, she signed off. They apparently hadn't received the news yet or hadn't chosen to spread it through the internet. Rose was hoping to be in Maine in five days. Too long, she thought. Driving cross country in a snowstorm was turning into a real problem. She picked up the phone book and scanned it. She dialed the number for Greyhound.

"Do you have service going east from Kellogg?" she asked.

"Yes mam," came the response.

"There's a snowstorm here right now in Kellogg, Idaho, is the bus through here still running?"

"We keep running as long as the roads are open...and so far the interstate is still open there as far as I know," was the reply.

"How long would it take to get to, let's say Cleveland from Kellogg if I caught a bus from here?"

"Just a minute mam," the young man said, coming back a few minutes later. "It could take about two days. If you caught the bus that comes through here tonight around eleven, you should get to Cleveland around noon on Thursday, with a transfer in Chicago."

"What is the charge?" she asked.

"Let's see.... it's $139.66..... and it leaves there around 11:10 this evening."

"And from Cleveland to let's say Maine....how long is that?"

"Another day," was the reply.

"Thank you," she said pawing through the phone book again and dialing a number for AAA Storage, the first ad in the car storage heading.

"Assume you store cars?" she asked of the man who answered.

"Store cars....uh yeah, we have a lot behind the storage units here," said the man.

"Do you tow?"

"Yeah, we do that too."

"Can I arrange to have a car towed there from the Lone Pine Inn if I pay you in advance for storage?" she asked.

"Sure, I guess," the man said tentatively. "When?"

"Tonight if possible," she replied.

"Yeah....uh, tonight? Uh...well I guess..... actually, I can see the motel sign from my office....well it's a little fuzzy now through the snow...."

"Good, I'll drop by in a little while and pay you for a month's storage".

"Uh, sure," he replied. "It's kind of piled up out there now...." He hesitated.

"But you can do it tonight?"

"Yeah, I guess....you can't wait until tomorrow?"

"Prefer tonight, I'm leaving on a bus tonight if the buses are still running."

"Oh, OK," he agreed with a pause. "But buses might not be running."

"I'm hoping."

"I'll do what I can....uh, what's the car?"

"A green Buick."

"OK, I can find that...don't think there are many at the motel."

"Thanks, now...what if I just leave the payment with the motel manager and save a trip over to your place in this weather?"

"Uh, sure, just leave the keys with the manager, Ethel, and I'll get that taken care of as soon as I can get over there. It's been a busy day with this white stuff. Oh, and the towing fee is twenty bucks... and storage is thirty five."

"Great, thanks," said Rose, hanging up the phone. She then picked it right back up and dialed the office.

"I'm going to take the bus home and have my car....." she began.

"I listened in honey," said Ethel.

"I'll be over there with the payment right away," said Rose. "How far is the Greyhound station from the motel?"

"Not that far, but Tex has a Jeep and can drop ya off with your stuff later."

"Tex? Uh...oh..... yes..... well, sure, that would be very nice," said Rose. "Thank you very much."

"No problem," said Ethel, hanging up.

Now I'll have to modify my plan thought Rose. Maine by approximately noon on Friday. So it would be Saturday instead of Monday to deal with the next one on the list. She pulled out the next file. Maxwell Snow. He was in failing health and was a widower who lived by himself in the country just outside of Portland, Maine. He had in-home care twice a week on Mondays and Thursdays. He visited the library on Tuesdays. That was in her previous plan. But Saturdays? Let's see, he watches college football with his son-in-law at home on Saturdays in the fall. Notre Dame was his team. That could be a challenge if the son-in-law is there. Is it still football season, she thought? Well into December. Maybe not, she wasn't sure. This was something she'd have to check into. She didn't want to inflict any more 'collateral' damage. That was never in the plan and was to be avoided now if at all possible, especially after Lopez Island. Maybe before the game. She could look up the times if games were still being played. And how would she get out there in the country to his place without a car? Couldn't take a cab. The cab driver would see her. Buy an old car? Perhaps. Yes, at an old used car lot. Or better, someone selling their own car. Whatever presented itself when she arrived. It would have to be a fast deal.

The other two marks on the Northeast swing were in New York and Pittsburgh, now also about two days early on the schedule. In one case it didn't matter. In the other, it could, and would have to be dealt with. The New York job should be a quick in-and-out takeout. She was familiar with the town, the man and his behavior pattern. Jeb Stewart was perhaps Judd's closest associate in the group and they had visited frequently. Jeb came to Judd's funeral and had consoled Rose afterward. Little did he know, she thought with a 'smirk, nor would he suspect anything.

Chapter 6

Rose sat on the long wooden bench in the Greyhound station. They were all so similar, she thought. Bus stations. Just a little ragged. They're not really dirty, but not really clean. People from all walks of life, especially those without the money to fly or drive themselves. Young people just starting out. College kids. Older people on small fixed incomes. Almost no yuppie types at all. None of the confident, casual individuals that flew and who always seemed to know exactly what was going on even if they didn't. These people were more subdued. Waiting. Afraid they would make a mistake. Bags were more tattered or were the new twenty dollar variety made in a Bangladesh sweat shop. They were black, or a dark color with lots of zippers and an unknown brand that was almost like a famous brand, but not quite. The talk was more homey, she thought, and was less sophisticated than in an airport or maybe she was stereotyping them based on her biases. She felt momentarily guilty for thinking those thoughts. Then, after looking around once again, she realized this was indeed a different culture than the one where she lived and felt comfortable in. She felt a little out of place. The woman next to her looked at her handbag, then her clothes.

"You ain't used to takin' the bus are you?" she said with a smile.

"No I'm not," Rose nodded, returning the smile. "I usually drive, but the storm kind of put a damper on my plans."

"You leavin' your car here in Kellogg?" she asked with raised eyebrow.

"I have to be someplace by this weekend and I'm not equipped to drive in this stuff."

"That's a bummer," said the woman.

"I know."

"Where do ya' hafta be?"

"Cleveland," she lied, not wanting to advertise where she was really destined for.

"Cleveland? Goodness me, how ya' gonna get back to rescue your car?"

"It's an old car. I may just sell it."

"Really? Ain't that somethin'? Just leave it behind..... man..... if I had a car, I'd never leave it no matter how old it was."

"I take it you don't have a car."

"Had one once but they made me take it off the road 'cause it smoked too much. Said I was polutin' the air. Shoot, it only smoked when I laid on the gas."

"Couldn't pass the emissions test?" asked Rose, not really caring what the answer was.

"There ain't no such tests out here. But they put up a stink

63

anyhow," she said, shaking her head and then looking blankly out the window at the snow in the glow of a streetlight that made the large flakes look like dark gobs of cotton.

"Did they say anything about whether the bus would leave on time?" asked Rose after looking out the window and realizing that the snow was beginning to pile up rather high.

"Reader board says 'on time', but until that sucker pulls in, I don't believe no reader board."

"This bus originated in Seattle?"

"That's what it sez in the schedule," the woman said waving a little folded up paper in her hand.

"What do you go by?" asked the woman.

"You mean my name?"

"Yeah."

"Gina," said Rose having thought about the next fake name she might use.

"Mine's Donna," said the woman reaching out her hand. "Nice to meet ya."

"Likewise," said Rose clasping it weakly with her fingers.

"I'm traveling to Chicago. Got famly there. Gonna spend the holidays with 'em. Don't particular like any of 'em, but it's better 'n spendin' it by myself here in this godforsaken hole."

"This seems like a nice little town."

"It's a fuckin' hole, scewz my French."

"Why do you live here then?"

"Lots of folk don't have no choice over where they live. They jes' live there cause that's where they are. Cain't afford to go nowheres else. Got nowheres else to go. So I jes' live here."

"Maybe someday you could move."

64

"My sister sent me these tickets, otherwise I couldn't afford ta go out to Chicago. I cain't really afford to do much of nothin', 'cept buy a few groceries and pay the rent on my trailer space. Too young for Medicaid. Don't have no health insurance nor nothin' like that. They take me as a house case or somethin' like that if I have a real emergency, otherwise they send me to Missoula General. Don't have no job. Too old and my knees don't work very well and I get dizzy spells. I got high blood pressure and diabetes so I need medicine. I get disability, but it's barely enough to pay bills. Jes' disappears. You?"

"Uh, oh.... me? Oh, I live by myself in a studio apartment," Rose replied, almost biting her tongue for having given out too much accurate information to a complete stranger.

"In Cleveland?"

"Yes, in Cleveland."

"You got a steady income of some kind? You look to be getting' soshal securty."

"I am, yes, and medicare and medicaid."

"Yeah, I got another four years. Another year til pension. Can't wait for thet. Thet'll be like a godsend but might lose my disability...don't know. I might even get a car with thet if I come out ahead. And a new big screen TV. Ya know, the kine thet fills a whole wall. Yeah...." The woman began staring out the window again.

"Is that the bus pulling off the highway?" asked Rose as she looked out the small side window to the highway.

"Only five minutes late," said Donna, getting up and limping over a few steps so she could see it pull up in front of the station. Rose picked up her handbag and walked with Donna over to the

65

line that was forming. Ten minutes later they were filing onto the bus, shaking off the snowflakes that had accumulated on their heads and shoulders. As they worked their way down the aisle, with those ahead taking empty seats, Rose wished desperately for a seat that was not next to Donna. As they approached the rear of the bus, only single aisle seats remained. She breathed a sigh of relief. Again, a slight pang of guilt swept over her for feeling that way, but this woman was from a different world than Rose's. Donna looked back at her and shrugged as she took a seat and Rose shrugged back. She then moved several seats past and sat down next to an attractive young man, probably a college student, she surmised.

"Hi," the young man nodded politely as she sat down.

"Hello," she acknowledged. He turned to stare out the window at the snow without introducing himself or saying anything more. Good, thought Rose, now she won't have to talk to anyone. She can read or sleep or watch something on the TV screens that lined the ceiling. This shouldn't be too bad at all. The engine on the bus roared and the bus pulled out onto the highway. It eventually re-entered the interstate that was surprisingly well graded considering the amount of snow that had fallen. She leaned back and closed her eyes.

"My name is Sean," said the young man just as she had settled into a deeply relaxed state. She opened her eyes and turned her head toward him.

"Gina," she replied with a smile.

"I joined the Army and I'm going to Billings to visit my brother before I go to boot camp," he offered.

"Will you spend the holidays with them?" she asked.

66

"No, just a few days."

"So, you'll spend Christmas in boot camp?" she asked.

"Well, yeah, it's no big deal really, just a holiday."

"I guess."

"Are you spending the holidays with your family?"

"Uh, yeah, I am," she replied, thinking about how she was really going to spend Christmas. Probably taking someone out with the gun she was carrying right now in the pocket of her jacket. Perhaps the Denver job looks like it could fall on or near Christmas.

"They take gays in the military if you don't tell them," Sean blurted out after looking out the window for a moment.

"They do?" asked Rose, guessing in her mind why he would bring up the subject.

"Yeah. Nobody needs to know."

"Are you gay?" she asked, suspecting by his comment that he was.

"Yeah," he said, still staring out the window.

"There's nothing ever to be ashamed of about that," she said.

"No, I know. You have children?"

"No, I don't," she replied, finding it hard to lie to him but doing it anyway.

"You were married though?"

"Yes, twice. Once when I was nineteen. That one lasted five years. Then right into another one that lasted twenty."

"Then nothing after that?"

"No. A few affairs. I've traveled. I enjoy the arts. I have my hobbies. I don't need to be married to be happy with my life."

"For a minute I thought you might be a lesbian when you

said you never had children."

"Some lesbians have children."

"I know, but you know what I mean."

"You were hoping for a kindred spirit."

"Yeah, I guess, something like that."

"No, I'm not a lesbian, although sometimes I get accused of being one."

"Because you don't wear makeup and wear stylish clothes and have short hair?"

"I don't know, is there a stereotype look for a lesbian?" she asked, feeling back at her bun and realizing she only appeared to have short hair.

"Well, I have short, neatly combed hair. I'm neatly shaven, very carefully and tastefully dressed. Some say gays do that."

"You don't have effeminate gestures."

"Many gay men don't have effeminate gestures."

"You're right, they don't. And all lesbians don't have short hair, designer clothes, and no makeup."

"Touche," he laughed, resuming his stare out the window at the dark mountains muted further in the gray-blue opaque of the falling snow.

"You can tell how hard it's snowing by looking at distant objects or hills," said Rose in an almost monotone.

"Must be really coming down because you can barely see the trees along the road."

"As long as we make it through these mountains before it piles up so high that we get snowbound."

"The snowplows keep the interstate open pretty well," said Sean.

"I hope so," she muttered worriedly.

"Anxious to get where you're going it sounds like."

"Anxious, yes," Rose nodded, thinking of the job she had to do when she got there and not at all what this young man must be thinking.

"I'm not in all that much of a hurry. When I get in it'll be hurry up and wait. That's what my dad used to say it was like in the Army."

"Your dad was in the Army? Was he in combat?"

"Vietnam."

"Did he talk about it a lot?"

"No, he never liked to talk about it very much. He said it was just something he did. Had he known what he was in for, he'd have never enlisted. He had volunteered for it, not drafted like so many who were there."

"I remember Vietnam," said Rose pensively, in an almost hollow voice.

"One of your husbands?"

"My brother."

"Was he killed?"

"No, he never even went in the service. He just railed on and on about how just it was and how communism had to be quashed."

"And you didn't agree with him?"

"I marched in the protest marches against our involvement there and distributed literature and even helped friends find ways to escape the draft."

"Wow, you were one of those."

"Yeah, one of 'those'," Rose smiled at him.

69

"So why didn't your brother go in if he felt so strongly about the war?"

"Like so many of the loud mouthed 'patriots', he was basically a coward. Some of the loud mouths claimed to have been in 'combat' only to find out later they really were stateside or in relatively safe places out of Harms Way. Out of the line of fire."

"All of what you call patriots aren't like that you know," said Sean.

"I know, but some are."

"And you don't think they have a right to express their opinion if they're not willing to put their lives on the line for their cause."

"If they're asking others -- young men like yourself, for example -- to pay the ultimate price, then I think they must be willing to do the same."

"They may have actually laid their life on the line in the past?"

"Perhaps....what do you think?"

"I guess you're right about some of them. My father laid his life on the line. It was not because he was carrying any great cause like your brother, but because he thought it was what he was supposed to do as a good American."

"He doesn't go around crowing about it now does he?"

"My father? No, just the opposite. He never talks about it or why he had to do it or whether it was a good or just cause. It was just something he did. He was not ashamed of it. In fact, he was proud of it. But it was obviously an experience he wouldn't want to have to repeat or see anyone else have to do."

"What did he tell you when you told him you were going into the Army?"

"He said he hoped like hell I'd never have to see combat."

"I think I'd like your father."

"Yeah, he's a great guy I suppose," said Sean quietly, leaning his head against the window as he stared out into the peaceful gray-white. A small cone of fog formed on the window below his nose.

Rose stared past him, her mind wandering to those days, more than thirty years ago, when she stood on that street in New York with a crowd of shouting, sign-toting protesters. She had looked up at the overpass and saw TV cameras and wondered if she would be on the evening news wondering whether her school administration would see her and put her tenure at the university in jeopardy. They had warned her about active participation and she received a formal warning after expressing her outspoken opinions in the classroom. She was told that she must cease the political speeches in her classical arts class. It wasn't the subject. Then her picture appeared so very prominently and clearly in the paper that evening. She had such an angry look on her face, her fist clenched and raised, and the sign directly behind her espousing her cause. After that it was a battle for her job. The inevitable confrontation with the Board. The arguments about free speech and anything done away from campus being on her time and not the university's. But an order was an order and she had broken it after being warned in writing not to. With her picture on the front page of a major newspaper, it left the Board with little recourse. An attorney friend of hers helped and she didn't lose her job, but she lost tenure and most of all 'face'. Yet she was a martyr to many. A kind of hero. But to others she was someone who was beaten down for her outspoken beliefs, including her glib brother who couldn't resist making phone calls to her to tell her how she had gotten exactly what she deserved. He told her that maybe now she would keep her big mouth shut and how unpatriotic she was. She was nothing more than a traitor and someone undermining the cause of worldwide democracy. Instead of standing by her as a brother should, regardless of her beliefs, he had treated her as he would any of those he reviled. Those who opposed the ultimate righteousness of his ideological cause. To him there was no friendly opposition. Just the enemy. The coldness of that moment left its indelible mark on her life. It sealed the shape of her relationship with her brother even though she had never dreamed that he could be involved with the group he was.

Montana was much bigger than Rose had imagined. It was seven hundred miles and over fifteen hours, including a dozen stops before they finally crossed into North Dakota. The snowstorm continued as they followed it eastward, but the huge amounts that fell before they were past Bozeman Pass were now much lighter even though the temperatures were lower and the wind was stronger. The bus pulled into Fargo at noon on Wednesday. It was about two hours behind schedule due to the weather and she was told that her connections in Chicago would have to be rescheduled. Already the new time schedule was sliding. Her Saturday morning 'date' at the country estate before the football game might still be viable she thought, but hope was fading.

After the stop in Minneapolis, Donna sat beside her for the trip to Chicago. Rose was half asleep after eating an unsatisfactory dinner with a tasteless wine and so she carelessly sat by a window instead of next to someone. Donna wasted no time and parked her rotund frame in the seat beside her, looking over with a big smile. Rose was crestfallen but tried not to show it in her returned smile.

"Finally get to sit together, Gina," she said, almost laughing.

"Yeah, it's been a long trip," Rose replied, almost having forgotten the name she was currently using and momentarily baffled by the name Gina.

"Seems odd leaving here at ten in the evenin', but that puts us in Chicago at seven in the mornin'. Only an hour behind I'm told. They really laid on it over that stretch from Fargo."

"Right," said Rose, not knowing what else to say and not wanting to say anything, but wanting to sleep.

"I'm wide-eyed now," said Donna. "Had two big mugs o' joe. Man, jes w'at I needed."

"That's good," said Rose. "I had a rather bland glass of what was shown on the menu as a Chardonay, but was most likely a very poor Zinfadel." Donna looked at her for a minute without speaking, seemingly trying to understand what she had said. There was a confused expression on her face.

"That so," she said finally and looked forward to a TV screen that was just rolling the titles of a movie. Rose closed her eyes and put her head back.

"Hot damn!" Donna said sharply enough to cut through Rose's nerves and make her jump. She glanced over at Donna who was looking at her with a wide grin on her face.

"Claude Van Damme!" she said enthusiastically, as if Rose knew who he was. Rose quietly shook her head and shrugged.

"Martial arts.... akshun.... this guy's amazin'..... I can't believe

I git ta watch it...."

"That's good," said Rose. "I'll just catch a little nap while you enjoy."

"Ya sure ya don't want to see this un? It's one of his best."

"I'm just too tired, I'm afraid I'll have to miss it."

"Too bad...." said Donna, as she turned again and focused intently on the opening scenes. She moved her body with the action on the screen and let out an occasional utterance from her mouth that sounded a little like a sick seagull. At first Rose opened one eye in annoyance, but then just tuned it out as part of the background hum of the bus as it rolled on toward Chicago.

The Chicago terminal was a zoo even at seven in the morning. People were wandering in every direction. Buses cancelled. Schedules changed. Her bus to Cleveland had been delayed due to mechanical problems. They were trying to get another bus to replace it, but with the pre Christmas rush and schedules full, it was taking more time than normal. As Rose sat calmly on the long bench in the terminal perusing the arrivals and departures board, she thought of an alternate plan. She would catch the bus to Columbus that was leaving in fifteen minutes, if it had room. Then catch another to Cleveland and buy a car. From Clancy, assuming she could find him again. She would go down to Euclid Ave like before and buy an untraceable used car from Clancy. For cash. Wouldn't tell anyone she was back. Then drive to Maine. It would be simpler and easier. She asked the lady next to her to watch her bags and went to a short line at the ticket window. They had only a few seats left and credited her with her existing ticket. Rose took the ticket, thanked the lady for watching her bag, and went to the line for the Columbus bus that was already beginning to load. Someone in the line told her that it was about six hours to Columbus. Good, she thought. That would put her there in the afternoon, before dark. The bus pulled out on time and, despite the snow that was still following her across the country, the roads were reasonably clear and she was off to Columbus.

Chapter 7

The bus was an hour behind schedule when it pulled into the terminal in Columbus. She went into the terminal and checked the schedule for Cleveland. An hour wait. Not so bad. A little over three hours later she was getting off the bus in Cleveland.

They retrieved her suitcase, sliding it onto the tarmac beside her. Until now, she had not really used the rollers on the bottom of it. They now came in handy as she wheeled it out onto the icy sidewalk and found herself again on Euclid Ave. How appropriate she thought. Apparently not far from where she wanted to be.... and unplanned. She hailed a cab and rode the mile or so to the little cafe where she had bought the gun from Clancy. She rolled the suitcase into the cafe with her backpack on her back. The lined jacket was not quite warm enough for the sub-freezing temperatures and she stood inside the door shivering.

"Well, well, well," came a familiar voice from the corner. She turned to see Clancy sitting at a table by himself with his hands folded across his chest. He motioned her to the empty chair and she came over, dragging her bag behind her.

"Just the man I want to see," she smiled. She was very glad to see him and amazed at how easily she made it from the bus station to the cafe, only to find him, in effect almost waiting for her.

"Tol' you if you need sumthin' els, to look me up," he nodded as he maneuvered the empty chair for her with one of his toes. She sat down.

"I need a car," she said.

"How much ya wanta spend?"

"I need something that will take me maybe five or six thousand miles and not break down."

"How much ya wanta spend?" he repeated.

"How much for a plain Ford or Chevy that is sound mechanically but not fancy and not new?"

"I dunno..... hmmm," he pondered, scratching his head and raising his eyebrows.

"Four grand?" she asked when he hesitated.

"Four grand? Hmmm. Maybe five. How soon do ya need it?"

"Right now."

"So you ain't interested in all those formalities with the title and licensing and all that paperwork stuff."

"No, none of that."

"What state would you like the plate to be from?"

"What state? Uh, I don't know. Could I get maybe two or three sets with different states?"

"Hmmmmm," he nodded. "For another grand, maybe."

"Maine, Pennsylvania, Florida," she said quickly.

"Maine? Shoot, that's not gonna be easy at all," he mumbled.

"OK, well anything in New England will do .... if you can't find Maine."

"I got maybe New Hampshire, I think."

"That'll do."

"How soon you say you need it?"

"Right now, if you can get it."

"Man, you always in a hurry, lady," he said shaking his head and grinning. "I could round it up in maybe two hours."

"Another five hundred if it's here in an hour."

"So that's five and a half large," he said with raised eyebrows.

"I think that's what it comes to.... but this car has to be dependable enough to get me to those states and then to the West coast."

"West coast? Hmmm. OK. And it'll be dependable all right. No problem. I'll get ya sumpin less than five years old."

"None of this can be traced?"

"No, not easily, but try not to get yosef stopped. If you do, the plates could trip you up. They're not stolen from other cars, but they never been registered with a car yet so the computers may trip you up if you're stopped."

"Where will you get....?.....oh never mind, I'll be careful...."

"Good, half now, half when I drive up in front with your new wheels." She unzipped a pocket on the backpack and peeled off twenty five one hundred dollar bills.

"Close enough.....I like doin' bisnis wif youuuu lady," he chuckled. She laughed as he folded the stack and put it in his pocket. He then struggled to his feet and lumbered out the door, waving to her as he left. Rose pulled her chair closer to the table and leaned back just as the waitress came up.

"Dinner?" said the blonde who was on duty the last time she was in. Rose nodded with a smile.

"Vegetarian?" she asked.

"Why yes," said Rose, holding her head back in surprise.

"And, let's see, a gin on the rocks," she nodded quite satisfied with remembering.

"Bombay Sapphire, if you have it," she smiled with a nod.

"Uhhh, yeah, Stoney next door has it, I think. I'll just duck over...."

"If it's no trouble," said Rose, somewhat apologetically.

"It's right next door, sweety," said the waitress.

"The Vegetarian Delight is actually good if you want to give it a go."

"That would be fine," said Rose, breathing a sigh of relief after eating at some of the places along the road from Kellogg. It was now Thursday evening, thought Rose. She had been on the road since Tuesday morning. If Clancy comes through, she could drive to Buffalo and stay overnight. She would get up early and make it to Portland by Friday evening, if all went well. She looked out the door at the lightly falling snow. It was only a few inches and the roads were fairly clear. She should make Buffalo by midnight, if Clancy got back when he said he would. She took her time with dinner and exactly one hour to the minute after he left, Clancy drove up in front of the cafe in a new small white sedan and got out. He wiped the hood with the sleeve of his coat with a dainty swipe, and sporting an ear to ear grin, lumbered in through the door. He stopped to catch Rose's eye as he pointed out the window and nodded. He then went over to her table.

"Four years old. About sixty five thousand miles. Just serviced. Has Maine plates now. Turns out I did have one. Pennsylvania and Florida under the mat in the rear. Pretty good deal huh?"

"What make is it?"

"Ford Focus. The basic car. Heat, air, am/fm, cruise, auto, air bags, etc."

"That IS a pretty good deal," she nodded.

"Real good. Ya gotta get it outa town right away, though."

"I will," she nodded. "I'm leaving now."

"I neva aks, but what's a nice lady like you doin wif a gun, and now a filed car?"

"Filed? Uh, never mind, I don't want to know.... I'm on vacation. I need the gun for protection and don't want my neighbors or friends to know where I'm at," she said, holding up her hands to indicate how obvious the answer was.

"Right," he nodded, looking at her with a serious nod, then bursting out into laughter and sliding the keys across the table. She slid the rest of the money across to him in a napkin and, without counting it, he folded it napkin and all and stuck it in his pocket, patting the pocket afterward. She got up, reached across the table and shook his hand. She then turned to leave dragging her suitcase behind. On her way out she handed the waitress two twenties. The waitress took one and tried to give it back, but Rose just smiled and held up her hand as she walked out.

She loaded her bag in the trunk and drove off. The soft, dry flakes of snow were flittering across the windshield, too cold to stick. Money, thought Rose as she drove eastward up Euclid toward the edge of town. She hadn't really thought about it when it was doled out in smaller amounts, but in big chunks like this, it made her consider her resources. Probably still had enough she thought. She had not worried about money before with well-to-do parents. She went to private schools and received a monthly stipend even when she was working. Then the inheritance changed her life when she was still in her forties. It was just after Nixon resigned. Her mother had preserved much of the estate left by her father ten years before. When she died, it all went to Judd and her. It was now much more than just a monthly stipend and it meant she would never have to work again. She had bought the building with the art studio upstairs, rented out the lower floors and had lived there for more than a quarter century. She had taught art at the community college for a few years after her mother's death. Then she traveled. That became her job. Her avocation. All over the states. All over the world. By car, by boat, by plane. No, she had never had to worry about money. Nor had Judd. And besides, he had been a successful real estate broker. He was very successful in his own right. His worth was close to a billion at one point. His kids will now inherit that. She was never in his will. Only his greedy, selfish kids. She had never liked them, nor they her. The son was just like his father, a staunch conservative and outspoken about it. The daughter was in and out of rehab for taking a wide variety of drugs. Sometimes, it took a while for them to even identify what she was on when she was admitted. Neither had married and so there were no nieces or nephews to worry about

81

liking or disliking. Although she suspected Judd Jr. of fathering several children and somehow escaping most of the financial responsibility. He kept true to his father's philosophy of looking out for himself first, last and always.

It was nearly midnight when she pulled into an unspectacular motel in Buffalo. The neon sign below the marquee was only partially lit, with just the 'vac' letters visible. She assumed there were vacancies, since only a few cars graced the snow-packed parking lot. There had been considerably more snow up here and it was increasing steadily as she had driven northeasterly on the interstate. As she pulled into a cleared spot on the lot, she realized the snow had been shoveled higher than her car. The door crunched into it as she opened it. Even though it was snowing only lightly now, it was extremely cold and Rose's medium weight jacket was just too light for the weather. She pulled the jacket in close to her body as she went to the darkened office and knocked on the glass. The door jiggled and she pushed it open and walked into the warm interior. Except for a night light on the side of the counter, it was totally dark. She walked slowly forward, spotting a bell near the night light. She pressed down hard. The bell rang out loudly and sharply, followed by a tremendous series of bangs and thuds. Then, there was a dull moan from somewhere behind the counter.

"Hello?" she said timidly, trying to lean forward enough to see over the counter, but her slight five foot three frame was too short.

"Oh myyy," came a weak male voice somewhere from the floor and out of sight.

"Are you all right?" she asked.

"Uhhh, yeah, just a minute. Have to get that chair fixed," came the mumble followed by a flurry of scuffing sounds and something falling on the floor with a tinkling sound. Momentarily, an overhead fluorescent light flickered, then came on with such intensity that Rose had to close her eyes until she could adjust to it. In front of her stood a tall blond man, probably in his early twenties, with a red plaid flannel shirt and blue jeans. He was lean, but was easily over two hundred pounds and, even under the flannel, she could see the muscles in his arms.

"I need a room for the night," said Rose, almost apologetically.

"Yes, mam," he nodded, reaching under the counter and pulling out a clipboard.

"King or queen?"

"Queen."

"Smoking or non."

"Non."

"Downstairs."

"Yes, please. How much?"

"Seventy."

"Which one?"

"135, just down at the end of this row," he pointed. "Right in front of.... I guess that must be your car."

"The white one, yes."

"Sign here." He slid the clipboard in front of her.

"Let's see....Cybil....here's the key, Cybil. I'm supposed to check ID but you look honest. Checkout is at noon. It's seventy eight with the tax. Will that be on a Visa?"

"No, cash," she said, producing four twenties. He dug under the counter for a change box and shuffled through it for a minute, producing two ones.

"That's close enough," said Rose, pushing the ones back into his hand.

"Oh, OK," he nodded.

"Are you a football player?" she asked, not able to resist the question.

"Yeah," he nodded with a little grin.

"What team?" she asked.

"Penn State," he said proudly.

"Really, don't you play Saturday?"

"No, we missed the bowls this year," he said shaking his head. "Had a tough year. Got probation."

"What ARE the big bowls this year anyhow," she asked. He excitedly ran down a list of the top bowl games, most of them on New Year's Day or the week after.

"Are there any big bowls on Saturday?"

"Nevada and Arizona," he answered quickly. "Tennessee and Michigan.....Po dunk bowls…"

"Po dunk?"

"Also ran bowls," he replied with snuff. "Didn't make the big times."

"When does the Arizona game begin?"

"Pregame in the afternoon I think since it's out west and kickoff maybe evening…. not sure."

Not Notre Dame but football. He liked football. And later in the day, not in the morning. The college season was over and they were playing bowl games. Fine. She'll get there early, just in case he invited his son-in-law over for the day.

"You a football fan?" he asked incredulously.

"I watch sometimes."

"Arizona fan?"

"I have a friend who's an alumni and he likes to watch them play."

"Oh, OK," he nodded.

"Well, I'll let you get back to..... I'll just go to my room now....." she said as she turned to leave. "I'll probably get out of here early if the roads are open."

"Where you headed?"

"New Hampshire," she lied.

"The Freeway is usually cleared and open," he said.

"Thanks," she said as she pushed open the glass door and left.

The next morning, her portable alarm was beeping and blinking. Rose sat up slowly. It had been a hectic week with spotty sleep and less than six hours last night. For the first time since she left for Seattle, she was feeling bone tired. The arthritis in her knees and ankles ached as she limped across the floor to the window and looked out. To her surprise, very little new snow had fallen. The forecast had been uncertain but held out the chance of clearing that day. She could see by the little crystals of ice on the corners of the window that it was bitter cold outside and she dug out an extra sweater to wear. After showering and eating the breakfast square that was left for her in the room, along with a cup of coffee from the little coffeemaker, she pulled on her jacket. She patted the pocket with the gun inside, and dragged the suitcase out the door and across the thin layer of fresh snow. It was so cold that it literally took her breath away. She got in and started the motor. Then, after trying the windshield wipers, dug the scraper out of the glove compartment and went out to clean the windshield. She got back into the car and put it in gear. It cracked and crunched as she backed up and started out of the lot. A large plume of steam came from the exhaust. It was a full ten minutes before the heater was able to warm the interior. She put the defroster on full force to keep the steam from forming and immediately freezing on the inside of the window. There were only a few cars on the road as she worked her way onto the interstate, traveling north for a short time before turning east. As she turned east, she saw a sign noting 475 miles to Boston. She would then have to travel another 100 miles from Boston to Portland, about twelve hours or more depending on how many stops she made. It would be another long day ahead.

Rose entered the Boston area at the peak of rush hour. It was after six before she finally noticed the first sign indicating how far it was to Portland. Ninety-seven miles. At least the snow had stopped and the temperatures had become a little milder. It was still below freezing, but not nearly as bitter as it had been in upstate New York. At exactly eight o'clock, she pulled into a motel on the outskirts of Portland. It was another semi-rundown motel of the type she had frequented so many times in the past week or so. This one had a New England motif which, probably at one point in its life, had been quite attractive. Now, the paint was weather worn and some of the features were broken, like the whale wind vane that hung uselessly at a precarious angle. The paint on the neon vacancy sign was showing white in places instead of what once was red. Half of a dozen cars were parked in the parking lot and a large yellow light shown down on the office sign that was not quite straight. She sat in the car a moment, the thought of getting a nicer motel crossing her mind as she looked at the frayed property. She finally got out and went inside, emerging a few minutes later with a key. Soon she was staring at the screen of the aging television set. She was still hungry, having stopped briefly only twice for food along the way. Her last stop was in Framingham just before she got to Route 95 near Boston.

The lady in the motel had said there was a Denny's less than a block away down the arterial and, after laying down for a few minutes to rest, she got up and trekked along the sidewalk to the cafe. This was not her usual choice, but it was close by and she was hungry.

"One for dinner?" asked the hostess as she walked in. Rose nodded and was seated in a small booth. It was warm in the cafe and she removed her jacket, feeling the weight of the gun as she laid it on the bench beside her.

"Cold," came the voice of a man sitting by himself in the booth across from her.

"Very," she turned to him and nodded with a polite smile, then looked away, not wanting to get into a conversation with anyone at the moment. He was perhaps sixty, she guessed.

"You traveling through?" he asked with a distinctive New England lilt to his words, lowering his head to try to get her to look toward him. She looked first through the corner of her eye, then turned slightly with a faint smile and nodded.

"I eat here pretty near every night and notice strangers," he continued. "Which way ya goin?"

"On up to Bangor," she lied, nodding. She then looked away trying to give him the hint again.

"Got kin up there myself," he pressed. Rose just raised her eyebrows to acknowledge the statement, but didn't answer.

"You?" he asked.

"Business," she replied.

"This near to the holidays and all," he commented.

"I'll be done by then."

"Right."

She didn't respond.

"Well, hope you enjoy your stay here," he nodded as he went back to his soup. She smiled and nodded as the waitress walked up with her pad.

"Don't bother 'bout him," she said under her breath. Rose smiled and shrugged.

"I heard that Darma," said the man.

"Don't bother the other customers, Ben," she said, shaking her pencil at him.

"I ain't botherin' people, I'm just bein' frenly," he whined.

"Let me do the being friendly part," the waitress said, turning back to Rose.

"Is this all mostly pre-prepared food," said Rose prying open the thick plastic menu with all of the food pictured at its greasy best.

"Well....not like airline food," she smiled.

"Let me try the vegetarian dish.... that one," Rose pointed. "And some kind of white wine."

"Wine's not that bad here," came Ben's voice from the other table. The waitress turned and looked at him ominously and he retreated back into his soup. Rose just smiled and shook her head, trying desperately not to look over at him. Most likely a man without close family or friends who is hungry for some kind of social contact, even if it means imposing his conversation on complete strangers. It wouldn't hurt to be friendly in return, yet it was virtually impossible for her to react that way, not knowing what kind of pest he may turn out to be. If it was just a casual conversation that didn't take up the whole evening, it might not be too bad. But he may turn out to be overly aggressive or impossible to get rid of once she extended a friendly hand. She decided to continue to ignore him. Too much about his behavior hinted at staying clear. She must not become too familiar with anyone on this trip. It would be risky. They might remember her if questioned. So, she finished her dinner in silence, without as much as a glance in his direction, and then waited until he had left before she asked for the check.

"Dangerous walking on these streets this time of night," came Ben's voice as Rose came out of the restaurant door.

"Look, if you want me to go back inside and call the police, I will," she replied, turning to face him.

"I was just...." he began.

"If you try to follow me or talk to me, I'm going to let out a scream that can be heard for six city blocks," she said in an ominous tone, folding her arms and putting her hand on the hard object in her jacket pocket. He stared at her in disappointment as the smile on his face faded. Then he nodded slightly and turned around and walked into the parking lot behind the restaurant. She then turned and walked briskly the half block back to the motel, looking back several times to make sure he wasn't following. Inside her room, she locked the door and put on the chain, then peeked out through the curtain toward the sidewalk. Traveling by herself for years had taught her to be very cautious about people who behaved like that, whether in the day or at night. She had had a harrowing experience in Atlanta twenty years before when she foolishly trusted the friendliness of a stranger, then had to run for her life when he trapped her in an alley. While she had no reason to suspect that Ben was dangerous, she knew that it wasn't possible to know what is going on in people's minds and what they're capable of doing, no matter how 'normal' they appear. She let out a little laugh. Take herself, for example. Tantamount to a serial killer....who appears to be a polite, well-educated, well-mannered elderly lady. Perhaps he was the one in danger she mumbled to herself as she clicked on the television with a wry grin, then sprawled out on the bed and almost immediately fell asleep.

Rose could hear the newsman announce the six o'clock morning news on the television. She had slept through without even waking up. Nearly eight hours. With her clothes on. She hadn't done that in so long that she couldn't remember the last time. Her normal pattern of sleeping was typically fitful and interrupted. Sometimes she would go for days without a restful sleep. She must have been very tired. It was Saturday morning. The map of the area was laid out on the table from when she had gone over it after she first arrived. She sat down at the table, still not fully awake, and groped for her reading glasses which she always seemed to misplace or forget where they were. Finally, she dug a folding backup pair out of one of her jacket pockets, unraveled them and put them on. It was about ten miles from the motel to the country home of her next target, Maxwell Snow. She would want to get there early. She remembered from the dossier that he arose very early each morning. How early is early, she thought. It would be probably a fifteen to twenty minute

90

drive out to his place. She thought for a moment, then decided to drive out there and see if a light was on and go from there. She quickly packed her things, toted her suitcase and backpack to the trunk of the car, scraped off the windshield, and then headed out onto the highway.

It took nearly a half hour to find the house. She missed two turns that weren't properly mapped and drove past it thinking it was too massive to be occupied by just one person. But a return past the house confirmed the address and also the fact that there was a light on in the wing leading to the gigantic garage that had doors for five cars and a tall one for, perhaps, a camper. The mansion was large. It was compacted into three stories with steeple topped spires on the pointy roofs of the main house and the garage which appeared to have rooms above. She quietly parked the car just off the road in an area cleared of snow in a grove of trees that had lost their leaves. It was light enough out by now, especially with the snow on the ground so she was able to leave the lights off on the approach to the house. The road looked to be very lightly used with only two sets of icy ruts in the snow. There was a small pile of snow along the edge to indicate that it had been plowed after the last snowfall. She sat in the car a moment to think through her next move.

Rose had put her warm sweater on under her jacket and now dug out the mittens that she had packed before leaving, never thinking that she might actually have to use them. They now came in handy in the subfreezing morning air as she quietly got out and closed the car door without slamming it, then moved behind a berm that ran across the field in front of the mansion. She saw a shed behind the house and decided to walk in the obscurity of the berm until she got to the shed. She then used the shed as a shield to the outer wall of the garage. Then along the back of the house until she could attempt to see where Max might be. Her assumption was that the backyard had private views of gardens or landscaping or something pleasant and that the windows would be without curtains.

Her feet were getting cold and even her hands inside the mittens were starting to stiffen up as she peeked around the garage into the backyard. The light from a window cast a plane of brightness across the snowy patio area with its fish pond, statues and evergreens. Little rivulets of steam rose from the water in the pond. It must be heated she thought, or it would be frozen over. She could not see into the window and so moved slowly and cautiously along the edge of the house. She looked back toward the garage when she saw movement. A dog door on one wall of the garage had swung slowly open and she could see the ears and eyes of a big dog. It was a very large brown short haired dog with a black nose, eyes and sharp tips on his ears. Perhaps a Doberman. She didn't know. The dog was studying her very carefully, steam emitting from his breathing into the cold morning air. She stood perfectly still and watched him. He did not come out, but was motionless in the partly open flap, eyes intently riveted on her. After what seemed a very long time the dog backed in and the flap came shut. She let out a little sigh but knew she would have to keep an eye on that door. She focused on the window again and crept closer, moving between the evergreen shrubs that framed the backyard and the house. As she reached the last stand of shrubs, she felt a presence behind her and turned her head slightly. Through the corner of her eye she could see the dog.

It seemed bigger than she was, and it's head was over three feet above the ground, with coal black eyes riveted on her. She had taken her hand out of her mitten and put it in the pocket around the gun earlier. So now she very slowly and with a minimum of movement took out the gun and held it in a ready position. One bare hand on the trigger, one mittened hand to steady she slowly turned around. At first the dog apparently didn't notice the gun. When it did, it began to move quickly toward her. She lowered the barrel and as the dog was only a matter of feet from her she calmly fired twice into its open mouth. The dog made a slight yelp and thudded to a heap on her toes. The weight of its huge body hitting the ground made more noise than either of the two shots or the tiny yelp. She then backed her toes out from under the quivering torso and turned around when she heard a sliding glass door open.

"Toby?" came a voice. "Toby?" it repeated. "Is that you, boy?" She stood perfectly still as she heard the shuffling and rattling of someone using a walker moving across the patio bricks. Through the foliage, she could see the light colored robe and barely make out the hunched-over figure of a man. She stepped out from behind the bush, looked past him into the house to make sure that nobody else was there, and seeing no one, looked around the patio area. Again, there was no one, and she finally focused on the old man.

"What the.....?" he sputtered, squinting at her as he tried to recognize her.

"Maxwell Snow," she said, recognizing his distinctive nose and ears even though she had not seen him in a number of years.

"Rose?" he managed. "Rose Baker? What....?"

"You're a member of the group," she said as she raised the gun.

"What are you doing...." he began, totally dumbfounded at her actions. It appeared as though he were about to welcome her with a warm greeting, but the smile froze into shock on his face.

"Your group of conspirators cannot get away with what you've done," she announced.

"I'm an old, dying man," he said, squinting his eyes in confusion.

"I know," she nodded. "But you cannot go to your grave peacefully. You must be aware that you have been caught and are now being punished for your part in the grand conspiracy of your group."

"But we never did anything illegal...."

"I know," she interrupted. "And that's why I must carry out the sentence, which is death by the same means your victims died."

"You can't....." he began as the shot struck him between the eyes, making them open wide in shock before he slumped onto his walker and fell forward. The walker flew out ahead of him and stopped against Rose's knees. She flipped it aside, turned quickly, and walked past the dog's carcass which she looked at to make sure it was dead. She then retraced her footsteps back to the car and drove away. During the entire trip out on the road, she had not seen a single car and did not see a car until she entered the highway to the interstate. Soon she was on the I-95 southbound. The sign showed 102 miles to Boston. It was seven fifteen. She would stop outside Boston for breakfast.

Chapter 8

It was eight o'clock when Rose pulled into a filling station in the Bronx.   She tried to remember what it had been like nearly fifty years earlier when she lived there for a short time before attending graduate school in Connecticut.   It was a bit like Euclid Avenue in Cleveland, only taller buildings and more people, she thought. She got out and went inside to pay before pumping the gas and then stood in line at the counter.

"You run outa gas o' sumpin' old lady," a thin black man with a goatee said, apparently addressing her even though his eyes were looking elsewhere.

"I lived in this neighborhood almost fifty years ago," she said, trying to make eye contact with the man.

"Tha' so," he nodded, finally looking at her, then quickly away.

"You know where the subway entrance is?" she asked.

"Two blocks that way," he pointed. "See the arch jes' pass the fruit stan'."

"Thanks.... you know of any hotels nearby that are fairly clean."

"Shhuuuuu...... hotelll....lady you gotta be kiddin'," he snickered.

"No, I'm entirely serious," she continued.

"There's a Days Inn back near the interstate," said a black woman in front of her in line.

"Off the 95?" she asked.

"Yeah, right near the Deegan Expressway exit," she replied.

"I must have missed it... that's where I got off."

"You from around here?" asked the woman.

"New Hampshire."

"Shuuuuu....." scoffed the black man behind her.

"You visiting?" the woman asked, giving the man a look that would wilt a steel wall.

"Yeah, I'm going to ride in on the subway down into Manhattan tomorrow morning to visit a friend. Then, I'll leave tomorrow night."

"You can drive down into Manhattan. It's not all that bad you know," said the woman.

"I prefer the subway," said Rose, thinking of her escape plan that would have her disappear into the crowd of the subway after the hit. She would then make her exit from New York City via I-95 here in the Bronx.

"Driving might actually be safer than the subway," she laughed.

"It's been a long time since I've ridden the subway," said Rose. "I guess I don't know what it's like now compared to when I rode it fifty years ago."

"Not the same….but that was likely back when my mama was a child so I sure wouldn't know myself," the lady laughed. The laugh was infectious and Rose laughed a little with her as the lady paid her gas, waved, then left.

"I'd drive, too," said the man behind her as she paid and turned to leave. She smiled at him as she walked out the door.

The din of street life made her feel somewhat safe as she made her way back toward the freeway exit looking for the Days Inn sign. Best to stick with a chain here, she thought. The possibility of a little mom and pop hotel that was clean and safe in this neighborhood seemed unlikely. She spotted the hotel sign a half block off the freeway, made the turn on the arterial and pulled into the drive. Free parking, cable TV, weekend special rates it said on the reader board. Inside the lobby it was very clean and quiet.

I'd like a room not facing the freeway," she said to the tall blonde woman behind the counter.

"All I have is a deluxe suite on the courtyard," she replied, still scanning the computer screen in front of her.

"That'll be fine. How much?" asked Rose.

"Two twenty five," the woman replied, looking at Rose in anticipation of her saying no. Instead Rose began peeling twenties. She handed her twelve bills. The lady counted them, handed rose a few ones in change and pushed the registration form in front of her. She signed it Hilary Bush, took the key, followed the directions for parking in the garage, and then went up to her room. It was a very large and well-appointed room with a lounge area, a bar, a living area and a separate bedroom.

The furnishings were not the usual chain hotel variety. This was the VIP suite. She smiled. Why not, she thought and maybe room service for dinner. She picked up the phone.

"Your gourmet vegetarian dinner and a Bombay Sapphire straight up with a twist of lemon," she ordered when she was finally connected to room service. A half hour later, as she sat in the overstuffed chair watching a Discovery Channel special, her meal and drink in front of her on the oak table. By ten o'clock she had fallen asleep in the chair. This was something she never did. But then this was not a usual routine for her.

It was a simple plan. She knew Jeb Stewart's routine. At noon, he would retire to his private salon for a light workout and a sauna before returning to his office for the afternoon. She would wait in the outer waiting room unannounced as some of Jeb's clients were known to do and then duck in the back entrance to his salon that only Jeb and a few close friends knew about. She would shoot him, then leave, and get back on the subway.

After a leisurely breakfast at a pancake house down the street, she walked to a subway station and rode the ten miles to lower Manhattan where Jeb worked. She arrived early, so she spent a half hour window shopping at the fine stores that lined Fifth Avenue. At exactly five minutes to twelve she entered the building and rode the elevator up to the thirty-third floor. Turning right as she left the elevator, she walked down a wide hallway to the end where upholstered benches lined both sides of the massive entry to the brokerage firm that Jeb owned. A man was seated on one of the benches typing on a notebook. She sat on the end and looked at her watch. Another five minutes, she thought as she smiled at the man who looked up for a second with a disinterested expression on his face. He went immediately back to his notebook. At ten after, Rose looked at her watch and got up, walked halfway up the hallway and disappeared down a narrow hallway marked private. On the left was an unmarked door which she tried. It was unlocked as usual so his lackeys could come in to pamper him about halfway through his routine. She carefully opened the door, reached her hand into the pocket with the gun, put her head inside and looked around. Seeing nothing, she proceeded past some exercise equipment to a large wooden door with a latch on it. She removed the gun and held it behind her, then slowly opened the door.

"I thought I told you twelve thir...." came Jeb's raspy voice, stopping when he recognized Rose's face.

"Rose...." he said loudly. "What on earth are you doing here....."

"Came to settle up the account," she said coolly.

"Account..... what account?" he sputtered, tugging on the towel he had pulled around himself when the door started to open.

"Baker's dozen," she said, finally using the term that she had thought of as Judd lay dead on the fireplace toolset.

"Baker's what?" he half laughed.

"The thirteen of you conservative conspirators."

"Conspirators.....oh my god...." his face went ashen and his eyes narrowed. "You....... Seattle......Lopez....it was you....." his voice nearly squeaking in terror.

"Yes," she nodded as she pulled the gun around and aimed it at his forehead. His eyes were now wide and he was past the point of being able to speak. He just shook his head, his eyes pleading. Then he shut his eyes. That's when Rose pulled the trigger and he jerked backward against the wooden slats. He then slumped forward into a heap on the floor, the white towel red with blood that was gushing from his face. She turned quickly and walked out. She closed the door and retraced her steps out into the narrow hallway and then out into the larger hall, not looking back toward the benches that were now empty. She smiled in mild surprise when she saw that, then strode calmly to the elevators and rode down to the street level. No witnesses she shrugged. She went out onto the crowded sidewalk and back to the subway station. A half hour later she was in the Bronx, walking along the sidewalk back to her hotel. It was almost one o'clock. Checkout time was supposedly noon. She had loaded her things in the car that morning before she left and now simply went to the garage, got into her car and a few minutes later was on the on ramp to the interstate. Clean, she thought. Although she had hoped that he would be more arrogant. Apparently, he had already heard about Brewster and Wes….and also Rex. So the word was spreading. It may not be as easy from now on. Maybe they would begin to take precautions. They might hire bodyguards or, maybe, it was just Jeb who is super on top of everything. Unless someone contacts the others, they may not know. She hoped at least her next victim had not been alerted.

Chapter 9

She saw the flashing lights in the rear view mirror but didn't hear the siren. Then, as the trooper pulled in behind her, he hit the siren briefly and motioned her over. A wave of panic swept over her. How could they have traced her? Maybe Jeb had a mic or camera in the sauna. Maybe the man in the hall. But even then, how would they find her? Or know who she was. Her mind was in a frenzy. The license plates. She was supposed to change them to New York but hadn't. What if they ran a trace? She rolled down the window as the officer walked up.

"May I see your driver's license please?" he asked. She reached into the backpack that was in the front seat, fished it out of her wallet and handed it to him.

"Ohio, and Maine plates?" he asked.

"Just moved up there," she lied. He looked at her carefully and nodded.

"You were going a little fast," he said.

"I thought it was 65," she said with a pained expression on her face.

"Goes down to 55 in through here," he said, leaning over and handing her license back to her. "I'm going to let you go with a verbal warning mam. Now you pay attention to the signs from now on."

"I will," she nodded in relief as he looked at her again, then retreated to his car. As he did he looked back at her license plate and wrote something down in a little notebook. Damn! She sat there for maybe thirty seconds then drove back into the freeway traffic. The sign ahead noted 102 miles to Pittsburgh. As she looked into her rearview mirror, she noticed the patrol car closing in on her. He had run a check, she thought. She anticipated the flashing lights again and slowed slightly, prepared to pull over. The patrol car sped past her, clearly in excess of the posted speed. She breathed a big sigh of relief. Wherever Clancy got those plates, it must have worked.... this time at least. She decided to just leave the Maine plates on for the time being. Maybe change to Pennsylvania plates after the little deed in Pittsburgh.

At eleven o'clock, Rose pulled into a Howard Johnson's near the freeway just outside of Pittsburgh near her next hit. Another chain motel she thought. She nodded with a smile. After staying in that nice suite in the Bronx, she decided to go a little more upscale for a while. As long as she pays cash and uses an alias, it shouldn't make any difference, she reasoned. Of course, they use computers now, and perhaps a clever detective could piece something together.....but she had no idea what. It was the Dozen that she was more worried about, and their piecing together the string of snuffs and either leaving town or hiring protection. Maybe even going after her if they knew who it was. Jeb had clearly begun to put it together but hadn't had time to act. He just assumed he was safe in his own well-monitored office building. He was wrong.

The room at Howard Johnson's was, of course, not nearly as elaborate as the last hotel in New York. She spread the dossier for the Pittsburgh conspirator on the table, together with a map of the city and a blowup map of where he lived. The computer street map program was able to provide enough detail for her to navigate even in an unfamiliar city. The house she was looking for was about three miles from the motel out in the suburbs south of the city.

This one could be quite difficult. Phil Oberg had a large family. There were apparently as many as eight people living in his home, including both his and his wife's mothers. Phil worked in the Golden Triangle, the downtown of Pittsburgh. Rose knew very little of the city, having only visited there a few times, and she wasn't comfortable with getting in and out of the congested center. Her plan was almost over the edge for this one. The only routine where she knew he would be alone was his confessional at a Catholic Church on Wednesday night. And this was Tuesday. Another happy coincidence despite being there ahead of schedule. The confessional would now have to be it... so find a Catholic church located near his home. The dossier did not say where. This could be a huge assumption and she hoped that there would not be several Catholic churches near his home. Only one Catholic church came up on the computer program near his home. It had to be the one.

Her idea was to park near the church until she saw Phil,

follow him inside and sit in a corner in the rear of the church. She would watch him go through the confession, then follow him outside in the dark. She would look for a darkened area and hope no one was around. It was extremely risky. She had no idea how many people would be in or around the church or whether there was a darkened area outside where she could operate. Something would likely present itself as it had so far. Her only other option was a sports bar he apparently frequented on the same night, usually with a group of other men he met there. That would likely be even more difficult. The option of doing him in his home would be virtually impossible. It was hard for Rose to imagine that option not involving a good deal of collateral damage. Except for the dog and the wife on Lopez, she had managed to keep that aspect of the effort in check. She shook her head at the thought. Whatever she did, she had to move quickly. If Jeb had begun to link the murders already, others likely would also know what was going on, which would seriously affect her ability to complete her mission. She just had to keep moving. She was still two days ahead in her schedule and, if she could accelerate that, she would.

Rose awoke early the next morning. After a quick donut and coffee in the lobby, she headed out for a drive-by of Phil's home, the church and the sports bar, 'the Lion's Lair' it said in the dossier. Phil lived in a walled community. The gate was open and a sign showed that the guard was on duty only at night. She drove past the address. The house was an elegant three-story white colonial with pillars twenty-five feet tall guarding the entry. There were several cars parked along the drive and behind she could see a garage with several doors and another car parked in front of one of the doors. She could see no movement through the windows as she drove by. The street had no large trees and it had tall light standards that appeared to provide ample light at night. Not a good setup, physically, to add to the fact that the house was occupied by a lot of people on potentially different schedules. She went back out through the gate. The church was just six blocks away and she could see its spire as she came over a rise. She parked just down the street and looked it over carefully. Only small shrubs decorated the front which was open and rose up to a wide set of steps from the street which had closely spaced streetlamps. If Phil parked on the street, there were no dark corridors. She followed the parking lot sign and wound her way behind the church into the church's lot. Better chance, she thought, if he parks here. A good stand of pine and oak shielded the lot. The oak trees were bare but the pine appeared to block a number of places from the few street lamps that were scattered across the lot. Not perfect, but better. Hopefully, he would park back here.

She then exited the lot and spent the next half hour trying to locate the sports bar, being careful not to ask questions of anyone. Finally, as she rounded a curved drive she could see a placard on the dirt shoulder with an arrow, 'Lion's Lair'. She turned into the gravel entry and past a thick stand of trees into a large gravel parking lot. There were old telephone poles lined up on the pavement to separate the parking spaces. Several cars were in the lot that appeared to have just two quaint lamps at either end to light it. She stopped at one end of the pole dividers, got out, looked around, then casually walked over to the end lamp, reached in, and unscrewed the bulb. She put it in her pocket, then got back into her car and drove away. Could be here, she nodded as she pulled back onto the street and aimed back toward the motel. The church first, then if that doesn't present a good opportunity, follow him to the bar and hope he parks nearer the lamp without the bulb.

There would probably not be enough time for a full speech with this one. Just announce who she was, why he must die, then pop him and leave. Quick in, quick out. The body would likely be discovered very soon afterwords and so she would need to be checked out of the motel and get back onto the interstate and on to Atlanta. That was the plan.

Rose sat in the little cafe in the corner finishing her dinner with a newspaper folded beside her plate. She checked her watch. Almost six. She wasn't sure when he came to confession. In the evening. Before going to the bar. Likely before seven she had surmised, but wasn't sure. Deciding to just go to the church and wait, she raised her hand for the waitress to bring the check. Outside in her car, she carefully took the gun out of her pocket to check it one last time. She pulled out the clip to make sure it was full. Then she felt in her pocket to make sure a few more loose bullets were there. She put the gun back in her pocket and drove to within a block of the church and parked under a row of oaks that must have provided near blackness in the summer when their leaves were full. Now, the nearby street lamp shown through brightly. She sat patiently. The snow that had blanketed the ground from Seattle to Maine had barely dusted Pittsburgh and only little white patches could be seen in the shade on nearby lawns. The temperatures remained below freezing and now, sitting in the car with the engine off, it was cold. She donned her

106

mittens and held her legs together to conserve heat as her breath steamed in front of her. Several people had entered the church. Four women and two men, emerging ten to fifteen minutes after they entered. One had stopped in front to let off a passenger before going back into the lot. The others all had parked in the lot and had come around on the sidewalk from the rear. At ten past seven a red Porsche pulled up into the loading zone in front of the church. A short, older bald man with a ruddy complexion and short black leather coat got out and walked briskly up the steps of the church. It was unmistakably Phil. She recognized him immediately, having run into him more than once when he visited Judd in Cleveland over the years. As he skittered up the steps, a police car entered the intersection in front of the church and the officer honked his horn. Phil turned just as he reached the church door to see the officer pointing to his Porche and shaking his head. Phil disgustingly held up his hands and shook his head, then trekked back to his car with a disconcerted gait. He ripped the door open and slammed it shut as he jerked it into gear, squealed the tires, roared down the street and up into the lot. Rose waited until he had disappeared, then drove down the street and into the lot. As she pulled in, she could see the dark shadow of Phil making his way down the sidewalk toward the front of the church. She spotted his red Porsche in the lot. She pulled into an empty space next to it, so closely that he would not be able to open his door. She sat with the motor running as the heat began to fill the cold interior. About fifteen minutes later, a door at the back of the church opened and a black and white clad priest held it open as Phil emerged, nodding to him, then turned and walked toward his car. The priest watched for a

107

moment, then went back inside. No one else was in sight. Rose removed her mittens and took out the pistol, placing it in her lap. A few feet from the front of his car, across the landscaping strip, Phil stopped and looked wide-eyed at how closely Rose had parked to his Porshe. She was not much more than a foot away, with only a few other cars in scattered locations in the lot. He hesitated a moment, then squeezed between the cars to her window as he was literally wedged between them. He stopped, tapped his fingers on her window deliberately not looking at her to show his disdain. She pulled the window lever back and the window came down. He looked down at her, his mouth open in surprise.

"Rose?" he uttered in an almost inaudible tone.

"Yes," she smiled. "It's your time." He furrowed his brow in confusion, then his eyes widened in horror as she quickly lifted the pistol to within inches of his face and pulled the trigger, hitting him in the forehead just above the bridge of his nose. He slumped down between the cars, sliding to the pavement and out of sight with a scraping sound as the buttons on his coat rubbed against her car. She put the car in reverse, feeling a bump as she must have run over his arm or leg backing out. She slowly drove out of the lot and turned right onto the street that led eventually to the highway. In a few minutes, she saw the interstate 70 on-ramp sign and was soon speeding at seventy miles per hour westbound. In less than an hour she would be on the 79 heading southwest toward Charleston, West Virginia where she planned to stop for the night.

It would be past midnight when she finally arrived at a Motel 6 just out of town. Half down, half to go, she thought, after pulling into the nearly empty parking lot and sitting in the stillness staring at the darkened entry. Including Judd, six. At length, she got out and went up to the glass door and peered in. In the dim light she could see the top of a woman's head sitting behind the counter. She tried to push the door open. As she was trying, she noticed a button to one side and pushed it. The woman stood up, laid the book down that she was reading and reached under the counter. A loud buzzer sounded and Rose pushed the door open.

"I'll assume from the nearly empty lot that you have vacancies," said Rose, half sarcastically.

"You'd be right," the woman smiled. "How many nights?"

"One."

"I can give you a deal on a second night," the woman added hopefully.

"Just the one," said Rose, picking up the pen that the woman handed her and filling out the form.

"Will that be on Visa, Mastercard or American Express.... miss Falkner?" asked the woman.

"Cash," said Rose, beginning to peel off twenties. "How much does that come to?"

"Thirty six forty five including tax," said the woman taking two bills from Rose as she pulled out a plastic card and handed it to her while she fished in the till for change. "Room 145 which is just down from your car, bottom floor," she said, pointing out the window. Rose nodded, took the card and walked out into the cool evening. It was not as bitter as farther north, she thought as she opened the trunk and fetched her suitcase. Inside the room, she quickly retrieved her laptop and plugged it in. She then

109

retrieved the next dossier from her suitcase. Placing a partially unfolded road map of the United States beside her she took out a pencil and circled Atlanta. Then she traced a pencil down to Orlando, circling it too. She hesitated, stopping to scratch her head and then stare at the map. After a moment, she unfolded the map all the way to show the western states, circling Denver, then Palm Springs, then Los Angeles. Finally, she ran the pencil off the bottom of the page with an arrow before turning back to place her finger on Atlanta.

Peter Bigelow, she nodded as she read through his file. Marietta, north of Atlanta. He was a lecturer three days a week at Georgia Tech near downtown. He rode the north line of the rail in from the park-and-ride to which he drove on Tuesdays, Thursdays and Fridays. She pulled up the map program and clicked on hotels. She would stay at a Comfort Inn just north of Georgia Tech right near the freeway and the rail line. Opportunities for the hit might be either at the park-and-ride station in Marietta or on campus. Probably on campus, in his office, if he had one. She could then use the rail for her access and getaway. She would check into the hotel, then visit the campus to check out the possibilities there first.

Tomorrow was Wednesday. If she left early, she would likely arrive in the afternoon. It was approximately a ten hour drive. She would check out the situation that afternoon, then possibly take him out on Thursday morning when he came in. A backup plan would then be to check out the park-and-ride and try again that evening or wait until Friday morning. If that didn't work out it may require the hit to be done in Marietta over the weekend. Her notes said he had an eight o'clock class. She'd get a train schedule and be on a train that arrived at the campus station at seven or a little after. Georgia Tech was the next station from the one near her hotel. Again, all of this depended on the circumstances. She would take the first available opportunity and have her escape route planned. The 75 freeway was nearby and she would be on it quickly from the hotel parking lot. She closed the laptop and lay out on the bed, feeling a lump in her pocket. It was the light bulb she had taken from the parking lot of the sports bar in Pittsburgh. An option she didn't have to exercise. But it was, nonetheless, an option she knew she needed. It would be the same in Atlanta. Think through several options, then take the first available. It would most likely be his office, if it appeared to be laid out in a favorable way, and if she could get in and out without being too conspicuous. She closed her eyes and fell asleep.

Chapter 10

An early start from Charleston had put her well on her way. She expected to stop in Charlotte for lunch getting into Atlanta by four or five at the latest. The weather had mellowed considerably and Rose could begin to feel the softness of the air outside as the heater was slowly turned down to its minimum. By the time the suburbs of Atlanta began to appear through the trees, it was almost like springtime in Ohio even though relatively chilly for those who lived in the South. As she looked for her exit, the traffic began to build and by the time she pulled into the hotel parking lot the congestion was very heavy. She slowly got out of the car, stiff from a long day behind the wheel. She knew she had more to do before the day was over. After checking in and insisting on a room that did not face the freeway, she stopped by the cafe/bar near the entrance to the parking lot and ordered her usual Bombay Sapphire. There was also a sign showing that they were famous for their hamburgers, so that was what she ordered.

By five thirty she was at the station waiting for the train, which was two blocks away.

"You visitin?" asked the young black man next to her.

"Yes," she smiled.

"Where you headin?" he asked.

"I thought I'd just ride a little ways to Georgia Tech to look around a little," she nodded.

"That place isn't any good after dark," he nodded back with a somber grit on his lip.

"Oh?" she asked, raising her eyebrows.

"Kinda mean neighborhood around there," he confirmed. "And it's gettin' dark already."

"I'll be careful," she assured him.

"No use bein' careful if you're alone," he shook his head with a tisk, looking away, then back at her.

"I'll be all right."

"Don't say I didn't warn ya."

"I've got a whistle," she lied, patting the pocket of her coat and feeling the hardness of the gun inside.

"Whistle?" he snickered, rolling his eyes. "You need an AK-47 not a whistle grammaw..."

"Thank you for your concern, young man," she said as the train pulled up and the doors swished open. He just shook his head and got in after her. A few minutes later the doors swished open again and she got out and looked around, trying to get her bearings.

"What do you want to see?" came the black man's voice from behind her. She turned her head in surprise.

"Are you following me?" she asked, folding her arms and

putting her hand on the hard form in her pocket.

"I'm not followin you, mam, I'm pratectin you," he shook his head.

"Is this where you get off or are you just doing me a favor?" she asked.

"This is my stop.... but I'm not lettin' you wander around here by yourself ....so just tell me what you want to check out and I'll stick around for a bit and keep the wolves off of you."

"Fine, I want to see the administration building."

"Over here," he pointed as they walked out of the station area and up a wide sidewalk. A minute later they were at the entrance. "It's open," he gestured. She entered as he held the door open for her. To her left was a black roster with white plastic letters spelling out names and numbers.

"You looking for someone in particular," he queried.

"No," she lied, scanning the list and finding Bigelow and a room number. "By the way, do you know where that hall is?" she pointed to the name of the building above Bigelow's room listing.

"Yeah, it's right next to this," he pointed.

"You seem awfully familiar with the campus," she said.

"I went here," he nodded.

"What was your major," she said.

"English Lit," he replied with a grin.

"Interesting," she said after a moment's hesitation. "Did you graduate?"

"Cum Laude," he snickered.

"Wow," she replied, squinting at him and wondering whether he was telling her the truth.

114

"Yeah," he nodded. "An me jes a black boy."

"I didn't….." she began, now feeling very guilty for what she had thought.

"Not to worry…."

"So…. do you have a job?"

"Yes," he nodded.

"English Lit? What….."

"I work on cars at a repair shop," he shrugged.

"You work on….cars….but what about…."

"Not to worry….now…. do you want me to show you that building," he asked.

"Uh, yes, thank you," she said, nodding as he once again held the door open for her and she started toward the building next door.

"I think it's still open," he muttered. "Night classes, I think." As they went in, Rose carefully looked down the dark halls, then went up one flight of stairs and down a hall, passing the closed door with the name Mr. Bigelow on it. It might work, she thought as she walked past.

"Are you looking for someone?" the young man asked.

"What's your name?" asked Rose, avoiding his question on the one hand and curious about this man on the other.

"Vincent," the young man replied.

"I'm Rose," she said before she remembered that she wasn't supposed to use her real name.

"Hi," he said, holding out his hand. "What else do you want to see, since you're obviously not going to tell me exactly why you came here."

"I don't know, just give me the cook's tour," she shrugged

with a smile. For the next half hour, Vincent led Rose around the campus describing each building or feature and its historic significance. He then escorted her to the train station and waited until a train came, then led her to the opened door.

"Thank you so much Vincent for uh...protecting me... and showing me the campus; I hope we meet again sometime," she said as she stepped into the car.

"Oh, I'm sure we will," he nodded with a smile as the doors swished closed and the train began to move. She waved to him through the windows as it pulled away and he nodded in return.

It was still dark the next morning as Rose stood in the rail station waiting for the next train. Only one other person was there with her, a young woman with a backpack who kept pacing back and forth nervously. Momentarily the train hummed to a halt and the doors squawked open and the young girl crowded in ahead of Rose through the same door. The train car was nearly full to Rose's surprise for this early hour. She chose to stand near the door rather than crowd in between riders for the short ride to the next station where she would get off. As she stood clinging to a post watching the early light of dawn that could be seen outside, she scanned the faces of some of the passengers. Her scan stopped abruptly on a man seated along the back bench seat. It was Peter reading a newspaper. She had met him only a few times and it had been a few years since the last time but she recognized his distinctive pointy features and impeccably neat hair and dress. She slowly turned around so that he couldn't see her face if he were to look up. She was still able to see him vaguely through a reflection in a side window against the still dark world outside. Next to Peter sat a large man who had his arms folded. Peter whispered something to him and, as the coach slowed to a stop at the next station, they both got up together and started for the opening door. Rose waited until the last minute, then turned and stepped quickly out behind them. She walked slowly after them as the train pulled away and silence suddenly surrounded her. Only the footsteps of Peter and the big man were heard just ahead of her in the dim light. This was a complication, thought Rose, as they approached the Physics Building. They both entered. She stopped for a moment, then followed them in the door. Upstairs she could hear their voices.

"After we check out my office, you can come back down and position yourself at the foot of the stairs," he said. A bodyguard, Rose thought. He knows. There has obviously been some communication among the group and they're beginning to suspect that something's wrong. She waited at the foot of the steps as the big man came down, nodding to her as she smiled.

Rose casually walked past him and up the stairs, taking the gun out of her pocket and tucking it into the half zipped fly of her coat as she reached the top of the steps and went down the hall. The door was still slightly ajar as she stopped in front of it and peeked through the slit. Seeing nothing, she stepped in. Ahead of her through an open doorway in the tiny office was a desk, behind which sat Peter, looking at her in stunned silence, unable to speak.

"Since you have a bodyguard, you obviously already know what this is all about," she said as she quickly pulled out the gun, aimed it and pulled the trigger as Peter was positioning himself to stand up. His eyes became wide as saucers and his mouth slightly agape in horror. He simply slumped back into his chair, tottered for a moment, then fell forward onto his desk without uttering a sound. Only the slap of his face on the surface made any appreciable noise. Rose turned, retraced her steps and then opened the door a crack to look down the hall. She walked out, going down the hall in the opposite direction and down the back staircase, hoping the back door would be unlocked. As she reached the bottom the back door was not easy to find. It took several turns in short, narrow halls before she spotted the green exit sign and pushed on the bar. The door opened and she found herself in a narrow alley between buildings. She hurried up the alley and out onto the sidewalk where there were now a number of students. She walked quickly toward the rail station. From her pocket, she pulled out the schedule which she scanned.

"Five more minutes," came a soft voice from just behind her. She spun around, a nervous look on her face.

"Vincent," she said after recognizing the smiling face.

"Can't stay away, huh?" he nodded.

"Right," she said, swallowing in the middle. "What are you....."

"Doing here?" he completed when she couldn't finish the question.

"Right," she nodded, still trying to be calm.

"It's my station. I live here in the hood, remember? I work out in the burbs where the man live. Remember?" he said in a lightly sarcastic voice.

"I forgot," she sighed, trying to smile.

"Train'll have you safely out of here in a few minutes," he said.

"I'm not in that big of a hurry," she shook her head.

"Right," he smiled with a nod. She nodded back and they stood without speaking until the train pulled in and the doors opened.

"You're probably wondering why I'm back here this early?" she stumbled.

"No," he replied, shrugging as they sat down together on a side bench in the nearly full coach.

"A lot of people heading back out," she noted.

"Jes po' foke lookin' afa dere massas," he mumbled.

"You said we'd meet again," she said quietly as the coach pulled away.

"And we may meet still again, who knows," he acknowledged.

"Yeah, who knows," she nodded. A few minutes later, she got up as the train pulled to a stop. She reached out her hand and shook his, then turned and stepped quickly out of the train and up the sidewalk toward her hotel. Having already paid for her room and loaded her car before she left that morning, she went directly to the lot, got into her car and was soon on the busy freeway. She slowly worked her way out of Atlanta as the morning sun reflected its bright rays off buildings that were contrasted against the dark green of the forests that seemed to fill in all the empty spaces between them.

They're definitely onto her, she thought. Private bodyguard. At least she didn't have to incur collateral damage. Since he had already hired a bodyguard, he knew he was in peril. But from whom? Obviously the bodyguard did not know that it was a woman they were looking for. An old woman. That much was still apparently unknown and in her favor. But now they know

119

they are in danger. All of those left are likely to have taken steps to protect themselves. Hopefully they wouldn't go into hiding or leave the country. The bodyguard did see her. That could pose a problem if he or someone else pieced things together. Or maybe not. They apparently hadn't mentioned the lady again in the Lopez Island case even though that was noted on the news before. Maybe that information wasn't passed along to the others in the dozen as relevant. It was too farfetched to believe that an elderly woman could in any way be involved. Nonetheless, she will have to assume from now on that they could be on the lookout for her. And she would proceed on that assumption. Next: Orlando and Dennis Conyer. Seven down, five to go.

Chapter 11

"Winter Park next exit", said the sign. This neighborhood is an artsy suburb just north of Orlando. Rose had made good time. Even with a half hour stop late morning for brunch and gas, she had made it there by four o'clock. She saw the sign for what appeared to be an upscale motel as she cruised down one of the main arterials. She pulled under the canopy and was promptly greeted by a young man dressed in a beige jumper with red trim with a small scull cap with the same color combination. He looked like the little Phillip Morris character that she remembered from many years ago as a child. She smiled as he walked up to her window.

"Checking in, mam?" he asked with a strange southern accent. Must be local Floridian she mused as she nodded to him and got out of the car.

"I assume you have vacancies," she asked.

"Yes, mam," he replied. "I'll wait until you check in then see you to your room."

"Thank you," she nodded as she tried her stiff legs and slowly began moving toward the lobby door with another similarly dressed but older man reaching to open the tall glass doors for her. She nodded her thanks to the man as she entered the darkened lobby with its deep red carpet and elegant crystal chandeliers. This one won't be inexpensive she thought as she walked up and put her elbows on the marble counter.

"And how many nights will you be staying with us?" came the greeting from an impeccably dressed middle-aged woman behind the counter.

"Just one I think," she replied, not having completely thought out the logistics of her job here in Orlando. "Maybe two," she added as she remembered the added complication of having to deal with the possibility- even probability- that they have all been alerted by now and will be more carefully guarded.

"Very good," said the woman. "Will a king opening onto the garden be all right?"

"Is it quiet?" asked Rose.

"Completely," the woman nodded as she pushed the marble framed register in front of her and Rose began to fill it out. When she was finished, she slid the register back toward the woman who glanced at it.

"And which credit card will you be using today Miss Gladstone?" asked the woman with a smile.

"I'll pay cash," said Rose, reaching into her handbag and fishing out a roll of bills, peeling down to the 100s and taking three from the top as she guessed the price. "How much is it for one night?"

"Two seventy five plus tax... that will come to two ninety nine," she smiled. Rose handed her the three bills with a shrug, knowing that it would be much higher than the motel chains she passed on the freeway before she exited. The woman handed her a plastic card key and a dollar bill. Rose went out the door, handing the doorman the dollar which he looked at disdainfully and then she held up the key so the man standing near her car could see the room number. He nodded and pointed to her trunk which she opened. A few minutes later he was showing her the room which was both large and exquisitely appointed. Some of the furnishings were legitimate antiques and the design and decor was well thought out. A pair of French doors opened onto a completely private patio adjoining a beautifully landscaped interior courtyard. She thanked the man and handed him a five.

"Bring my car keys to me when you've parked the car, I will want to take it out later," she said as he left.

"Very good, mam," he bowed as he closed the door.

Pretty posh, she laughed to herself as she slumped into one of the comfortable arm chairs. She stared out into the courtyard at the flowers that almost glowed in the waning light that reflected off the alabaster walls of the building. She was definitely becoming spoiled, having gradually worked her way up from the fleabag motels to this. This was not as good as some of the world class hotels she had been in over the years, but for the price, it was actually quite elegant. A few minutes later there was a knock on her door and the man handed her the car keys. She thanked him and went to her suitcase to retrieve the laptop and set it up on the intricately inlaid writing desk. Then she pulled the dossier of Dennis I. Conyer from her suitcase. When she had originally reviewed his case, she had thought it might be easier to do the job at his home here in Winter Park, since he lived alone with his wife, who was away much of the time in Europe at their summer home. There would probably be just the servants, if he had any. He worked at an office in Universal Studios, a theme park south of Orlando. That might be a better option. There would be crowds to disappear into. The home is likely to be guarded. It would be more difficult to provide total protection in the crowded conditions of a theme park. She decided to drive by his home to look it over before she made a definite plan. The home was on Oceola Drive. It was just down the street where the arterial makes a big turn she noted from the street map on her computer map program. First, however, she was hungry. She studied the dossier a few minutes longer, then put the car keys in her pocket, pulled on her jacket and started to leave. She then remembered it was warm outside. She was in Florida. She quickly dug out a lightweight sweater, then tried to rethink where she would carry her gun. After some thought, she decided to leave it in the room.

Impossible, thought Rose as she neared the turn in the arterial and looked off to her right at the lakefront villa. The house was way too exposed. There was also too much traffic on the arterial and there was a gated drive. An approach by boat would be too easily seen as well. It was an exposed property. It was not a good site for what she had to do. She continued on and stopped at a restaurant just down the road. She asked for a corner table and sat with her back to the wall while she waited for the Bombay Sapphire to arrive. A tall, well-dressed elderly man with silver hair and an obviously dyed black mustache came in and was seated by the hostess at the empty table across from her. She saw him unfold his newspaper and start to read an article. Momentarily, he looked over toward Rose who was trying to avoid his stare.

"You from out of town?" he asked, waiting for her to look his way. She hesitated a moment so he might get the hint that she wasn't interested in a conversation with him. She could feel his smile and his raised eyebrows and she eventually looked his way. Deja vu, she thought. He was another man at a table next to her in a restaurant wanting to be friendly. Where was the last one? Denny's? Where was that? She couldn't remember this happening at all in her many years of traveling alone. Now, how many times already on this trip?

"Yes," she nodded, finally, looking down at the table in front of her with a passive nod.

"Me too," he replied, the brightness of his smile almost glowing across at her. She finally turned toward him and smiled slightly, giving in to his warmth.

"Have you seen the theme parks?" he asked.

"No," she smiled, shaking her head then looking out the window. "No, I haven't."

"Me neither, not really much fun by yourself.... especially at my age," he snickered.

"Yeah," she nodded with a little chuckle as the waitress arrived with her drink.

"Bombay Sapphire.... straight up with a twist of lemon," the man said. She looked at him and nodded.

"I don't drink anymore," he said after waiting for her to reply.

"Oh," she acknowledged politely but dispassionately, focusing

125

on her drink.

"Yeah, it's been almost fifteen years now," he confided.

"Was it a problem for you?" she asked after hesitating for a moment, then looked his way.

"Alcoholism," he nodded solemnly.

"Good for you then," she nodded with a smile.

"It was a bit hard at first, but I just learned never to touch the stuff... not any of it."

"It can certainly control your life if you're not careful.... I limit myself to just one drink a day."

"Never been a problem for you?"

"No."

"You're lucky. It just built up for me over the years until one day I woke up and realized I was addicted to it. I realized it was ruining my life. It was killing me and driving me to depression."

"You seem together now," she said, still showing little interest in her voice, not wanting to get into a friendly conversation with him and hoping he would just go back to reading his paper. He could sense her coolness and picked up the paper again and began to read. She took a sip of her drink and stared out the window at the passing cars, her mind going over the possibilities for tomorrow. Perhaps even tonight, she thought.

"Is Universal Studios open at night?" she found herself asking, hoping he would not suggest that they go together.

"Yes," he said, still reading. "Til midnight I think."

"Hmmm."

"Funny you'd ask.... I was planning to go down there tonight just to look around.... understand it's spectacular in the evening."

"I imagine," she replied, trying to avoid encouraging him.

"In fact, I've got two free passes," he offered, still not looking up from his paper.

"Really?"

"You're welcome to join me if you wish. I hate going to those places alone."

Rose started to say no and to make up an excuse for why but thought for a second and realized it might actually make a good cover. She looked over at him with a cautious grin.

"Sure, why not," she said finally, surprising herself at accepting without more thought about the actual logistics of having someone with her as she cased the scene of her next hit.

"My name's Steve," said the man, picking up his newspaper and moving to her table, then holding his hand out for her to shake. He was a big man. Imposing. Maybe six two or three and probably at least two hundred. He was not overweight but had a definite stomach that hung over his belt. He had a very clean, well shaven face and was very good looking for what she guessed was a man in his late sixties.

"Estelle," said Rose, taking his hand and shaking.

"Pleased to meet you.....I ate here last night and the ribs are excellent," he said in one breath.

"I'm not a ribs fan," she replied, flipping open the menu.

"They say the pork chops are good too."

"I might try that, yes," she nodded as she scanned the menu.

"You got a car I presume?" he asked.

"Yes."

"We can take mine. Drop your's off wherever you're staying."

"Devonshire," she offered.

"Hmmm.... really.... nice place..... a bit steep, but nice."

127

"Yes it is..... both of those.... nice and also a bit steep."

"Hope you don't mind riding in a sports car."

"No, I don't mind. Why, what kind do you have?"

"Morgan."

"Morgan? Isn't that kind of an open-air car?"

"It's a little Spartan.... like you can sometimes see the pavement through the floorboards. But it does have a rag top if it gets cold."

"I don't think I've ever actually ridden in one of those, but my brother has friends who collect rare cars and I've seen them before," she laughed.

"I play with cars, it's just one of my toys."

"Why a Morgan?"

"Basic car. I like simple things. No electric windows or automatic transmissions. This one doesn't even have a radio."

"Sounds quaint," she nodded. "I guess we're in Florida and it's supposed to be warm.

"It actually freezes around here in the winter sometimes, though now it's quite mild, but can get chilly in the evenings this time of year."

"Yeah, it is mild here compared to up north," she mused, studying him for a moment and trying to assess the wisdom of her decision to go with him to a theme park at night.

They talked through dinner and afterward wandered out into the parking lot where they surveyed Steve's Morgan. Then Rose got into her car and he followed her to her hotel where she parked in the garage. She then went to her room to get her jacket, which she carried rather than wore, and came out and got into his car. The gun was in one pocket.

"Spartan is a good description," she laughed as she sat in the firm seat and looked at the archaic-looking dash and interior holding the jacket in her lap to hide the outline of the gun.

"Basic sports car," he smiled as he raced the engine, then sped out of the drive slowing only to duck between cars as they nearly tilted onto two wheels whipping into a lane. Rose hung on tightly and groped for the seatbelt, then quickly secured it keeping one hand on the grip above the glove compartment and one hand on the door-rest handle. It was a fast ride down the 4 past Orlando's downtown and off the exit to Universal Studios. At the gate, Steve showed the man the passes and they proceeded to the parking area where they hailed a tram to the main gate.

It was far more crowded than Rose had expected in the evening. Lines waited at virtually all rides. Some lines were several hundred strong. Her next mark, Dennis, apparently worked in an office within the theme park. She wasn't sure where nor was she at all sure how she would find out where the offices might be located in such a complex. They would likely be a bit out of the flow of the crowd. Maybe up one of the alleys that she could see as they walked around. Besides, this was just to case the place, certainly her man would not be there this evening. Steve guided her to a line and they stood to wait.

"Back to the Future," he nodded. "Great ride."

"You've been here before."

"I've never actually been inside the park before."

"How do you know it's a great ride then?"

"My grandson fills me in…. he apparently rides it at least twice every time he comes," he laughed. "He told me to go here first if I ever came."

"How old is he?"

"Ten."

"I guess a ten year old would know," said Rose, scanning the buildings on either side, looking for signs of doors and windows that might indicate something other than maintenance access or where facades were mocked up as part of a ride. In the distance she saw a street that appeared to lead between buildings and none of the crowds were there. She'd check that out after Back to the Future.

"That was a fun ride," said Rose as they came out.

"Where next?" asked Steve.

"I think I'd like to find a restroom first," said Rose looking around then pointing toward the street that she wanted to check out.

"Me too….over there," said Steve as he pointed to a street in the distance. Rose stopped, looked ahead to see if she could spot one closer to her destination.

"OK," she capitulated, heading toward the women's as Steve headed for the men's. She hesitated at the door and when he entered, she quickly scurried up the promenade toward the other street a block away. As she stepped onto the street she knew this was likely the office area as she could see no lines, no signs and an occasional person going in or coming out of a door. Higher up she saw lights from windows. Then she turned and hurried back toward the bathroom where she had left Steve. He came out just as she arrived.

"How about that ride?" she asked, pointing to a large gorilla.

"That one's on Greg's list too," he nodded. "Might as well."

As they attached themselves to the end of the lineup at the

ride a phalanx of men in suits crossed in front of them. In the middle, was the unmistakable face of Dennis. Round, ruddy, red hair that was clearly dyed considering his wrinkled face, freckles, and close set eyes. He had a rotund frame in a suit that was a little too small.... and that rolling limp. She remembered that. She watched intently while holding her hand to her face as if to scratch her nose. They continued past them into the street where the offices were apparently located. On the far side, four of the six entered a bright red door, two of the entourage remained posted by the door. He's there, she thought. And fully guarded. Six of them. As they waited in line she watched as a light came on in the second floor of the brick facade that formed the alley-like streetscape.

"Strange bunch, those," said Steve, following the activity with Rose.

"Must be execs or something," said Rose, shrugging.

"You forget that there is business going on here in pretend land."

"Apparently," Rose mused passively.

After the ride which included a twenty minute wait in line, Rose and Steve wandered back out into the crowded promenade. Rose took the lead and moved them past the office street where Dennis had gone. One guard still stood at the red door. Steve pointed at a nearby restroom sign.

"My plumbing requires frequent draining," he laughed.

"Mine too," Rose smiled as her mind raced with an impromptu plan. Again, she watched Steve enter the Men's door and then she moved quickly down the street toward the man standing at the door. She approached with a panicked look on her face.

131

"My husband is up there and I don't have his key," she said, rushing up to him, trying the knob which she knew was locked and pointing up at the lighted window.

"I'm sorry mam, I can't let anyone......" he began to say.

"Are you serious?" she shrugged, giving him a facial expression that would indicate that he was a complete idiot.

"Do you know who my husband is?" she said stepping a little closer.

"All right," he nodded, cowering beneath her glare and reached into his pocket for the key.

Inside, she saw an elevator. Down the long hall she saw another door that seemed to exit the other side of the building. She pushed the button to the elevator. A moment later the door opened and she stepped in and pushed the second floor button. The door opened and she entered a hallway. There was no one in sight. Down the hall was a row of doors with light shining through the windows onto the light green carpet. She walked quickly toward the first door, taking the gun out of the pocket of her jacket that she was still carrying over her arm and sliding it underneath. She stopped before walking in front of the first door's window and peeked carefully in. She could see the backs of two men in suits and moved past to the second door. As she approached she could see the back of Dennis' head as he sat at a computer. Moving forward to get a better view, she could not see anyone else. She very carefully opened the door a crack and aimed at the back of Dennis's head just behind the ear and pulled the trigger. Dennis sat up in a bolt, his body trying to stand up, but his arms fell to his side as he slumped downward, slowly, in the chair with barely a sound. He finally rolled to the floor in an almost fluid motion, his chair sliding backward, quietly, across the carpet coming to a stop against a wall. She closed the door and continued down the hall, coming to an exit sign at the opposite end from where she had entered. Through the door was a stairway which she quickly descended to the first floor. Down a short hall was another sign that said emergency exit only. She pushed the bar and found herself inside a large enclosure that looked like the back of a ride. She worked her way up the side of the enclosure until she came to another door. She pushed the bar and it opened. Outside she found herself in the midst of a line for a ride to the curious glances of some of those there. She calmly pushed her way through the line and out into the crowded promenade and finally located the entrances to the bathrooms where she spotted Steve who was waiting patiently near the women's entrance.

"I think I'm ready to call it a night," said Rose from behind.

"Oh, I thought......" said Steve, turning in surprise then looking at the door to the women's bathroom, then back at her. "Uh, sure, it's kind of a circus tonight anyhow. And we can come back tomorrow if you like."

"I might just do that," said Rose, nodding. "I've been driving all day and am suddenly very tired."

"I'll bet," said Steve, studying her for a moment then pointing through the throngs toward the exit and motioning her that way. Five minutes later they were on a tram and soon in the rustic old car behind a line of cars making their way out. As they pulled onto the main road, sirens could be heard to their right and Steve pulled over. Soon a police car with lights flashing and siren wailing sped past and squealed around the corner they had just

133

rounded. As they waited, two more police cars roared past and teetered around the corner with smoke rising from the burning rubber.

"Must be something big," said Steve, watching the phalanx of flashing lights disappear through the trees.

"Obviously," said Rose, nodding casually as she watched.

"Just think, if we'd have stayed a few minutes longer we could have seen all the excitement," said Steve with a little laugh as he put the Morgan in gear and let out on the clutch, throwing a spray of gravel behind them and ending in a little chirp as the spinning wheel came onto the pavement.

"I think Back to the Future was excitement enough for me for tonight," said Rose. They must have discovered the scene of the crime rather quickly, she thought as Steve continued talking to her and she looked at him with a nod, not even hearing what he had said. And obviously they are still not looking for an elderly woman. Unless the guard puts two and two together, which he might. Advantage could still be on her side. If and for how long she did not know. But now her focus would be on the next leg in her mission. The long road to Denver.

After stopping for an evening snack at the International House of Pancakes, Steve dropped Rose off in front of her hotel.

"Tomorrow then?" he asked optimistically, tilting his head and smiling broadly.

"Unless I decide to get an early start out of here, Steve," she nodded. "Either way, I want to thank you again for a lovely evening. I had a wonderful time and I'm sorry I had to cut it off early, but I really am a bit tired after the long drive earlier today."

"More reason to stay another night and rest," he said with

raised eyebrows.

"You may be right, but I am expected in Miami and I'm already way behind schedule," she smiled.

"Can I at least get your phone number at your daughter's in Miami?" he begged.

"Just ask for information, Miami, South Beach, Miriam Zeman," she replied, making up the name and location on the spur of the moment.

"Miriam Zeman.... thanks Estelle.... it was a distinct pleasure, and I hope you decide to stay and go with me to one of the other theme parks tomorrow. My treat."

"I appreciate that Steve," said Rose. "You're a sweet man. If I don't see you tomorrow, I'm sure we'll meet again."

"I'm sure of it," said Steve as he put it in gear and pulled away, waving one last time to her as he sped out onto the arterial.

Where have I heard that before, thought Rose as she stood in the mild evening air watching the Morgan disappear. Wasn't it the guy in Atlanta? I wonder if they're right? It might actually be interesting to revisit these places sometime in the future after it had all settled down. Unless they catch up to her before then she smiled. Oh, and change the license tags to Florida.... the thought suddenly came to her. Just as an added precaution. She would get an early start tomorrow morning. Mobile. Then Dallas. Then perhaps, Denver? Long segments, but she needed to keep going fast. Christmas Eve was only four days away. She wanted to be in Denver before then. Maybe Clay Darling would die on Christmas Day. There may be more opportunities for that to happen on the actual day. He was a devout Christian. Small family circle. Large, remotely located home. And he liked to go

135

skiing on Christmas Eve. That may be the opportunity. On the ski slopes. A chance to see if she could still manage to ski. It had been a few years now since she had been on the slopes. Perhaps there. Again, opportunity would be the deciding factor.

The holidays had almost become invisible to her as Christmas approached. All of the decorations and festivities seemed so distant and unimportant. This was unlike most of the Christmases she had known which were usually spent with her daughter whom, incidentally, she would have to call on Christmas Eve to prevent curious inquiries. If she remembered and if she could, depending upon circumstances.

Her goal now was to complete her work before the New Year. That would be a tall order. Things would have to continue to go well. And things had gone very well up to now. Actually, easier and faster than she had imagined. The many things that could have gone wrong had not gone wrong. Second options had not been necessary. All of the men had been there and not out of town. Nobody had suspected her as far as she knew. She wondered whether someone on the investigating team, if there was an investigating team, would eventually tie her visit to Seattle with the murders. They might question it or, perhaps, they were even now seeking her for questioning. Or they have no suspicions whatsoever of her possible involvement. That would seem incredible, but possible. Whatever the reason, the fact that none of the bodyguards she encountered in the last two hits seemed to be at all suspicious of her.... or even had a clue who she was. They're obviously looking for hit men or a hit man. Certainly a man not a woman. The traditional stereotype killer, or executioner. She didn't fit that mold. She was not just a woman, but an elderly woman. An elderly woman with Gucci shoes, an Armani blouse, designer haircut and Nordstrom makeup. She was cultured, with manners and an air of sophistication. A cultured elderly woman with an incredibly well-suited weapon from Clancy of Euclid Avenue. A weapon both very quiet and very deadly. An elderly woman with an apparently untraceable car and plates. Using cash and traveling by auto and using entirely random fictitious names and addresses at hotels without advance reservations. So far it was working. Four more to go. On to Denver.

Chapter 12

Three days. Three long days of driving from dawn well into the night. She had made New Orleans the first day and then Wichita Falls. Now she was in Lamar, Colorado, still 150 miles from Denver and was tired. The grueling pace was continuing to take its toll. She would sleep in tomorrow, she thought, as she pulled into the parking lot of a motel that was encircled with a small wall of snow even though the pavement was black and dry under the light standards. A dozen other cars were sprinkled around the oversized lot. It was a rather inauspicious motel. It was not run down, but well worn, even through a layer of new pale green paint that had been applied over virtually everything, then trimmed in dark green. It was not the Devonshire, that was certain, but it would do. It was just before midnight. She could see movement inside the lobby as she walked stiffly toward the entrance, feeling the pain in her knees and ankles from sitting for hours on end at the wheel. It was warm inside, almost too warm in sharp contrast to the freezing temperature outside.

"Good evening," came the greeting from a smiling woman with flaming red hair and a round pretty face.

"Good evening," Rose replied.

"Do you have a reservation?" asked the woman brightly as she pulled a clipboard toward her and scanned with her finger.

"Is that a problem?" asked Rose with a cynical shrug as she glanced out the window at the sparsely filled lot.

"No," the woman replied, pushing the clipboard out and following Rose's obvious gesture out the window. "We have vacancies."

"When is the peak season here?" asked Rose in a somewhat disinterested tone, walking up to the counter and reaching for a pen.

"Summer, I guess," said the woman tentatively, handing Rose a registration form. Rose nodded and began filling it out as the woman watched.

"I've heard that name somewhere before.... are you..... famous?" asked the woman watching Rose write.

"No, I think I had the name before the song," Rose snickered.

"Is that English....? Elenore Rigby?"

"My grandfather came over on the Mayflower," Rose replied with a straight face. "He was one of the criminals sent off to the penal colony called America." The woman looked at her for a second, then burst out laughing.

"Yeah," she nodded, still laughing.

"When is checkout time?" asked Rose as the woman continued to laugh.

"Uhhh, eleven...." said the woman seeing Rose's sober face

and quickly retrieving a key from a drawer and handing it to her. "Number 162, just a few doors down from here." Rose took the key with a smile and walked out as the woman stared after her, not sure whether to continue the conversation. As the door closed Rose could hear a muffled salutation from inside.

She entered the unit and surveyed the room. At a desk on one wall was a computer. She took a double take, then walked up to it. A computer, she mused, reaching down and switching it on. A moment later, an internet explorer icon appeared within a forest of others. She clicked on it and sat down in the chair, typing in Baker's Dozen's address and password. She clicked on 'mail' and scanned the e-mail titles seeing there were dozens by now. She then clicked on the latest entry entitled 'Orlando' and opened the mail.

"No clue," it began. "Someone went right in past bodyguards and shot Dennis. Must have been in the building when he and his guards arrived. That is the most likely scenario. It was done right in front of them and none of them saw anything. They quickly sealed off the building after Dennis was discovered, apparently minutes after he was shot, and no suspects were found. Several maintenance employees in the building are being held for further questioning. Nobody even looking suspicious had been seen going in or coming out. There was only an elderly woman in her seventies that went in earlier, and she is being sought for questioning as she may have seen something. So far they have not located her. My advice is to leave the country or go into deep hiding. Bodyguards seem not to be a deterrent. Whoever he is, he knows a lot about each of us. He knows where we will be. Our homes. Our work places. Not sure who will be next but the pattern seems to be in a track from Washington in the Northwest across to the Northeast, then down to the Southeast. Possibly looping back to the West Coast. With that track, Denver is likely the next stop. Clay, be on the lookout. Then, perhaps, Palm Springs. John, be ready. Would advise both of you to disappear immediately if you can arrange it, despite the fact that it's almost Christmas. We're not even sure if this website is secure. Direct communication from now on is advised so we all might be well advised to avoid this address."

She stared at the screen for a moment then signed off, hesitating at the 'sign back on' box. She reflected a moment, then looked back at the dossier, recalling the small penciled notes along the edge of one page. What looked like an email address and a password. She then typed: 'claypidgeon@range.com' and the password 'pull' from the notes and waited. A welcome window appeared and she went to 'mail', scanning for the latest message under 'sent'. It was entitled 'laying low' and addressed to 'Chipster'. Chip, his son, lived in Los Angeles. Santa Monica.

It went: "Going to Vail for Christmas Eve, then off to Fiji for a few weeks. Taking two muscles along for both. Some of our associates have been killed so we're a bit wary right now. The family doesn't know what's going on and have been asking who the two men are. I've told them they are some of my business associates. I'm not going to alarm them."

Under that another email addressed to the remaining three members of the group: "We need to get out of town. Pronto. He's heading out west and we're next. I have an inkling to just go straight to Fiji right now, but the annual ski trip with the family is a decades-old tradition and they are so looking forward to it.

It's not a likely place for a hit anyhow. Too many people. Too crowded. I'll be extra careful. By the way, wasn't there a middle-aged woman referenced in the Lopez Island hit, and an elderly one also seen in Orlando? Does anyone suspect a middle-aged or elderly woman? Or more likely a man dressed as a woman. I'd put a bet on that being the case. Chances of an elderly woman pulling this off is next to nil. However, might be alert to the possibility of a man dressed as a woman. The sightings could be just a coincidence but we have to cover all bases. Keep me informed if any additional info comes in."

Rose signed off, then sat back in her chair and smiled in amusement mixed with concern. She might be marked now based on Clay's comment. A man dressed as a woman. Same thing. They'd see an elderly woman and be suspicious. So now it would clearly be more difficult. No more walking past the muscle with a dainty smile and fast line. It would have to be direct contact with the target, possibly in a crowded situation. Or an isolated opportunity if one presented itself. Maybe collateral damage again as much as she regretted doing that. It was doubtful that what remained of the dozen would have shared very much, if anything, of what they know with the authorities. Whatever the authorities were doing with regard to solving the chain of killings -- if in fact they had even linked them at all -- was likely on their own with only minimum input from what was now left of the group.   And how much they could get from family members would be likely minimal as well. If family members knew, they wouldn't talk. If they didn't know, they wouldn't know about it. On the other hand would it make sense to maintain secrecy now with nine of the thirteen already cut down? Yes they would.

They would protect their secrecy to the last man even though in so doing it would make it much more difficult to identify who was picking them off one by one. This gave her a slight advantage. Hopefully, a slight advantage would be all she would need to finish the job.

Vail. That was Clay's traditional Christmas Eve retreat and it was still on according to his email. He was still an active skier despite his advancing age, and the family tradition of skiing together was still on and Christmas Eve was tomorrow night. She was still four hours from Denver and another two or three up into the mountains on the 70 to Vail. It would be an early start in the morning, making Vail by late afternoon. Hopefully sooner, she hoped. The last hit was in Florida and she had Florida plates. She would change to Pennsylvania, or maybe Maine again, before leaving the motel just in case anyone had made a connection. She wished she had Colorado plates. But what she had would have to be good. This one wouldn't be easy. She lay back on the bed and fell asleep.

The snow was piled high along the roadway as Rose wound her way up into the Rockies. She had made very good time, stopping only once near Limon for a late breakfast and gas. Ahead was the Westin sign where she planned to take a room even though she may or may not stay the night. Clay and family were likely at one of the condominiums nearby since he had mentioned staying in them in previous communications in the dossier. She planned to look for him at the Lodge and near the lifts. Rose had not skied in years and was not comfortable doing it now even though she knew she might have to. Her once agile body was not as strong or docile as it used to be. She would rent skis, get a lift ticket and carry the skis around while looking for Clay. Hopefully she would not have to ski down the hill.

The man at the hotel welcomed her. He said she was very lucky since it was Christmas Eve and they had been booked for weeks, but a cancellation had just came in a few minutes before she walked in and she would have a room for the night. Something Rose had not really considered even though she should have. Another incredible stroke of luck and, again, very timely. Once checked in, Rose rented skis and equipment, including a ski suit. She caught the shuttle and was soon at the hill that Clay had mentioned in earlier correspondence. It seemed less crowded than some of the more popular hills as she trundled out of the shuttle and headed toward a crowd near the lift. She felt a bit like a mummy in the one-piece ski suit, her skis over her shoulder and poles in one hand. The heavy gloves would be a problem she thought. As she reached the crowd she stopped and practiced removing one glove, unzipping the top of her suit and reaching inside to the pocket of her jacket for the trusty gun. It would be difficult. She tried pulling her right arm inside the bulky suit leaving an empty sleeve hanging. That would look a bit strange she mused.

"Cold?" came a man's voice from just behind her.

"Oh…uh… no…. just trying to adjust this darn sweater," she lied as she pushed her arm back out through the sleeve and put on the glove.

"Been skiing a long time, I assume?" asked the man in obvious reference to her age.

"Over fifty years," she nodded with a smile. "Though not

recently."

"Forty for me," he chuckled, straightening up and beating himself on the chest. "And not recently for me either."

"Forty... really?" asked Rose beginning to glance around to look for familiar faces. "You don't look that old."

"Sixty-one," he said proudly. "Looking for your party?"

"No, I'm here alone," she said, still looking around. "Sometimes spot a familiar face."

"Yeah, guess you've been up here a lot."

"A few times years ago," she nodded while still studying the crowd, trying to see past people. She was looking for that familiar silver haired, tall slim figure with the penetrating blue eyes.

"You going all the way up?" he asked.

"Yes, but I may just be a bystander. I don't know right now," said Rose swinging her skis to the ground and clicking her boots into them.

"A bystander? No way," he scoffed reaching down to secure the fasteners on his skis.

"My knees have been acting up so I'm not sure how I'll feel on the skis. If it doesn't feel right, I may just doodle around on top and ride the lift down."

"Mind if I doodle with you?" he asked encouragingly.

"I prefer by myself."

"Sure," he smiled with a shrug as the line now placed them near the swinging chairs. She spotted an empty one and maneuvered out, then backed in as it came around. Her poles were laying in her lap. The man caught the lift behind her.

"The ride up is worth the price," he shouted from behind as the darkening evening mountain scene stretched out before

145

them.

"Nice," she yelled back.

"Do you like night skiing better?" he asked, now with a softer voice once he realized they could hear each other.

"Sometimes," she lied, having never night skied before.

"It'll be dark in a little less than an hour," he said glancing at his watch. "It's almost four thirty."

She looked at her watch. It had taken her longer to check in, rent skis and shuttle over. But she was sure that Clay skied at night. That was part of the celebration and this was the only hill with full lighting. She had asked about that. It was mentioned in the dossier, so this must be the hill he and his family would ski. His family.... and bodyguards...she remembered. 'Business associates' to his family who apparently did not know about the Dozen. There were a lot of other people, she thought, as she watched the lift in front of her and the ample scattering of skiers on the slopes below. As they approached the summit, she braced herself. She had not ridden a lift in more than five years, nor had she been on a pair of skis since then either. More like six or seven. As she touched, she swung out of the seat and glided effortlessly toward the skiers who were congregated in little groups ahead. The man fell in behind her and did not try to catch up, having given up on conversation well down on the lift. She stole a quick peek back to see if he was following and noticed he was angling off to another area. There were two young men with armbands ahead.

"Is there a gentle way down?" she asked with a smile as she approached.

"First time up here?" asked one of them, seeing her aged face and sounding somewhat apprehensive.

"I've been skiing for decades but am probably not up to the rigors of the big hill," she admitted.

"There's a section down the side over there," one of the men pointed. "You lose the good light in spots but some people go down at night. Were you going down now before it gets really dark?"

"I might," she nodded.

"That would be my advice," he said, giving her an animated nod in return. "Go while it's still a little light out."

"Thanks," she said with a little wave and slowly began to glide toward the area he had pointed to, all the while scanning the little groups for Clay and his clan. Off to her right she could see what appeared to be an extended family gathered around in a cluster. She aimed toward it but as she approached, she did not see his familiar face, so she continued on. Back toward the lift was a red and blue striped canopy with fold-up chairs and perhaps a dozen people of all ages laughing and milling around a table covered with bottles and containers of food. She glided in that direction and as she reached the cover of a tree, she could see them turn almost in unison in one direction as an elderly man trundled toward them with a red bag over his shoulder. He had on a red Santa's hat, but under the red and white felt was that distinctive nose and tiny cleft mustache. It was Clay. The group let out a cheer and began clapping as he strode up, the pillow under his red coat falling out just as he arrived in front of them. This resulted in uproarious laughter that seemed to echo across the entire hilltop. She could see other people stop to look toward the canopied party to see what was going on. Then they went

147

back to what they were doing. Behind and above the canopy was a snack bar with a large plate glass window. It overlooked the little party and Rose nodded to herself as she made a wide berth on her way to the group. She clicked off her skis and leaned them against the wall. She then went in. A seat was available at a bar against the window. She sat down and deposited her gloves, hat and goggles on the bar. She then went to the counter and returned a few minutes later with two hot dogs and a bottle of beer. She sat them down in front of her and stared at them for a moment before smiling. This was not exactly the type of meal she was used to, she mumbled to herself, as she squeezed mustard onto one of the hot dogs. But she was hungry and hadn't had time to stop running until now. The hot dogs were surprisingly good. Maybe, she was hungry, or maybe it was just because of where she was. The beer, which she almost never drank, actually tasted good.

It was the better part of an hour before she could see signs that the party under the striped canopy was breaking up. By then she had consumed the hot dogs and beer and gone on to a cup of hot chocolate and some kind of glazed roll in cellophane that tasted like nothing it was supposed to be. She collected her things and went outside. It was now noticeably colder and almost entirely dark. The floodlights on the white snow made the hill glow and created deep shadows where trees blocked them. Several men in white coveralls were busily boxing up what was left of the party. Most likely caterers she concluded since the main group was now migrating very slowly toward the hill. She followed, taking care to stay in the shadows as she did. As they neared the hill, Clay and two men started off to her left. Everyone stopped and a discussion ensued that appeared heated at times. Finally, Clay and the two men started to move away again, leaving the main group standing in a semi-circle. At length, they waved to Clay pointing toward the big hill as they began to move toward it. Clay waved them off and he and the two men continued in the other direction toward the easy hill. Rose followed Clay and the men. One was in front of Clay, the other behind. Bodyguards of course. She wondered how she would get past two husky young men who appeared to be excellent skiers and who would likely have Clay sandwiched between them on their way down the hill. Collateral damage she thought. There may be no other option. Otherwise, it was wait for another opportunity. No, she would play this one out. Up until now, the opportunities came quickly and cleanly and she had been able to take advantage of them. Perhaps she had been lucky before. She had been largely invisible because nobody suspected someone like her. Now it could be different. She would do her best. However, a big unknown at this moment was her skiing ability. It had been over five years since she'd been on the slopes. Seven if she was honest. Even though she exercised regularly and worked out at a gym, she knew she was not nearly as strong or agile as she had been years before, especially her ankles and knees that were critical on skis. But she would try.

Rose glided along behind them a good distance back. She looked down to adjust a strap on her poles and when she looked up she found she was closing in on them quickly. They had pulled to a halt and were huddled ahead talking. She smoothly and nonchalantly swung out in a wide berth along the wide approach to the back hill, well away from them. She kept her face nestled down and out of sight behind the collar of her outfit. What now, she thought catching a glimpse of them through the corner of her eye as she slid past and down into the first big, easy turn. She picked up speed and soon was coasting effortlessly down the hill. It was surprisingly easy, though the hill was gentle and the snow powdery.

As she made the turn, she glanced quickly back up the hill and could see the three breaking up and starting down the hill. Another glance a moment later saw the three beginning to spread out a bit. Maybe there was a hidden corner somewhere she thought as she scanned the area ahead. She straightened out on a long hill and sped up. She was going faster than she felt comfortable with but as she entered a flatter area she leaned into it with the edges and began cutting sweeps to slow down. The ruts jolted her knees and she began to feel the weakness that she knew she would have, although she didn't feel in danger of falling. Ahead was a sharp switchback flanked on all sides by tall, snow laden trees that cast dark shadows along the edges. The scattered light standards barely provided ample light to the area. She looked back and, not seeing them yet, hooked to a halt well up into the shade of a stand of trees. She held out her arm to see how bright her suit was in the shade, then nodded as she took off one glove, unzipped the top of her suit and reached in to put her hand around the pistol, keeping her hand inside as she scanned the hill for the oncoming trio. Hopefully, others would not venture down the hill this early. She thought about her next move. Maybe follow them. It depended on how close they were. What order? She spotted the top of a head. No cap. Gray hair. It was Clay. He was going first. Cautiously slow. Behind, the two men rocked back and forth, cutting S's in the hill, weaving their way down, carrying on some kind of conversation. She could hear their voices through the almost deafening silence of the snow. As they passed, she slowly fell in behind, keeping her distance. To her left, a break through the trees. A shortcut that would cut off the next big switchback ahead. She could see the lighted hill below through the dark corridor. In the center of the shortcut entrance, she saw a skier working his way down, trying to slow his ascent by making sharp turns. Off to her right she could see the backs of the two bodyguards disappearing down toward the main switchback. It could be Clay taking the shortcut. They could have missed his swerve as they chatted and could not easily get back to the Y. She turned quickly and tucked down, firing down the hill toward the man and catching up to him quickly. Her right hand was in her partly unzipped suit, the gun now in her hand, her pole cradled under her left arm. Ahead she could see the gray hair even in the pale light that filtered in from the standards on the main route. Orange suit. It had to be Clay. And this would have to be fast since she would pass him quickly. He was going half as fast as she and swooshing to her right. She aimed at the spot he would be, holding the gun out with her right hand, aiming at the gray head ahead. She was now almost upon him as he began to slowly make a turn which she matched. The gun was almost touching his head when she pulled the trigger, seeing red splash out into the pure white landscape like pieces of a smashed tomato as she shot past brushing his shoulder and feeling her skis pass over the back of his as he tumbled in a mass of poles, skis and body parts.

She placed the gun back, zipped up her suit and secured the

151

other pole as she aimed downhill, her glove still dangling from its tie, the cold air making her right hand almost numb. She was literally flying as the wind whistled past her head. She was going faster than she could ever remember, even when she was young and strong. Any unexpected bump or break in the snow would likely send her into a nasty tailspin. The main hill was just ahead through the shadows. She couldn't look back as she curved out onto the brightly lighted main route, feeling the ruts of other skiers rattling the edges of the skis as she began to swing into a wide curve to slow down. As she curved back, she glanced back up the hill and could see two dots farther up. Then, she took a double take and nearly fell as she could now see a third figure in front of them. A third. Had she just shot the WRONG person. She refocused on getting down the hill without ending up in a broken heap as she cut large sweeping curves to lower her speed. She was careful not to slow too much. A quick glance over her shoulder and she saw the three dots on the hill now converged at the Y with the shortcut route. Another glance and one of the figures was starting down the hill. A few minutes later she could see the figure getting much closer in a tuck position aiming directly down the hill toward her. She straightened her course to pick up speed again but another glance a moment later told her he was gaining fast. She was sure she could not outrun him and began to think about what would happen when he caught up. Just as she heard the scraping of his skis on the snow behind her, a figure appeared to her right from behind a tree. This was followed by the loud cutting of ski blades, a loud thumping noise, the sound of skis scraping and bodies thumping into the snow. Then a lot of shouting. A quick glance back saw two men tangled in the ice and snow, their skis shooting aimlessly in all directions. The lodge was just ahead and she was entering the lower slope where a scattering of beginners were slowly angling about, toe in with the skis. Around the lodge the shuttle was loading passengers. In an instant she was there, clicking out of her skis and now seated in the shuttle, looking constantly at the corner of the lodge for signs of the pursuing skier. The shuttle pulled away.

"Got nicked a little did you?" asked the young woman next to her.

"What?" asked Rose, not sure what the woman was referring to.

"See you got a few spots of blood on your nice white suit," she pointed as Rose looked down onto her left shoulder and could see the spray of blood that obviously came from Clay's head.

"Oh, look at that," said Rose in surprise. "Nosebleed."

"How......?" the woman began.

"I get them up here and the wind does weird things when you're going fast and the blood is gushing," Rose manufactured.

"Hmmm," the woman said raising her eyebrows and looking away. "Try soda water when you get back to your hotel."

"Thanks, I will," said Rose thinking quickly of the problem of when she returned the rental with the blood stains. I'll just throw them away, she thought. Already paid the deposit in cash. Skis too. No, I'll put the skis in the car. No, too awkward. I'll just leave them in my room. Room service will know what to do with them. Others have forgotten to return their skis. It wouldn't attract attention.

A half hour later Rose was sitting in her car. The suit was put

153

into a black laundry bag and deposited in the big dumpster behind the parking garage. She had given the license plate number to the hotel so she could park in the garage. She got out, opened the trunk and with a screwdriver took off the Pennsylvania plates and put on the Maine plates, then got back in and was soon back on the 70 heading west.

Again, too easy, she thought. Literally the first opportunity. But had she taken out the right man? It certainly looked like Clay. But who was the third man on the slope with the two bodyguards? Another bodyguard? A stand-in….someone dressed up to look like Clay. Why had one of them suddenly started after her at full tilt? And who was the person who seemed to wander out of nowhere to trip up the pursuer? It was all very strange. And once again she was able to get away quickly and smoothly. Too smoothly. She turned on the radio.

"This just in," came the voice about a half hour later, interrupting a news broadcast. "There has been a shooting on the slopes at Vail. Witnesses say an elderly man was fatally shot shortly after five thirty PM as he skied down the mountain. Sources say he was pronounced dead at the scene apparently from a bullet wound to the head from a small caliber pistol. The name of the victim is being withheld pending notification of next of kin. Officials at the scene had no comment on possible motive or suspects or whether the killer was still in the area. A roadblock has been set up on Interstate 70, both eastbound and westbound."

Rose clicked off the radio, looking intently ahead to see if she could see the red tail lights from braking cars. Fifteen minutes. Still no road block. Where is it, she thought. It had been over forty five minutes since she pulled out of the parking garage. The body must have been discovered before she left. The three men on the slope knew something had happened, even without working their way back up to the shortcut. That's why one of them came after her. So the police must have set up the roadblock quickly. But where? She was almost fifty miles from Vail by now. Perhaps it had been behind her somewhere and she was past it. She smiled and leaned back. But all of a sudden, ahead, she saw a sea of red tail lights. The roadblock.

Rose looked frantically for a side road to pull onto. There was no way off the highway with its wall of snow lining both sides. She fumbled with the radio dial, scanning for some station.... and getting nothing. Slowing, she looked for room on the side of the road to pull over. Sweat was beginning to form on her brow. Her mind was racing. Did she have anything in the car that was incriminating. The gun, of course. She could feel it in her pocket next to her breast. Registration on the car. What was it? What if they asked? Her driver's license, Ohio. Plates, Maine. Same lie as in Pennsylvania. But the roadblock. They must know who they're looking for. Man dressed as a woman? No, that was an email from one of the group. Did the authorities suspect a man dressed as a woman? Why else would they put up a roadblock? She was at the end of the line of cars. Stopped. There were cars now behind her, blocking her. She was trapped. It was too late now. A rap on the window caused her to jump. She looked up. It was the man she had met in the line for the lift. She pushed the button to put down the window a crack.

"You," she said, acknowledging that they had met on the slopes.

"I've got a favor to ask," he said sheepishly.

"I don't understand," said Rose, shaking her head. Her mind was still racing. She was focused on her dilemma.

"My significant other refuses to ride with me another minute....," he said motioning back to the car behind with his thumb. "I need a ride..... I mean..... if you don't mind.....?"

"Uhhh," Rose stumbled, looking ahead as the line began to move. She then looked back out at him and finally nodded.

"Only if you'll drive," she said, quickly, just as he started around to the other side.

"Uh, sure," he nodded, getting in as she struggled to move across the console into the passenger seat. A moment later they were settled.

"Thanks, I really appreciate this," he said, seeing the traffic ahead begin to move and putting it in gear.

"Sure," she replied, knowing that it was her who owed the thanks.

"And at the checkpoint, I'm your what?" the man shrugged with a smile.

"Where are you from?" she asked.

"A very long way off," he snickered as he moved forward again with the line.

"Where?" she insisted.

"New York," he said, looking at her.

"Perfect," she nodded.

"What's going on up ahead anyway?" he asked, trying to see past the long line to the front that was perhaps fifty cars and an eighth of a mile ahead.

"I'm not sure but it looks like some kind of inspection or

156

something."

"Interesting."

"So, who do I say I am?" he asked.

"I'm your new significant other."

"OK," he nodded, looking at her for a moment.

"I'm ten years older than you…."

"A well preserved ten," he smiled.

"If I close my eyes, turn my head and pretend I'm asleep, I think I might look much younger," she suggested. He watched her with a serious expression, then nodded as he looked ahead and moved forward with the line.

"OK."

"I don't want to embarrass you."

"Sure, I can handle the interview…. whatever it involves….. uh, let's see, we came together across the country. We're on our way to Las Vegas, then Los Angeles. We live together…. where?"

"Maine."

"I still have a business in New York."

"That's good."

"You're totally exhausted from a long day and we're trying to make it to St. George for the night."

"OK…. what's your name."

"Henry."

"Rose," she said without thinking. But she had to tell him. She couldn't use an alias. It was on her driver's license. She dug out the registration for the car and read it. Rose Baker. She stared at it for a moment in surprise. Clancy was very thorough. Amazing since she did not recall giving him that information. Perhaps she did. She must have. Didn't matter now. But her real name could be a problem. It was too late now to do anything about it.

"OK, Rose, so is that where we're going for the night? Las Vegas."

"First things first," she said. "Tell me if I look a lot younger when I scrunch down and turn my head to tighten the skin on my cheek and neck."

"Yeah, you do.... very good," he said after she had situated herself and he had an opportunity to see her. "You look forty."

"Don't try to flatter me," she mumbled without opening her eyes.

"Actually, I'm not.... you look forty.... you look very, very good...."

"I'm going to stay like this until we get through. If they ask for my I.D., I'll leave my purse open on the console. My wallet is just inside. Show them my driver's license. My picture was taken ten years ago and it was a very flattering picture then....talked the lady at the DMV into keeping it."

"I wouldn't be embarrassed if they thought you were older," he commented.

"Just go with it," she said abruptly.

"You got it," he said.

A few minutes later Rose could hear the window lowering and voices. One of the officers shined a flashlight on her and she could see the brightness through her eyelids.

"OK, drive carefully, there's a new storm on the way," came the officer's voice and she could feel the car moving forward. A moment later they were at freeway speed and she sat up.

"Did they say what it was all about?" she asked.

"No they didn't," he said. "You don't mind if I ride with you as far as Vegas do you?"

"Not at all," she sighed, feeling the weight of the crisis lifting from her shoulders.

"It was going downhill for some time," he said.

"What was?"

"My relationship."

"Is that why you were by yourself on the slopes."

"Yeah. She's twenty years younger than me, you know."

"No, I didn't know."

"She just went to the lodge when I was on the slopes. She was at the bar."

"Oh."

"I saw it coming, I guess. Just too many things not in common. Except, well, you know...."

"No, what?"

"Uh, well, in bed.... we had that....."

"OK...got it.....you don't have to...."

"Well, at least I thought it was."

"So what are you going to do now?"

"I don't know, maybe spend a few days in Vegas, then catch a plane back to the Apple."

"Why don't we just try to drive through to Vegas without stopping,"

She asked.

"That's sort of what I figured, too," he nodded. "I mean.... I really appreciate this. It was.... uh, shall we say, rather convenient of you to just be there and me.... well, needing a ride like that."

"Yes, convenient," said Rose, staring at the highway ahead,

159

brownish black against the white all around. Convenient. Very convenient. Another coincidence? Henry showing up just when she needed a cover. At exactly the right moment, there he was. Convenient. Too convenient. Her mind raced with the possibilities. But who? And why? How could anyone know what she was doing or know her plan or even know who was on her list. How could someone, anyone, manage to be there, follow her, or stay close enough to be there at the right moment. Then there was the mysterious skier who just happened to get in front of the pursuing bodyguard. Then Henry. All to essentially help her to get away with it. It was not just this time but also in Florida. And before? Was all that a coincidence? Perhaps. Atlanta. The young black guy. He was there at just the right time. Even the patrol car in Pennsylvania. Perhaps. Perhaps not. Maybe all of this IS just a coincidence. It's possible. But whatever was going on, she no longer had the luxury of anonymity, at least to what was left of the Dozen and now probably the authorities. Another case where a woman could have been involved somehow. They could know who they're looking for or at least have a description. A thin elderly woman. Or man dressed as a woman. What if they were piecing it together and were actually looking for Judd Baker's sister? Rose. Her. Knowing that she might match the description of someone seen at some of the crime scenes. And what if they had tried to contact her and weren't able to find her. More suspicion? She had clearly been seen in Florida. In New York...maybe that man with the laptop in the hall could have noticed her and reported it. Then at Vail. Probably not in Pittsburgh nor Maine. She was there with the wives of the two she took out in Seattle. That has to be suspicious. There were a

160

lot of pieces that could add up for even an average investigator, if there is an investigator and if they had connected the killings as the Dozen had in their emails. It was still possible that they hadn't done that yet even though the Dozen were eventually well aware of what was going on. Were the authorities? Had they confided their plight with the authorities? Clearly they should have. No, again, pride, arrogance and the honor of the secret society and its purpose most likely would have kept them from going to the authorities. This she knew. Her mind was spinning. There were too many questions and no clear answers. Her only strategy was to continue and be more cautious, knowing that they are likely looking for a thin elderly woman matching her description. Or equally bad, a man dressed up like an elderly woman. Just as damning. Maybe a disguise would be in order. But what? A younger woman, perhaps. That would be a trick. How would she hide all the wrinkles and her stiffness? How about dressing like a man? A beard. Hat. Men's clothes? An old woman dressed up like an old man! Yes, that's what she would try to do in Vegas. She would get a hotel and disappear into the lights and noise. She would find a disguise. There should be costume stores in Vegas.

"We can trade off at the wheel every few hours," said Rose.

"Sounds reasonable....I think it's about 400 miles from here, plus or minus," said Henry.

"So what's that, six or seven hours with stops for food and gas?"

"Something like that. We should be there just before dawn if we go all night."

"That's fine with me," said Rose. "Let's just push on. Nobody cares in Vegas what time you get in, so wee hours is not a problem. Everything is twenty four seven."

A few hours later Henry pulled onto the shoulder and asked Rose to drive for a while. She slid behind the wheel and they continued on.

"I'm going to try to catch a nap," he said, slumping down in the seat and closing his eyes. She studied him for a moment, then stared ahead into the monotony of the highway at night.

Chapter 13

It was just before five in the morning when Henry pulled the car into the entry drive of a large hotel shaped like a pyramid. Luxor, said the banner. He had taken over driving again just an hour earlier and felt refreshed. Rose was asleep. A doorman came out and opened the passenger side door as Rose awoke with a start, then began clearing the sleep from her eyes.

"Thank you," she said, hesitating a moment, then slowly stepped out into the cool morning air and zipped up her jacket in response to the chill.

"Do you have reservations?" he asked, still holding the door, looking first at Henry who looked away, then at her.

"No we don't... why, is the hotel full?" asked Rose as she walked past the man.

"Uh....I don't...." The man shrugged as he turned to face her back as she walked away.

She went up the long entryway, pushed through the large

double glass doors and walked toward a large counter straight ahead over an unusually large expanse where the ceiling rose over 100 feet above. Henry trailed behind after instructing the doorman to park their car for them.

"We need a room," she announced as she reached the counter.

"Yes mam," said the man positioning himself behind a computer screen. Henry came up behind her and stood at her shoulder, his tall six foot four frame suddenly apparent to Rose for the first time as he loomed above.

"Will that be a King or two doubles?" asked the man behind the counter looking first at Rose, then at Henry.

"Two separate rooms," said Rose.

"Actually, I won't be able to stay," said Henry, shrugging as she turned to look up at him. "The place has some bad memories for me."

"Oh, I see.....well, I'm sorry," said Rose somewhat apologetically. "Can I drive you....."

"No, actually, there's a nice place just across the way that I've stayed at before called the MGM Grand. I'll just walk over," he said pointing toward a long, wide corridor that disappeared out the end of the massive room.

"Are you sure?" asked Rose.

"Yeah, I'm sure. And I thank you so much for the ride. You saved my life, quite literally."

"Well....no.....thank YOU," said Rose, nodding. She knew it was he who actually saved her from being detained and likely caught. In a very strange way, she was sad to see him leave as he turned with a little salute and slowly faded into the light crowd in the corridor. She stared after him for a moment before turning to sign in. This time it would be Sandra. Sandra Brent.

In her room Rose pulled out her computer but decided not to access Clay's email site. By now, someone would likely have changed the site or password or both and what if they could somehow trace her to the hotel if she were able to sign on. Instead she opened the dossier of her next target, John Becket, Palm Springs. He was in poor health. He lived with his daughter and an in-home nurse. Somewhat of a recluse. Rarely left home, which was a forty-acre ranch on the outskirts of town. She wondered if he had heeded the warnings that must have reached him by now. Warnings that he could possibly be next. His profile suggested that he would likely dig in rather than run. Stay at home. Maybe hire extra bodyguards. Perhaps arm himself. He was a decorated Army colonel. Full bird. A gun collector and still active in a gun club. She wondered how he did that in such poor health. He apparently used a cane and sometimes a wheelchair. He was likely very stubborn. She had only met him once years before at a function in Kansas City. He had a crew cut then. He was not a tall man. Maybe five six. Slim. But a look that was tough as nails. Yeah, he would dig in. He wasn't going to run anywhere. The question was, how was she going to get to him, especially now that her innocent old lady cover was likely blown. She would give the little-old-man-with-a-beard disguise a try and come up with a scheme. But she had to do it fast. There was no time to sit around and carefully plan anything. She had a few more stops on her mission. John Becket was just the next on her list. Number ten.

It was noon before Rose awoke. She had slept for six hours. She had not eaten since the all-night Burger King back somewhere on the 15 around midnight except, of course, for the chocolate donut she picked up in the lobby of the hotel on her way to her room. She dialed room service and a while later a full breakfast was delivered. As she sat sipping her coffee, she looked through the yellow pages, finally stopping at a costume shop. She finished her breakfast, showered and walked down to the lobby, a page that she had torn from the phone book in her pocket. She asked for her car and while it was being delivered inquired about the cross streets where the costume shop was located. A moment later she was off down the strip toward the older part of town. After what seemed a long drive through first the newer resort areas, then past the older casinos, she spotted the logo that was in the phone book and pulled up outside.

"May I help you?" asked a young woman with wire rimmed glasses and a harsh face with thin lips that glistened with a bright red lipstick.

"Looking for a beard, nose and prospector's outfit for my brother."

"Prospector's outfit," the woman repeated, furrowing her brow in thought. "OK. I can do the beard and the nose. I might have to do some substitution on the prospector's duds, though."

"Let's see what you've got…make it small size," said Rose with a shrug. The woman nodded and walked down an isle stacked high on both sides with boxes full of masks and other costume paraphernalia. A moment later she threw a selection of beards, rubber noses, hats, coats and trousers on the counter.

"Wow," said Rose looking at the collection and beginning to paw through it. "Do you have glue or something to make the beard and the nose stick?"

"Yes, and something to make the nose blend too," said the woman. Rose nodded.

"I like the plaid shirt and trousers with the red suspenders but do you have some even smaller sizes. My brother isn't much bigger than I am."

"I think I might, but you might do better at Target or one of the department stores on the clothes," the woman admitted.

"No, I'll take this beard, this nose, a shirt like this in the smallest size you have, this pair of trousers with the suspenders, also in your smallest size and how about that scruffy jeans jacket?"

"I got that in a small somewhere," said the woman.

"Great," Rose nodded.

"Anything else?"

"No, that's fine," said Rose, peeling off bills as she surveyed the tags on each of the items while adding up the total in her head.

Back in the car, she drove toward the outskirts of town looking for used car lots. Off to her right was a lot with a row of pickup trucks. She pulled over, got out and walked to a red Ford that looked at least twenty years old, scrapes along one side, faded paint, gun rack in the rear window, mud flaps and sheepskin covers on the seats.

"Nice little truck," came a voice from beside her. She hadn't seen the salesman sneak up on her and started a bit in surprise.

"It's a little beat....no, it's a lot beat....what's it worth?" she asked.

"Do you got a trade?" he asked.

"That Ford Focus there. Only four years old with low miles. Worth a lot more than this truck, but I need a truck. I don't need the Focus."

"For a few thou difference, you could drive off in that truck."

"Me pay you? You have to be kidding....you do know how to make people laugh don't you?" she scoffed.

"Well how much would you be willing to pay....?"

"Nada," she said, shaking her head. "I was thinking you would owe me."

"I don't really do business that way," he shuffled. "This is a very nice little truck and trucks hold their value much better than cars, especially a Focus."

"Don't get me pissed off," she shot back. "Fords do well with value....I think straight across would be the best deal you've had in here in the past year, especially for this old wreck."

"Straight across?" he asked, taking a little step back from her.

"Yeah, I'd be willing to sacrifice. Mine's worth twice what this truck is worth. No, three times...straight across or I walk."

"Hmmmm. You got a title?"

"I got a title," she nodded, having spotted the forged title in the glove compartment. It was the title that Clancy had somehow manufactured instantaneously.

"What is it....Maine?"

"Ohio."

"Maine plates, Ohio title?"

"That's right," she nodded without explanation.

"Get the title, come in the office and we'll work a deal," said the man, pointing to a green roofed shack near the back of the lot. She nodded, went to the car and retrieved the title that Clancy had placed in the glove box, then went to the trunk and wrapped the two sets of license plates in a rag and put them in her bag. A half hour later she rattled out onto the strip in her red pickup sporting a temporary Nevada sticker with her suitcase piled in the back. This will do, just in case they are looking for the white Focus, she thought. Very soon it will be driven by a wiry old man with a beard in bib overalls with red suspenders.... and a scruffy jeans jacket.

Rose parked the truck in the hotel self park lot and walked, carrying her bag with the disguise. The red pickup was her new transportation, and the fewer who knew of it the better. In her room she sat in front of a mirror at a dressing table and began experimenting with the nose and beard. She trimmed the beard a little with fingernail clippers and then tied her hair back in a bun. She also needed a hat. Perhaps, a baseball cap. She carefully removed the nose and beard and went down into the lobby to the gift shop. She returned a while later with a plain blue Dodger's cap that had been pre-faded to look worn. It matched well with the faded jean's jacket. She then tied a small blanket around her midriff just below her breasts and above her hips. It filled out her torso and provided a more straight-bodied masculine shape. It would work, she mused looking in the full length mirror on the closet door.

It was four o'clock. Maybe too late to leave tonight. Palm Springs was about a five hour drive. She would leave the next morning. No, why not leave now? Catch a quick dinner on the way out of town and make it there before midnight. Then be ready to go the next morning. She packed up her disguise and her bag and went downstairs and out the back door to the covered lot, slinging the suitcase into the back of the pickup when she reached it. Just out of town, she pulled over to the side of the road and put on the Florida plates that she had retrieved from her car after she traded it. Hopefully she would not be stopped since there would be no match between plates and vehicle. A half hour later she was eating a pre-frozen dinner at a little chain diner.

*****

Rose had never stopped in Palm Springs before despite having traveled through it on the freeway a number of times in the past. She expected it to be alive with nightlife but it was eerily quiet as she cruised down the main street at just past eleven that evening. The red truck had proven to be a relatively comfortable vehicle for the trip which was a pleasant surprise. She had traveled mostly on secondary highways to Palm Springs, since there were no major routes directly from Vegas, just the last stretch on I-10. She was, nonetheless, ready for a motel room. A loop back through town on the one-way couplet turned up an inauspicious little place just off the arterial with a vacancy sign blinking. It took several loud knocks to raise the night clerk, but the elderly man finally came out, obviously awakened from a nap. In a little while she was pulling her red truck into the carport alongside one of the semi-detached units. An old-fashioned western motel she thought, remembering much earlier times when she had seen one like it near Yellowstone on a vacation. It seemed to fit the red pickup and also the old bearded man with the Dodger's cap who would be driving it tomorrow.

Inside, Rose reviewed the dossier again, studying a map of the town that she had picked up at a filling station off the freeway. She then located his address and her motel on her laptop. Google maps was a godsend on this adventure. It appeared to be about seven miles from where she was now. She would do a reconnaissance run in the morning just to get a feel for the area and the approaches to the ranch. On the drive down from Vegas, she had contrived an approach for getting close to Becket's spread. She knew he had a cousin, about seventy, who lived in Lone Pine California, up in the high country of the eastern Sierra. He lived alone. Jake Carmody was his name. One approach would be to say she was Jake Carmody and was just dropping through and wanted to visit with John while he was here. She wasn't sure if John Becket had seen him recently and was relatively sure that his bodyguards, if he had any, would not have. The dossier gave no indication of when or even if they had ever visited one another. She doubted it, but she would just have to assume that he hadn't recently. Although, on the other hand, they are likely to be suspicious of just about anything out of the ordinary and would, for sure, be on the lookout regardless of what tactic she chose. She knew she couldn't just drive up and pretend she were lost. That was too obvious. She could try to sneak up through the desert, but she was not physically capable of those kinds of maneuvers anymore. He apparently didn't leave the grounds often so she would have to come to him. He could not come to her. The Carmody scenario was worth a try.

The next morning, Rose got up at sunrise and drove down the road that went past Becket's ranch. The main buildings were more than a quarter mile from the highway, nestled in a low area that was green with vegetation, contrasting sharply with the desert landscape that surrounded the compound. Even from this distance she could see three cars outside and assumed other cars too in what looked like two detached garages. There appeared to be an entrance gate with a small guardhouse about halfway down the long drive. She started down the drive and stopped just below the rise and out of sight of the ranch and the guardhouse. She looked at her watch. It was seven thirty. Why not, she thought. Why come back later? It would either work or it wouldn't work. Waiting an hour or two shouldn't matter.

Beside the road, using the rearview mirror, Rose donned the beard, the nose and the rest of the disguise and then got out to straighten up. The tennis shoes were the only thing that didn't work very well, but overall it seemed good. Her voice was naturally raspy so it might not be an immediate giveaway. She practiced a few lines. Maybe just naturally, without trying to modify it. That sounded better than attempting to deepen it. Deeping it sounded fake. She checked herself in the side mirror, then started over the rise in the truck. A minute later she pulled up to the locked gate in front of the guardhouse. A man who was slumped low in the guardhouse sat up when he heard her approach, then walked out to greet her as she pulled up.

"Can I help you?" asked the man in a thick latino accent, a sidearm strapped to his beltline.

"Is this the John Becket ranch?" she asked.

"Yes, do you have business here?" he asked.

"I'm his cousin Jake from up in Lone Pine," she smiled, pointing north and nodding.

"Is Mr. Becket expecting you?" he asked.

"No, no, I'm just down this way and wanted to look him up before he kicks the bucket," she laughed. The guard furled his brow and gave her a forced smile back, raising his eyebrow.

"Could you let him know I'm here?" she asked, shrugging.

172

"Uhh, I'll call down," said the guard, hesitating a moment before walking back into the shack and picking up a phone. After a short conversation, he returned.

"Mr. Becket's at breakfast and can't be disturbed," he said.

"What do you mean.....he's just eatin' breakfast and can't even acknowledge his cousin?" she asked incredulously.

"He's strict about not being disturbed at breakfast time," he nodded.

"Call back and tell him I'm hungry and ask if I can join him for breakfast..... Jake.....cousin Jake from Californ eye ay."

"Californ eye ay," the guard repeated, slowly retreating to the shack and delivering the message. He returned shaking his head.

"Someuns comin' out to escort you in," he said as if disappointed in the outcome. It was a full ten minutes before a van with blackened windows pulled up and a stubby man with tight curly hair got out and started her way. He waddled as he came up to her.

"You cousin Jake?" he asked. She nodded.

"Come with me," he gestured, pointing to his open van where another man sat in the passenger's seat. Both had side arms that were clearly visible. She followed him and got into the back seat as he slid the door open and pointed. She got in, feeling the pistol in her hand inside the jean's jacket pocket. As they drove down a corridor of tall grass and shrubs that abutted the road, Rose pulled out the gun and put it to the head of the man in the passenger's seat and pulled the trigger. Then quickly turned it to the driver's head, just as he turned toward the bloody mess beside him. She pulled the trigger, simultaneously grabbing the slumping body by the shoulder and pulling him back from

173

the wheel as the van drifted into the pampas grass. It thudded to a halt against a bed of large rocks with a tin bending crunch. She calmly got out of the van and started down the road on foot. Necessary collateral damage she thought as she strode quickly along. Ahead she could see the open area in front of the main structures of the ranch. One white car was parked by itself on the circular road. To her left was a thicket of bougainvillea stretching nearly to the porch of what looked like the main house that sprawled in a semi-circle with seemingly no windows. There was just a rose colored stucco facade, broken with half walls, planting boxes and landscaping of desert plants. There was no entrance in front that she could see.

Rose walked behind the bougainvillea on a strip of bare earth, wet from a morning watering. When she reached the end of the house, a narrow nearly overgrown walkway was visible leading to the back. She followed it to a gate. Beyond, across a garden area bounded by fish ponds, was a red door with ornate extruded brass hinges. She slipped through the gate, across the garden with its quaint wooden bridge to the door. She slowly turned the knob and opened it a crack, peeking in and listening. When she heard nothing she opened it more, poking her head in. The bright cream-tiled vestibule was empty and she could not hear a sound. She tiptoed in. To her right was a hallway. Ahead, there were two doors. She started quietly but quickly down the hall. As she moved forward she began to hear noises and soon could make out voices somewhere in the distance. Ahead was a large room and as she approached, she could see shadows and what appeared to be a conversation between a man and a woman. The man's voice was quiet, almost weak. The woman's voice was soft, but strong. Rose stopped short of the room, then crept forward, stopping again as a figure came into view. It was the back of a man sitting in a wheelchair. He was a slight man with a bow in his back. It had to be Becket. Across the room, a woman was standing looking out the window into a courtyard holding a cup. She put the cup down and walked across the room, opening a door, going in and shutting the door behind her. From the mirror inside, Rose guessed it was a bathroom. Rose moved quickly and quietly forward with the gun drawn. When she was a foot away, she squeezed off two shots. Blood spattered forward onto the man's bright blue and white blanket, his body slumped to a doubled up position, head on his knees, but not falling out of his wheelchair. She turned immediately and retraced her steps down the hall, running through the red door, out through the garden, back up the overgrown sidewalk to the corner of the house.

A white Lincoln Town car sat in the drive. She looked both ways to see if anyone was present, seeing no one she walked to the car and opened the door. It was unlocked. A keychain with keys lay in the front seat. How convenient she thought, almost shaking her head at how convenient it really was. She got in, looked for the Ford logo on the keys, started it and drove back out past the van with the two dead bodyguards in it. As she approached the guardhouse, the gate the guard jumped up, looking confused, then squinted to try to see who was behind the wheel. Gun in hand, Rose lowered the window as the gate guard came over to her side. He obviously could not make out who she was through the dark windows. As he walked up, a surprised look came over his face, but it was the last thought he would have. The bullet went through his forehead and he just staggered back and fell into the shallow ditch on the side of the road across from the guardhouse. Rose got out, climbed into her red truck and drove away. Three items of collateral damage she said to herself, shaking her head. It could be like that for the final two. Only two left. One in Los Angeles - the other in Mexico. Or perhaps they had fled. Surely these last two will flee and not stick around after finding out about Becket and three of his guards. At least she hadn't had to take out the woman who was with him. She was his daughter, most likely, according to the dossier. She visited often and seemed about the right age or, perhaps, she was the in-home caregiver. In any event, she was spared by the call of nature.

Rose drove back toward town. On the way she passed two police cars with sirens and lights flashing, followed a moment later by a Medic One truck racing after them. She drove coolly through town and out onto the 10 toward Los Angeles, only a few hours away. Next stop, Marina del Rey. George Bundy. Number twelve.

Chapter 14

The room was poorly lighted with a single window high near the end. There was a dark curtain over the window. In the middle of the room was a large rosewood table surrounded by molded swivel chairs upholstered in a plain blue fabric. Seven men and a woman sat at the table. Against the wall, sitting at the end of a row of gray fold-up chairs, was an eighth man smoking a cigarette. He seemed to be shielding it from view as he drew in the smoke and blew it through the side of his mouth off toward the wall at the end of the room. The thin man at the head of the table looked up at the row of yellow ceiling lights and, noticing the blue cloud drifting across the glow, turned to the man with the cigarette.

"Jesus Christ, Chuck, you know fucking well there's no smoking in here!" he bellowed in a deep voice that seemed to careen off the bare walls and echo to every corner.

"I didn't think...." Chuck began after having looked up with a nervous jerk.

"If you want to kill yourself for god's sake, stick your fucking head in a paper bag with that goddamn cigarette and suffocate.... but leave the rest of us out of it," the thin man shot back before Chuck could finish his reply.

"Uh, yeah... fine...." said Chuck, quickly dropping the cigarette to the floor and grinding it into the gold carpet with his heel.

"Fuck! fuck! fuck!" yelled the thin man turning around and glaring at Chuck whose eyes were now wide open in confusion about what he had done now.

"The goddamn carpet you moron!" said the thin man, pointing to the black smudge on the gold carpet. "The goddamn carpet!" he repeated.

"Oh, geez," said Chuck with a pained expression, shrugging and shaking his head then reaching down to try to rub out the black spot with his thumb.

"Why don't you come to the table and join the rest of us now that you've destroyed the carpet and fouled the air in here," the thin man grumbled, turning back to the table. All eyes were on Chuck, a few with smiles at the little foray. Chuck got up hesitatingly and walked over to the table, sitting at the far end from the thin man who shook his head in disgust.

"I think we can assume at this point that it's more than one person," said the thin man after Chuck was settled.

"Possibly," said the woman with a raised eyebrow.

"How could one person do what they've done without some help?" asked the man next to her who had stopped chewing his gum long enough to speak.

"Someone with inside knowledge of the victims... someone who knew the victims well enough to know their habits and patterns," she replied reaching for the glass of water in front of her.

"I agree it's possible," said the thin man. "But it could be a man disguised as an elderly woman."

"Why is that?" asked the woman.

"What better disguise?" he shrugged. "And have you ever heard of a sweet little old lady doing something like this?"

"OK, right, yes, this is clearly not a sweet little old lady," said the woman. "It's someone with a purpose, determination and ability to carry it out."

"It's classic gangland assassination," said a ruddy-faced man with short blonde hair, his body bulging from a suit that was a size too small.

"Maybe," said the woman. "Or maybe someone who is very meticulous about what they do. Very careful and also very very clever."

"All of those," said the thin man. "But I'm convinced it's a man in disguise."

"Why a 22 caliber handgun?" asked the woman.

"Just a weapon of choice I suppose," said the thin man.

"Well, whoever it is, man or woman, they seem to be one step ahead of us and we have no idea where they're going to strike next," said the man with the ruddy complexion.

"Most likely West Coast next if we follow the path, but where?" asked the thin man, nodding. "And who? We still can't seem to connect the victims except for some kind of conservative club thing that we've managed to find out about."

"The conservative club thing may well be our common element," said the woman. "Question is, how big is this 'club'?" she hung her fingers in a quote sign. "We seem to be short on details about who they are and what they do."

"Is it important? This club thing?" asked the thin man.

"Might be a clue to the motive," said the woman.

"So you've got a theory, Cathy?" asked the thin man.

"I don't have one right now, but someone who knows these victims must be able to tell us more than they have," she shrugged. "We've gotten nothing about the group from the family members and almost nothing from the two wives in Seattle. Just that it's some kind of conservative club. I believe they know a lot more than what we've gotten so far from them."

"We haven't gotten dick from them, so far," said the thin man. "The one has had a nervous breakdown, and is now living with the other one, and she's protecting her like a mother hen."

"I agree they must know more," said the man with the ruddy complexion. "Those first murders were different than the rest. It was almost as if someone were on the boat with them that they knew. It's a stretch to imagine someone in a diving outfit climbing aboard and then just getting away like that. Something is fishy there."

"I tend to agree," the thin man nodded pensively. "Cathy, get back up there and try that interview again. Maybe you can get through to them. Ed here wasn't able to get anywhere on two separate occasions."

"Hey, I could only do so much," said the man with the ruddy complexion. "They refused, and I couldn't break their door down. I had help from the local authorities too, so it wasn't just me. I did all I could do..."

"I'm not indicting you, Ed. I'm just reassigning the job to someone else," said the thin man. "Maybe a different face, a different approach....a woman.... I don't know...."

"I know," Ed huffed, looking away.

"Chuck, you go with Cathy," said the thin man. Chuck nodded. "I want something to go on, we're running out of time. This maniac is likely to strike at any moment and we have no clue who we're looking for or where he or she will hit next."

"Maybe Los Angeles," said Chuck with a shrug.

"Right, there's only fifteen million people there so we can go door to door," said the thin man sarcastically.

"We need a list of people on that conservative club," said Cathy. "I'm completely amazed that we haven't been able to come up with a list. Why haven't the victims' family members given it to us? What's so secret about it?"

"They don't seem to know, or more likely won't tell," the thin man shrugged.

"So these guys -- the victims -- are all members of some conservative group...club....whatever....and the only way we have to find out who else is next on the list is to wait for the victim to get toe-tagged?" asked Chuck, finally chiming in.

"The Seattle wives obviously know about the group, but seem to be silent about how big it is or even a single member's name," said Ed.

"And none of the other family members that we've managed to contact don't know either?" asked Chuck.

"Correct, it seems to be a secret group, yet they must know something about the other members," said the thin man shaking his head. "I absolutely cannot believe that they are totally in the dark. Not for one minute. They're all holding out information. The spouses HAVE to know something."

"What are we going to do torture them until they tell us?" asked Chuck. "They're not talking."

"It's like the mob or something," said the man with the ruddy complexion.

"It is," said the thin man. "Exactly like the mob. Apparently sacred honor and all of that. Right down to the family members."

"Maybe it IS the mob," said a man sitting next to Chuck.

"No way, not this one," said Cathy. "These people are not in the mob. They're very distinguished, upstanding citizens. Backgrounds on the deceased indicate nothing of the sort. But something is truly odd here. Surely whatever they do couldn't be so important and secretive that it cannot be revealed even if it costs its members their lives..... could it?"

"I don't know, but so far it seems to be and that's why we need to get more information," said the thin man.

"Someone will eventually spill," said Cathy. "I'm hoping it's one of the two widows up in Seattle. I hope they spill not only about who the group is and what they do-- or did-- but give us a lead as to who it is that's out there trying to eliminate them."

"What bothers me most about this whole thing is that the victims are all old," said the thin man. "They are in their late sixties, seventies and eighties. Some of them are even disabled due to age and disease. So why now? They're all mostly retired and they couldn't be that active in whatever it might have been that they were involved with. So why now? I don't get it."

"I don't either," said Cathy. "But there's obviously something that they may have done in the past that has pissed someone off a whole lot....enough to pay them back by executing them...that's pretty pissed off!"

"Agreed.... well, see what you can dig up in Seattle and do it ASAP, we've got to move quickly on this thing," said the thin man. "The clock is ticking on us. We don't know how many more lives are at stake." With that he stood, prompting everyone else to get up and within minutes the room was empty except for Cathy and the thin man.

"Can you get up there this evening?" he asked.

"I plan to, yes."

"You need to get back to me on this thing by tomorrow at this time."

"I'll try."

"Don't try, you have to do it."

"Right, I'll do it," she smiled as she turned to leave.

"By this time tomorrow," he reaffirmed.

"I'll call you before three Seattle time."

"I'll be waiting," he smiled as they walked out the door and turned down the hall. Chuck was leaning against a wall a short distance away and fell in behind them as they passed. At the end of the hall the tall thin man turned left and Cathy and Chuck turned right and into the corridor with the elevators. A few minutes later they were in the garage sitting in their car.

"He's a tough motherfucker," said Chuck staring out the window.

"Who?"

"You know who."

"Jack is Jack," she shrugged as she started the motor.

"I'm actually a good agent," said Chuck dejectedly.

"That's why you're assigned to come with me," she snorted as they drove out onto the street.

"Yeah, right."

"What's your take on this thing by the way?"

"I guess it could be an elderly woman with a vendetta of some kind. She'd have to be very clever, very calculating, very careful. The possibility that it's a man dressed as a woman does make sense however. What better disguise. Who would suspect an elderly woman?"

"Question is, even if we got a positive ID on who he or she is, could we stop him or her from completing their mission, whatever that mission is?"

"If we could get a list of the members of the group we might," said Chuck.

"I know. Names. Addresses. Whereabouts. We don't even know how many more targets are left. The way he's going he could leave another half dozen in his wake."

"I don't think so," said Chuck.

"Why not?"

"Pattern of crimes. West Coast, across to Northeast, down the seaboard to Florida, across to the west and likely to the West coast again. I'd say it ends on the West Coast."

"You mean you think that he's down to the last victim?"

"Could be, yeah."

"If you're right we'd better find out something on this trip or we may never know who the killer is."

"I think we should have been digging a lot more aggressively before now, actually."

"We didn't know.... we've been piecing....."

"We knew that someone in one of the families must know more than they say... or don't say...."

"The FBI didn't get into this until we had half a dozen corpses, so we really haven't been on it that long," she defended.

"I think we wasted a lot of time initially just rehashing and not acting."

"Well, be that as it may, we are where we are on the case. So let's just take it from here and not beat ourselves up over what we should have done."

"I know, I know."

"We'll just leave the car at National and pick it up on the return," said Cathy.

"We need to go to LA after Seattle," said Chuck in a matter of fact way.

"If we're sent."

"We need to go to LA after Seattle. I know that. This case isn't going anywhere unless we get into it Cathy."

"We'll see what happens," she replied, looking at him apprehensively.

"Let's put it this way... I'm going to LA after Seattle," he said, reaching into his shirt pocket and pulling out a pack of cigarettes, looking at her with questioning eyes.

"No to both the cigarette and LA," she shot back firmly.

"You'll come," he said, jamming the pack back into his pocket and then drumming his fingers on the arm rest in nervous frustration.

"We'll see...."

"We have to take this case and run with it because there isn't enough time to do anything else."

"We have agents in Los...."

"Not with as much knowledge about the case as we do, especially after Seattle."

"We don't know that we'll get anything new in Seattle, Chuck..."

"Oh, we'll get it... we'll get it..... if we have to beat it out of them."

"We're not beating anything out of anyone."

"Maybe not, but we'll get the information."

"I hope you're right, Chuck," she said studying him as they paused at a stop light. "I do hope you're right."

Chapter 15

The line at the Avis window was several deep as Chuck and Cathy stood patiently. It had been a long flight from Washington to the other Washington and a little turbulent at times. They both managed to nap for a few hours, and as the big clock behind the clerk clicked to six o'clock, Pacific Time, they were ready for a night's work. It was nine back in Washington, but they were used to all-hours assignments and were mentally prepared.

"I'm not sure if we'll be able to complete the interview tonight," said Cathy, reconsidering the decision they had discussed on the plane.

"Perfect time," said Chuck with a shrug. "We should get out to Bellevue and be at their door before seven."

"But if it goes late...."

"Late? Geez..... late? Oh yeah, you're the health nut who gets up at dawn and runs around the park.... everybody else reads, sips beer and watches TV until midnight, then sleeps in. People haven't gone to bed at nine since the fifties."

"That's just you, Chuck, but you're right we have to get this thing taken care of…. so whatever it takes."

"A nice after dinner chat," he nodded confidently. "Even though we haven't had dinner."

"What if they ask us to come back tomorrow?"

"We won't take no for an answer."

"You're right, of course," she said, shaking her head. "Time is running out, especially if our killer is down to his last victim."

"Now you're talking," he nodded. "We hit the bell. We have to practice our urgent plea lines again. Ten killed. How many more have to die? We have evidence that suggests you, in fact, know who the killer is as well as who their next victims are, etc., etc."

"How long does it take to drive to Bellevue from here?" Cathy asked the clerk as her turn came up and she stepped up to the counter.

"This time of night, on the 405, maybe a half hour if you get through the traffic. It would be a lot longer if you don't. Just go onto the freeway and directly onto the 405 which goes right through Bellevue. What part of Bellevue are you going to?"

"Hunts Point," said Chuck.

"Actually Hunts Point is a separate town next to Bellevue. You go past downtown Bellevue and swing off onto the 520 headed west toward the Evergreen Point Bridge, then take the first exit."

"OK, that sounds easy," said Cathy "We have a GPS and an address so will just follow the voice."

"All the paperwork for your car was taken care of ahead of

time so here are the keys. It's just out the door and to your right."

"Whatever happened to agency cars with agents waiting at the curb?" said Chuck as they hurried out through the automatic swinging glass doors.

"Budget cuts. I don't know. We do this sometimes. Sometimes they send a car. This time we get a rental."

"Yeah, I know, but in the movies...."

"This isn't the movies Chuck," she laughed. "I wish it were the movies... then I could walk out at the end and know it wasn't real."

"You know you like this shit," he said as they got into the car.

"Some of it," she nodded. She started the car, quickly backed up, then darted out onto the ramp toward the freeway.

"It's more than just a job, isn't it?" he pressed.

"It can be," she admitted.

"Like the rush you get now in anticipation of a break in a big case."

"I hope it's a break."

"I feel it. Guess that's why I stick with it. I could do other things you know."

"Like what?"

"I have a degree in Economics from a respectable university."

"You call UCLA a respectable university?"

"It's better than Smith College or whatever puke pink, sissy, sorority shit school you went to."

"But what does one do with a degree in Economics? Tell me that? Take that degree and a dollar and it'll get you a cup of coffee."

"What did you major in, basket weaving?"

"No, but I'm no better off. History."

"History. Jesus. We're both fucked. Working for the feds. Civil service. Unsuited for other work. Protecting the general populous from criminals. Except we have someone with a 22 pistol going around the country assassinating old men, one after the other, and we haven't a goddamn clue who he is, where he is, what he looks like or who he'll bonk next. Some protectors we are, huh?"

"Yeah, well we just keep trying."

"I know."

The drive to Hunts Point took a little over half an hour. After driving through the winding streets, it was a quarter to seven when they pulled up in front of a stately Northwest contemporary home that stepped down to the edge of Lake Washington. Over the shake rooftop, they could see the mast of a sailboat moored below. Lights were on in several rooms of the house and they walked up to the front door.

"I'm going to do something a little different here," said Chuck, holding up his finger.

"Chuck..." Cathy began, a concerned expression on her face.

"It's OK, I'm going to slip around behind as you ring the doorbell. I want to see if I can see what's going on inside as they answer."

"We didn't discuss this Chuck and....."

"Same procedure we discussed, except I'm going to observe from behind.... I want to see what's going on in there."

"There could be a burglar alarm or guard dog or something."

"Maybe. I'll be careful."

"I'm not sure...."

"Just give me thirty seconds, then ring the bell," he said, turning and scurrying off through the shrubbery. She held up her hand as if to stop him, then shook her head and looked down at her watch. Thirty seconds later she stepped forward and rang the bell. After a moment's wait, she rang again. A light came on in the foyer, coming through the two narrow floor-to-ceiling windows that flanked the huge carved door. A woman's face appeared in one of the windows. Then the door opened a crack.

"Yes? What do you want?" came the sturdy voice.

"FBI. This is urgent and we must ask you a few questions."

"Let me see your ID." Cathy handed her the badge and identification card and the woman looked it over carefully, then handed it back.

"I've answered your questions," she said curtly. "I can't help you."

"Please, let me come in for just a minute, it is most urgent that I speak with you."

"You can speak with me through the door. I've told your other agent all that I know, which is nothing. I don't know who this person is and I don't know how these deaths are connected."

"But what about Mrs. Dunfrey?

"She's had a nervous breakdown and is under the strict care of a professional. She cannot answer any of your questions. I thought we made that perfectly clear."

"But we have evidence now that one or both of you, in fact, know the killer and the other victims." There was a brief hesitation.

"What evidence?" said the woman, glaring intently at Cathy

191

through the crack.

"I'm not at liberty to divulge that to you, but we want to offer you the opportunity to volunteer to cooperate with us."

"What evidence? You don't have any evidence. That's a bluff."

"I assure you, it's no bluff."

"Yeah, well get the evidence together and present it in a court of law and we'll just see how convincing it is."

"We don't have time to do that."

"So why aren't you here with a court order if you have this so-called evidence."

"Again, we want to offer you an opportunity to volunteer the information.... and quite frankly, there just isn't time. More lives are in danger even as we speak. Please, please let us talk with Mrs Dunfrey if you don't know any more than you've shared with us so far....maybe she does..."

"I doubt whether you have any evidence at all. You're just desperate. As I've told your other agent, I have nothing more to offer. So you're wasting your time."

"Please be reasonable, we need your help desperately," Cathy pleaded.

"Sorry, I can't help you, now go away," she said, slamming the door shut.

"Look, maybe if I showed you the list of victims it would jog your memory," said Cathy loudly through the door as she pulled out a sheaf of papers from the leather folder under her arm.

"Go away or I'll call the police," the woman shouted through the door.

"We ARE the police," said Cathy.

192

"I know my rights," she shouted back. "You have no warrant, you're trespassing, now get out."

"Please, we need your help," she pleaded.

"If you're not out of here in thirty seconds, the local police will be here and you'll have to sort this out with them," the woman shouted as she turned off the light in the foyer and disappeared. Cathy stood at the door for a moment before turning slowly to walk back to the car. As she did, she scanned the shrubbery where Chuck had disappeared, wondering where he was and what he had seen. She stood near the car waiting for him to return, finally getting into the car and sitting as she watched the bushes for any sign of movement. Just as she was about to get out of the car to go look for him, he burst from the landscaping, his clothes rumpled and a tear in his overcoat. He quickly climbed into the car and pointed ahead. She started the engine and pulled away.

"What?" she asked expectantly.

"A lot.... I think," he nodded. "Let's get to the airport pronto. Midnight special to LA."

"They might not have a midnight special," she replied watching him pull out his cigarettes and light one up but not stopping him. "Now fill me in on what you found out?"

"Well, she thinks it's a man dressed up like a woman as we suspected. They're not sure exactly why this man is killing everyone but she did fill me in on who these victims are. There were thirteen of them. Apparently a man named Baker, who died in an accident in November, was the current leader of a group of conservatives whose purpose it was to encourage others to do assassinations of prominent liberals. Eleven are dead."

"Eleven including this Baker guy?"

193

"Yes."

"And Baker was an accident? I wonder."

"Uh, yeah, seems like too much of coincidence considering. But at least ten have been killed by this assassin? Ten victims. Possibly eleven if Baker's 'accident' was in fact another killing. And so two remain of the thirteen."

"Correct. Anyway, this group met annually in different parts of the country over the past forty or more years. She says that Mrs. Freidhopf told her that they somehow gave moral support or something to potential assassins of prominent liberals. She is sure that they did nothing illegal. So she believes that someone thinks they did a whole lot more than they actually did and is out there paying them back. She thinks that it's most likely a man dressed like a woman. Didn't say why she thought that. And she has no idea who this man is. After the death of her husband Mrs. Dunfrey faked a nervous breakdown to keep all of this a secret."

"So why did she tell you anything now?"

"Because in the back of her mind she says she is still skeptical about what her husband's group was purported to have done. She didn't think it could have been as evil as this hit man seems to think. And I think the real reason is that years ago she had an affair with one of the last two men on the list and didn't want him hurt even if he had been part of some kind of conspiracy."

"Wow, well hopefully you got the truth from her."

"Hopefully, yes….you never know of course….they've been very reluctant to give us anything before so I'm not one hundred percent confident in her info, but we've gotta get to LA. pronto in any case."

"So you got the name and address of this man she purportedly had an affair with?"

"Yes, George M. Bundy, 4744 W. Anchor Lane, Marina del Rey."

"Great….but how do you remember all of this?" asked Cathy. "And how did you get so much from this woman in such a short time?"

"I'm fast and have an incredible memory."

"I'm not even going to ask how you were able to get in and talk to her without her making a scene."

"I have ways."

"Right. So you have the name and address of the last one too, the twelfth potential victim?"

"She was not sure of his name…thought it was John something …..but apparently he lives somewhere in Puerto Vallarta. Apparently has time shares or something there and in other places."

"He lives there? And what other places? Did she say?"

"Hawaii. No addresses there either. He's back and forth. Mostly in Mexico according to what she knows of him."

"Hopefully we'll make it to Los Angeles in time to save number eleven."

"This assassin has several days on us, and if past performances are any indication, we will either be just in time to save Bundy or just in time to find his body."

"Yeah, I know," said Cathy. "Get on the cell and call headquarters, give them the address in Marina del Rey and have them start poking around down in Puerto Vallarta to see what they can find out…. and tell them we're on our way down there too after we go to LA."

"They'll likely tell us not to go down you know," said Chuck.

"Just tell them we're on our way down," said Cathy. "We won't ask. We'll just go."

"Now you're talking," said Chuck, taking the cell phone out of the holster in his belt and dialing a number. "Yeah."

Chapter 16

"How far did you say it was to Marina del Rey from here at LAX?" asked Cathy as they hurried across the busy ramp traffic to the rental car.

"Fifteen minutes..... better let me drive. I know the area and driving in LA is not for newcomers," said Chuck holding his hand out for the keys which Cathy gladly handed to him.

"Go for it."

"We'll take a shortcut. Marina del Rey is just a nine iron from here," said Chuck, yanking open the car door, leaping in and putting the car in reverse before Cathy could even close her door. She quickly grabbed the seat belt and struggled to snap it in place as Chuck squealed around the first corner. He shot through a light that had long since gone past yellow, eliciting a few horns and one squeal of a tire from the other traffic. He lurched out onto the highway, weaving in and out of traffic, clearly over the posted speed.

"Do they issue traffic tickets in this city?" asked Cathy, holding onto the seat with both hands.

"Sometimes, when someone really fucks up bad."

"Aren't you going a little over the limit?"

"Everyone here drives over the limit. I'm just a click or two ahead of them." Ten minutes later they were in heavy traffic. Chuck spun a quick left and down a side street, through a parking lot and out onto Admiralty Way, the main arterial in Marina del Rey. "We'll be there in less than five."

"I'm sure of it," she said, still hanging on.

A few minutes later they were snaking their way through a canyon of very large three and four story townhouses arranged on narrow cobble streets. Chuck was craning his neck to read the street signs.

"I think it's on or near the beach toward the breakwater."

"These must all be million dollar townhouses," quipped Cathy as she looked up at the structures.

"Several times that at least. Some are obscenely priced. Mr. Bundy's place no doubt," said Chuck, making a right turn, then slowing to a near halt. Up ahead were several police cars and a small crowd of people. An officer with a notepad was writing something as they slowly pulled up. Chuck rolled down his window and held out his badge.

"I see we're late," said Chuck, hanging his badge out the window.

"Happened this afternoon sometime," the officer concurred. "You know about this?"

"We do....so he came right in and shot him?" asked Cathy, leaning across.

"Yeah, apparently," said the officer. "What do you know that we don't?"

"Haven't you been briefed?"

"About what?"

"We notified the LA bureau about the possibility of this and gave them the address earlier. They should have passed that on to you," said Cathy.

"They might have, but I just got here. The body was discovered about four hours ago down at the marina."

"In the marina?" Chuck mumbled with a squint of disbelief as he looked at his watch. "And you said it was done in the afternoon?"

"He just disappeared around noon and nobody could find him. Didn't think to check in his boat until this evening," shrugged the officer.

"His boat was for sale," said Chuck in a matter of fact manner, nodding to himself.

"Uh, well, yes it was," said the officer. "How did you know?"

"This assassin called him to have him show it to him, broke into the boat, then shot him.... and walked away.... again," he speculated with a nod, holding up his hands in a shrug.

"Uh, well, yes, that's a good possibility....but how did you...?," the officer stammered, dropping his pad to his side and coming up to the window, bending down to stare at Chuck.

"Educated guess," said Chuck shaking his head. The officer continued to look at him with a puzzled expression.

Through the crowd a man emerged wearing a dark blue suit and red tie with jet black hair plastered back on his head. He came straight to their car.

"Hastings," he said as he arrived, flopping his FBI badge as he came to a stop just to the side of the officer who looked first at him, then at Chuck.

"You didn't pass on the scoop on this gig because the deed was already done," said Chuck, anticipating Hasting's line.

"Exactly. By the time we got down here the street was lined with blacks and whites."

"What about Puerto Vallarta?" asked Cathy, craning her head down to look Hastings in the eye.

"A team is on their way down there right now," he nodded.

"Jesus," said Chuck, leaning back in his seat and closing his eyes. "This guy is fucking good. He's really fucking good."

"Lucky too," said Hastings. "Boat for sale. Calling him. Walks out past body guards with their fucking hands in their pockets. Don't even ask where he's going. Of course it's only a couple blocks from his home to his boat, so he doesn't even think that anything is out of the ordinary. How many things could have gone wrong in that scenario?"

"This guy has MADE his opportunities, Hastings," said Chuck with his head still back and eyes closed. "If it hadn't been that ploy, it would have been another. He's so fucking clever and unpredictable that we're all looking like a bunch of goddamn amateurs. It's all essentially unplanned. There's no extensive pre-planning or plotting. Just walks in, assesses the opportunities and goes right in and does the dirty work. Just goes right fucking in. Wherever it is. Right past everyone. Just bold as fucking hell. Jesus, there isn't a hit man in the world with balls that big. This guy is fearless. He has pure ice water in his veins."

"Just determined," said Cathy. "He's committed to what he's

doing and has obviously decided that he's going to carry out these assassinations and doesn't really care about the consequences. He probably doesn't even care if he eventually gets caught. So, to that extent, yes, he is fearless."

"The last one, number twelve, might be a doozy," said Chuck, turning his head to look at Cathy.

"Why?"

"Something that Judy told me that didn't make sense at the time, but now that I think about it, it might just be significant.... very significant."

"Like what?" asked Hastings.

"She said this last guy was considered the 'closer'. He was not really part of the grand conspiracy of the good old boys, but maybe like the trigger man or something like that. He was the guy who made the contacts. That he may even have helped arrange things. He was not really part of the gang per se and therefore not traceable back to them. I think she said he wasn't privy to their closed door meetings, and contact with him was kept on the QT. That's why the name and address are not known."

"So he wasn't really part of the conspiracy or whatever it was," said Cathy.

"He was part of it, yes, but not in the same way as the others. He was a critical part, actually. Another thing Judy said...."

"OK?" prompted Cathy when Chuck hesitated.

"She said that this hit man may not have known his role in this whole thing. Judy only found out about the special role, inadvertently, by snooping through some of her husband's tossed notes after he was killed. So he may not actually realize that this last guy was different, and not just a stuffy old conservative sitting around cooking up hate about liberals... but an active player...a professional."

"You mean, perhaps someone who can and will fight back?" asked Hastings.

"This last guy must have been aware of and kept track of the assassination binge and knows he's on the list. So he's got to be ready and not just with some hired thugs. He's likely to be a tall order, even for someone as clever and cunning as this hit man."

"I guess we're going down to Mexico right away," said Chuck, looking at Cathy. She nodded.

"Have the bureau try to dig up whatever they can on this last guy... we think his first name might be John," said Cathy, again craning her head down to make eye contact with Hastings.

"You said he might be in the timeshare business in Mexico and Hawaii?"

"That's what we think based on what we found out in Seattle," said Chuck.

"Probably should do some checking in both places, but not very much at all to go on," said Hastings.

"Hawaii," Chuck mumbled while staring blankly ahead.

"What are you thinking?" asked Cathy.

"I think I need to go to Hawaii," said Chuck. "And you're going to Mexico."

"Nope, I'm going to Hawaii with you.... I think I have the same feeling about this one as you do."

"Hastings, we're on our way to the airport. Keep us informed about anything you turn up in Puerto Vallarta. We're going to catch the next flight to Hawaii."

"What shall I tell the chief?"

"Tell Jack that we're playing a hunch," said Cathy.

"A hunch?" Hastings snickered.

"Yeah, a hunch," she affirmed. "With this case I think we have to start using our intuition. And maybe do a little guessing too."

"I'll have a bulletin issued to check all flights to Puerto Vallarta and Hawaii," Hastings said, writing something on a notepad. "But, again, who the fuck are we looking for?"

"Don't have a clue…but it could be a man dressed as a woman," said Chuck.

"A what?" asked Hastings in disbelief.

"That's a theory that one of the wives in Seattle thought might be the case….and we thought of it too…..so it's always a possibility….there were elderly women spotted at some of the hits. And it would be hard to believe that an elderly woman could actually pull this off."

"Well, I certainly agree with that…. OK, I'll pass that on," said Hastings.

"And if this guy crossed into Mexico he'd cross at Tijuana or another border town by car…. not fly." Said Chuck. "You're never going to catch him crossing. And that's a two to three day drive down to Puerto Vallarta so we might have some time if he does that. He obviously has dossiers on all of these characters and knows that this last guy has a condo in Hawaii. At least we'll assume he does. But my guess is he's gone to Hawaii and will figure how to lure him there. If this last guy is the type of operative that we think he is the hunted will very gladly become the hunter if he thinks this hit man is there. That's what I think."

"I agree, so let's do it," said Cathy. "Get us to the airport."

She pointed. The car was already in reverse and a couple of quick maneuvers had them screeching out the narrow road with the officer and Hastings staring at their departure.

Chapter 17

"All right, I need to move out of here for a while. Bundy's been offed," said John, slapping the lid shut on the cell phone and flinging it onto the sofa.

"How in the....." began a slender blonde woman at the other end of the sofa.

"In his boat."

"In his boat? For god sakes he had a half dozen body guards. How...?."

"I don't know how. This guy figured out a way as he has so easily done right across the country.... he just did, that's all," he snapped, placing his hand on his neck and leaning his head back.

"Where are you going to go?"

"Don't know that, I'm thinking. I figured once the FBI was on the case that he'd be caught."

"But you've dealt with far worse than hit men before," she said almost sarcastically.

"Yeah, but I know what to expect from other professionals. I can think like them. I can anticipate them. But this is different, he's been entirely unpredictable and he's very clever. He doesn't seem to have any inhibitions whatsoever about anyone who happens to be in the way."

"How about Cancun?" she asked. "I like it there."

"You're not coming," he said curtly.

"Why not? I always go where you go."

"Not this time."

"He wouldn't shoot me. I haven't done anything."

"He's managed to shoot anyone and everyone who is in the room at the time. So, yes, he would shoot you. It doesn't matter whether you've done anything or not..... I haven't done anything either. I'm just a facilitator. I've never shot anyone or harmed anyone in my life."

"I know that darling," she said softly. "Is it because you've been mixed up with those intellectual politicos, or whatever they were?"

"None of us ever actually did anything. Either them or me. We just encouraged those who wanted to do something to go ahead and do it. There's really nothing illegal or immoral about that. A lot of people wish other people were dead. Especially those whose ideas are a danger to one's way of life."

"I know you've never done anything wrong. But you said...."

"I said we discussed a lot of things that ended up coming true such as the assassinations of dangerous liberals, but this hit man, whoever he is, THINKS that we did a lot more than we actually did. I know we didn't, because I was the one who actually made contact with those who did the assassinations. I can tell you that we didn't give them guns. We didn't give them inside information. We didn't really give them anything."

"Except a pep talk."

"What's wrong with that? They still had to do the work. We didn't. We just wished and talked. That's all."

"What was that you once mentioned about hypnosis?"

"That.... that was just talk. We didn't actually..... well, not in any real clinical sense......"

"But you did sort of give them suggestions."

"That's all we did. Just forget about that hypnosis part. It wasn't really hypnosis. It was..... just forget it. And if anyone ever asks you, don't ever mention it. It was nothing. I can promise you that. It was nothing."

"OK, I won't mention it again," she shrugged.

"Hey boss, I've got the info on airplane reservations and went ahead and got you some tickets," said a short stocky man with a head full of stubby blonde hair who poked his head around the corner.

"What've you got?" asked John.

"Fastest way out is to LAX with a connecting flight to Hawaii. Plane leaving here soon, then a charter leaving LAX later in the evening. Flight here leaves in about an hour and a half so you'd have to hustle. I got you tickets already as I said. I assumed that is what you wanted to do but if you want to do something else there's a flight in three hours to Mexico City connecting to Cancun. Then, later still, there's one to Houston, connecting to Miami."

"Question is, what would this hit man guess," he pondered. "He's most likely coming here....I'm pretty confident of that based on his previous moves....so anywhere I go will be OK for the time being."

"Why do you think he's coming here?" asked the man.

"Like I said, that's what he's done with each and every one of the others. He came right to their primary residence."

"We have four properties in Hawaii, so that should confuse the situation even more even if he does go there," he said. "Which property?"

"Maui."

"Wailea or Lahaina?"

"Uh.... Wailea."

"Actually we have two in the Wailea area."

"The one on the beach."

"Down in Makena, got it. I'll punch it in."

"Have the car outside in fifteen minutes, Cody."

"Right."

"Are you sure I can't go with you?" the woman whined.

"No, Monica. If things get settled, I'll send for you."

"You mean if they catch him?"

"Exactly."

"The FBI is on this, you said."

"Yeah, they'll get him."

"You said once that the FBI was populated with a bunch of stumbling oafs who couldn't tell their asses from holes in the ground."

"Yeah, well, maybe I was exaggerating."

"Be careful."

"I will, don't worry," he said. "Besides, he won't be able to take his little 22 on an airplane without getting caught. Security is way too tight for that."

"Can't he check it through?"

"They'd catch that, too."

"Once you said there were ways..."

"All right, it's possible, but he wouldn't know how."

"Maybe you're right. There isn't any other way to Hawaii, is there?"

"Flying is it. He's not about to go by boat."

"But he could."

"Go by boat?"

"Yes, by boat."

"That's ridiculous, he can fly there in five hours. Why would he take a boat when it's over two thousand miles from LA. It would take four or five days to get there on even the fastest ship."

"You said he's unpredictable."

"I know..... besides, he's coming down here first, so the whole discussion about how he gets to Hawaii is mute. If he goes there, he'll fly. And they'll be looking for him. Now I've gotta get packed and get out of here. Ride to the airport with me, hon."

"Oh sure, I wouldn't miss seeing my sweetie off for anything."

Chapter 18

Rose sat in the large circular waiting area watching the monitors. Her departure had been delayed more than two hours because the plane was a continuation flight from Denver and was late due to weather conditions. She looked at her watch. It was almost eleven. Eight in Hawaii. It would be one AM when she arrived there. An unusual time for an arrival. But during the crowded holiday season flights were full and she felt lucky to be able to book a seat at all. She used her regular ID. Rose Baker. There was no other choice. Security was too tight to do anything else. Every time anyone with a uniform entered, she would watch them through the corner of her eye even though she was fairly sure that she still had not been identified.

"Now boarding flight 101, Air Republic, gate number six B." Rose got up slowly and walked to the line that was forming. As she did, a figure with a vaguely familiar face approached the counter ahead of her. Even though she had never met him, she had seen his photo when she went through Judd's things. It was John Averill. On this flight! She smiled, shaking her head in amazement after having correctly guessed to which island he would run, and she also knew that they had never met before so he would have no idea who she was. Apparently by himself. Too bad she couldn't have taken the gun onto the airplane, but of course that would have been impossible. If she could she could have finished him off right then and there. She had disassembled the gun and checked it through, hoping that it would be OK. She had not flown in over ten years and had never encountered the tight inspections that were now in place, nor had any idea whether someone could check an unloaded gun through with luggage or not. She had to take the chance. There was no other choice. She packed the silencer and a handful of bullets in a sack of nickels that she picked up at the bank on her way to the airport. Ten rolls of nickels, five opened and just poured into the sack. Then just placed the empty pistol on top of her clothes in the suitcase. Might work. She didn't know. At this point though, with twelve down and just the final member to go, she somehow wasn't as concerned about being caught as before. This last member was supposed to be more of a messenger boy anyhow according to the dossier. He was not really part of the inner circle of hard-core hate mongers. He was perhaps in his early seventies, maybe her age, she didn't know. He was a good looking man she thought as she watched him talk with the woman at the counter. The lady nodded and handed him a packet and he turned and walked past her, close enough to touch. Too bad, she mused as she watched him go by. No, he was part of Baker's Dozen. An important part actually. A dedicated professional who obviously

211

knew what he was doing. Knew the consequences of his actions. In some ways more guilty than the others, even though probably not philosophically committed to the cause. John Averill could be working for any political affiliation, or none. His job was to carry out orders. Convince. Foment. Incite what often were unstable people. He was obviously good at his job. Whatever or however he had assisted them, it had been remarkably helpful. He had very skillfully covered up his actions with not a trace of involvement detectable. So, yes, he must die too.

The line began to move and a few minutes later, Rose was settling into her seat near the rear of the plane, an aisle seat. She stood, slowly removing her jacket, folding it carefully and stowing it in the overhead bin while watching where John Averill was seated. He was about midway forward. Also, an aisle seat. He was definitely alone. No body guard. Interesting. But he was obviously confident that she would go directly to Puerto Vallarta, so this bizarre coincidence would be unanticipated. Now at least she knew which island even though she did not know which condo complex. She would have to follow him, probably in a rental car, she assumed. That would take time to do the paperwork. The logistics of that would be a challenge. Maybe it would be best to wait, watch what he did and then take a cab and follow him. It would be late at night so there would not be a lot of traffic. Easier to follow.

She sat down and began reading the magazine from the back of the seat. Time passed. She looked at her watch. It had been nearly twenty minutes since they boarded and there was no sign of activity. She signaled for a steward to come over.

"What's the delay?" she asked.

"There was a delay in getting here as you know, and now we're having some difficulty locating a tour group that had gone to dinner, but they're outside now and once they're boarded, we should be underway."

"Thank you."

She watched the remaining passengers straggle in, dressed in very casual clothing, some in shorts and T-shirts, except for one couple. They were dressed in nice, though somewhat rumpled, suits. The woman had a briefcase, and the man needed a shave. They were probably on some kind of business and didn't appear to be on vacation. She could see the outline of a pack of cigarettes in his pocket as they came by and sat in the seats ahead of her. They were talking, and in the otherwise quiet of the plane, she leaned forward to listen.

"I wonder if the hit man is on this plane?" asked the man.

"That would be something," said the woman. "But at least we alerted the airlines that he could be dressed like an elderly lady."

"Somehow I doubt if he could actually get away with that on a flight," said the man. "Or even try it."

"I guess it's not as easy to do as it used to be. Now with the scanners and x-rays. If it were a man dressed as a woman he would have been found out. And we alerted the airlines to be on the lookout for just this situation."

"Whoever he is he could be sitting right near us and we'd never know."

"By the way do we have a hotel?" asked the woman.

"Are you kidding Cathy? We stumbled onto this flight and jumped on. No baggage. Nothing. We didn't have time to do jack," he scoffed.

"And we don't have a location for this last guy's condo either."

"Correct, plus we don't even have an island."

"Nor do we have any idea what he looks like," she laughed.

"Not only are we flying blind but to top that he has had ample experience at changing identities, so even if we did know more we might not be able to spot him."

"This flight is going to Maui so it's as good a place to start as any. And this time we'll have an agent meet us at the airport."

"More company flying blind with us. We have a whole lot of shit to figure out when we get there. A first name. Maybe. That's not much. Everyone is named John."

"Of course, he may not have even come here. The hit man may be down in Puerto Vallarta right now knocking him off."

"We have people down there," she said.

"Which means dick!" he scoffed. "They're flying just as blind as we are. But at least we'll have someone there to help put him in a body bag. Not to worry, this last guy will be here," he said confidently.

"What if the hit man came directly here too? Guessing like us?"

"I know. Exciting huh?" he chuckled.

Interesting, Rose mused, sitting back and closing her eyes. John Averill on the flight, plus what sounds like two government law enforcement agents, probably FBI, and her. All on the same plane. All heading for the same place. Except the FBI is a step behind since they don't seem to know who she is or who John is nor where he's going. So, it will take them a while to sort out the unknowns. A man dressed like an elderly woman? Interesting.

I'm sure they assume that an elderly woman could never pull this off. In any case, regardless of what they know, it may have to be done as quickly as possible. That part she would have to work on and she most likely will have to seize whatever opportunity presents itself. Hopefully she'll have her gun when she lands, and not a bunch of authorities questioning her about the contents of her bag.

The plane ride was over five hours. And the trip seemed even longer knowing she had to maintain a low profile and not appear nervous or unduly suspicious to either the agents or John. At one point, on her way back from the bathroom, the woman agent turned and asked her when she thought they would be served the evening meal. Rose, very politely said she didn't know and promptly flagged down a stewardess and asked. The agent was grateful and thanked her, hesitating for just a second to seemingly assess her. Rose calmly shook it off with a nod and returned to her seat. A few minutes later the woman turned around in her seat again and asked her if she were traveling alone. Rose told her that her husband had gone ahead the day before and was waiting at the airport in Maui for her. There had been an illness in the family and Rose had to tend to that before she left Minnesota. She also expressed concern that the lateness of the flight would likely cause her husband fits since he didn't like to wait. The woman laughed. She seemed to buy it. To Rose's relief there were no further exchanges.

It was just past one in the morning, Hawaii time, when the door finally opened and passengers began trundling down the steps into the mellow evening breeze. It was much warmer than when they left Los Angeles, but it was still cool enough to require a light jacket. The baggage area was a lengthy walk through a staging area and Rose decided to boldly charge ahead of everyone rather than lag behind. They would all end up in the same location and besides, she had a plan for dealing with John Averill. Her aging legs carried her spryly along and she arrived ahead of most of the other passengers. There were a few younger passengers with only carry-ons in front but John and the agents were not among them. Rose went immediately out to the ramp to find a cab. There were none parked in front. She flagged down a porter and asked about cabs. He explained that some would arrive soon but this was an unusual hour for an arrival and none were on hand at the moment. Across the way on the other side was an older beige cab with weather worn paint and a pale light on top. It sat empty, the driver's head was back on the headrest with his eyes closed. Rose walked across and reached in the open window, putting her hand on his arm. He jerked to attention.

"Uh….oh…. need a cab?" he inquired, fumbling forward and attempting to turn the key.

"In a moment, yes," she nodded, as he finally blinked away the sleep and focused on her. "There will be a tall elderly gentleman with dark hair and graying temples, wearing a dark blue sweater and black slacks…. with a large, expensive-looking gold wristwatch and a large gold link chain around his neck. I want you to do a U-turn to the other side the minute he steps onto the sidewalk near the curb and tell him that you were sent here to pick him up. Ask him if his name is Mr. Averill. Do you have all that?"

"OK…cut a Uee across when this guy with the blue sweater

and gold chain comes out. Ask him if his name is Mr. Averill," he repeated sluggishly.

"And you have never seen me before, so when I come up to the cab after he's in, you pretend you've never seen me before, nor heard my story," she added. "Got that?"

"Pretend I've never seen nor heard your story before," he repeated again.

"Correct, so just be ready," she concluded as she flipped a one hundred dollar bill in the window to his raised eyebrows.

"OK...OK," he said shaking his head and smiling while folding the bill and stuffing it into his shirt pocket.

She continued back across the empty ramp to the baggage area that was now filling up with people.

It was fully ten minutes before the bags finally began tumbling out of the chute and down onto the rotating trough. She spotted her suitcase and pulled it off, noticing that it was partially unzipped. She zipped it shut without looking inside and wheeled it over to the sidewalk within a short distance of the cab that had now made a U-turn and had worked its way slowly over in front of the baggage area. John was now on the curb in front of her and the driver had managed to attract his attention with a little chirp on the horn. He then called John's name through the passenger window. Acting somewhat surprised, but shrugging, John put his two suitcases on the sidewalk in front of the cab. The cab driver was now out and had the trunk open, helped by a porter who hoisted John's bags in. Rose picked up her suitcase and, just as John was comfortably in the back seat, arrived at the passenger side window and poked her head in to speak with the driver.

"My husband was supposed to pick me up and there doesn't seem to be any cabs this time of night.... are you going toward Wailea?" she asked, having overheard John tell the driver where he was going.

The driver turned around and looked at John as if asking. John shrugged, then nodded.

"Do you mind?" she asked, looking at John. He nodded in appeasement, clearly not wanting company, but not able to put up a cogent argument at this hour. She opened the front door, sat down and pulled the heavy suitcase onto her lap. The driver looked at her for a moment, opened his mouth and began to point toward the trunk as if to ask if she wouldn't prefer to put it back there. He thought about the hundred in his pocket, closed his mouth, turned around and drove away.

"I just need to get something out of it on the way," she said to the driver, pulling the zipper open and lifting the lid slightly so she could peek in. She could see the pistol lying on top of the clothes where she had placed it. Great! Another stroke of luck she thought. He looked at her through the corner of his eyes and shrugged as he wound his way out onto the highway.

Chapter 19

"I thought an agent was supposed to meet us here?" asked Cathy as they stood at the curb.

"I've only seen one cab since we arrived. Everyone else seems to be pretty much in the same boat as we are. At least the rental car agencies seem to be having a landmark day. We've been standing here for over fifteen minutes."

"Perhaps they had cars reserved," she offered.

"Is that a white unmarked full-sized domestic car I see," said Chuck sarcastically, pointing to a car making its way around the circle toward them.

"Gotta be an agency car," she nodded as the car pulled up and a short, slight woman with a dark tan, blonde hair and a dark gray suit that fit very tightly got out and walked toward them. She was carrying a piece of paper in one hand.

"Must be our man in Maui," said Chuck, holding out his hand to the woman in greeting.

"Agent Cole, Vivian Cole," said the woman, clasping Chuck's hand strongly, then reached for Cathy's.

"Hi, I'm Chuck.... this is Cathy," Chuck waved, first toward himself, then toward Cathy.

"Got big news," she declared. "I'm late because I was waiting for this to print out in the car."

"What have you got," asked Chuck expectantly.

"Rose Baker," said Vivian. "We think the assassin might be Rose Baker, not a man dressed up like a woman."

"Baker?" asked Cathy. "Isn't that...."

"Judd Baker's sister," said Vivian. "Baker apparently died in November before all of this killing started."

"Right, Baker, the name was mentioned by the Seattle widow....yes, he died....so she killed her brother too?" asked Chuck.

"Don't know but it was classified as an accident, but considering what else has happened......"

"She actually killed her brother?" asked Cathy.

"We don't know that, but he's dead and was part of the conservative group that she seems to have gone about eliminating."

"So how did you find out about Rose Baker?" asked Chuck.

"We were able to get more from one of the wives in Seattle."

"So she held out on me," said Chuck. "Or lied?"

"Probably both. We went back to the Dunfrey lady with a warrant and were able to interview her more thoroughly. Apparently she had an affair with this Bundy character in LA and was now more interested in talking. Seems this twelfth guy, or thirteenth if you include Baker, was always a bit invisible in this group, confirming what she told you. They never really ever met with him. Seemed to take orders from them though. He would help them 'facilitate' their plans. Whatever their plans were. This Rose Baker was on the boat the night their husbands were killed. And an older woman is consistent too with sightings in some of the other killings. So it's a good possibility. Improbable as it may seem. But it's a lead. In any event, here's the photo of her...." she held up the piece of paper she had in her hand under the street light. Cathy looked at Chuck whose eyes were wide as saucers as he looked at the photo.

"Jesus Christ!" he bellowed as people around them turned their heads at his outburst. "Jesus Christ!" he repeated in an equally shrill tone.

"She had a little different nose," said Cathy. "but...."

"And some extra makeup," added Chuck.

"And wasn't that her getting into the cab with someone earlier," said Cathy, pointing down the street. "You don't suppose that someone is........"

"Of fucking course I suppose!......of fucking course I suppose!....... Jesus Christ, and right under our goddamed noses!......again....again....right the fuck under our goddamned noses!....."

"What are you two?...." Vivian sputtered in confusion.

"She was right behind us on the plane. For one moment on the plane.....for one moment..... I thought...... I hesitated..... could it be, I thought....."

"I never even fucking thought!...... never even fucking thought!....." shouted Chuck.

"What's going on?" asked Vivian excitedly. "You've seen her, obviously....on the plane?"

"Number twelve, or perhaps now it's thirteen, is likely in the books..... where did that cab go?" yelled Chuck.

"Where did that cab go?" repeated Cathy, grabbing a porter firmly by the arm and pointing toward the street.

"There's only been one cab here and that was at least twenty minutes ago," he shrugged, trying to wrest free of her grasp. "Man and a woman."

"Right....of course....and could you tell if they were together?" Chuck asked.

"No they weren't... I think she slipped the cabby some money, then after the guy got into the cab a few minutes later she came back and got in after asking if she could ride with them....I overheard some of the conversation...."

"Where did it go?" asked Cathy, now pulling on the porter's shirt, jerking him toward her. He pulled free with an angry look on his face as she reached into her briefcase and pulled out her badge and ID, dangling it in his face. He pulled back, holding up his hands.

"I don't know, honest to God, I don't know. I had walked away by that time."

"Who does? Can we call his cab company?"

"He ain't got no cab company.... he's an independent."

"Surely he has a radio.... all cabs have radios...."

"Not all the independents.... and probably not Ralphy. Ralphy don't do nothin' he don't gotta do and if he don't have to have no radio he ain't got no radio. I don't even think he has a cell phone."

"Where does that road go?"

"Well, assumin' Ralphy went on towards the resorts, could

either go west to Lahaina and Kaanapali and beyond..... or south tord Kihei and Wailea."

"What's most likely?"

"Either one's most likely, lots of hotels and stuff both ways. Maybe more action toward Lahaina and Kaanapali depending on what you like."

"We need to get on the horn and alert the local police to get a make on Ralphy's cab. Also, the license number and have them look ...... anywhere..... have them send out an all-points bulletin. What color was the car? What make? What year? And what's his last name, we'll look him up with DMV."

"Brownish," said the porter. "Sort of brownish. Light. Maybe yellowish. Older Chevy, could have been a Ford. Maybe 92 or 93..... yeah, Chevy, full-sized Chevy. Four door. Name.... uh....don't really know...just Ralphy is all I know."

"Got that? Light brown four door Chevy, early 90s, cab emblem on the side.... thing on top..... what did it say?"

"Maui Island Cab, I think," said the porter.

"Maui Island Cab. And make it a code three. A homicide is in progress, possibly already taken place."

"I'm on it," said Vivian, already in her car with the mic in her hand.

"What can we do?" asked Cathy, shrugging at Chuck.

"I say we get in Vivian's car and head for Wailea," I have a hunch that's where they went."

"What's the hunch based on?" asked Cathy.

"Read about it on the plane in their magazine."

"Good a place as any to start I guess....any thoughts of where in Wailea?" she nodded, starting for the car.

"I'll grab a couple of those tourist magazines in that display and we'll see what's advertised," he said, running over to a colorful display of local commercial attractions and grabbing a couple of tourist magazines, then darting for the car.

"We're trying Wailea first," said Chuck climbing in.

"Wailea is closer, yes," said Vivian as she quickly drove past several parked cars and sped onto the highway. The traffic was light and she flew very fast across the barren countryside. Ten minutes later she was racing along a freeway that was parallel to some of the resort areas near the ocean. "That's Kehei we're passing. Condos there too."

"Uh, I'm guessing the more upscale area for this guy," said Chuck. "Wailea looks like the more upscale area in South Maui."

"You never know," said Vivian. "Might be a good cover to stay in a modest area."

"Nah, this guy is likely used to luxury," said Chuck.

"Whatever you say….how do you want to go about this?" asked Vivian. "As I mentioned back at the airport, the bureau came up with a big fat nothing on our mystery man other than what we were able to get from the Dunfrey widow. Possibly name of John. Not much help. And she said that she had no pictures or even a description of him since she'd never seen nor met him. Somehow I know that someone in that group must have his picture. More than likely Baker since he was apparently their leader. So it's likely that Rose has his picture and that's how she has managed to tag onto him."

"They may still be lying, covering up," said Cathy.

"I know and I have no suggestions regarding who we're looking for or what he looks like, or where he's staying," said

Chuck with a shrug. "Do you remember anything else from the latest interview with the widow that might give us a hint as to who he might be?"

"No," said Vivian. "Other than what we already know.... that this guy was apparently some kind of messenger for the group.... or something to that effect. Look, here's a condo that looks upscale, let's start there. Wailea Surf."

"What do we ask by the way?" asked Cathy.

"Ask if someone who has a condo here also has other condos, like Puerto Vallarta," said Chuck.

"We do know what Rose looks like now so we can at least show them her picture," said Vivian.

"Yeah right..... like she's going to check into the condo AFTER she offs our mystery man?" said Chuck sarcastically. "I think our only hope is the APB that was sent out."

"Do you really think the Maui police are all out in force combing the streets looking for this independent cab in the old brown Chevy?" Cathy quipped.

"No, but at least someone might know the cabby," said Chuck. "This is a small community in many ways."

"Actually, in reality, it's not that small, especially with literally millions of tourists filling the roads, condos, restaurants, shops and everything," said Vivian. "The native population isn't that big, true, but the tourist population is huge, especially now during the holiday season."

"We don't have a lot of other options," said Chuck. "I guess we just have to keep checking condos."

"I know, we're quite literally flying blind right now," said Cathy. "They may well be half an hour or more in the other

225

direction."

"Or even out toward Hana," said Vivian.

"Hana? You mean there's another direction?"

"Well, not a lot of resort activity out there, but it's a direction that they could have taken," she replied.

"Ohhh mannn," groaned Chuck, shaking his head as he leafed through the magazines. "After the Surf, we'll try the Outrigger Wailea. They have a big ad in here. And of course we can also look for that old cab parked outside."

"As if the cabby would stick around after letting them off," said Cathy.

"OK....not likely unless she asked him to wait," said Vivian. "I think the Outrigger is just down the road from the Surf, but I'm not sure if it is a time share," said Vivian, squealing around a big bend and down a hill toward the ocean and the resorts. In a few minutes, they pulled up into the spacious drive of the Surf. A lonely attendant hurried out of a little hut and ran up to the driver's door.

"Checking in?" he inquired.

"FBI," said Vivian, hanging her badge and ID out the window. He drew back. "Has anyone been here to check in the last fifteen minutes or so?"

"You're the first in more than an hour," the man said, shaking his head.

"If you see this woman.... at all.... notify us immediately at the phone number on this card, or call the police.... she is armed and very dangerous," Chuck said handing him his card.

"This elderly woman?" the man said in disbelief, looking at the photo.

"Just do it," said Vivian, flooring the gas and racing away. They repeated the routine at three other resorts with much the same result. Nobody had checked in within the last half hour, nor seen Rose.

"They went the other way most likely," said Cathy as they sat in the car following the last stop, waiting for Chuck to direct them to the next.

"They might have taken the lonely road around the south end to do the job," said Vivian.

"Lonely road?" asked Cathy.

"The highway just fades away into a twisted, bumpy, rolly, rocky narrow road as it goes farther around to the southern tip of the island."

"You think she hijacked the cab and our mystery victim and took them to some remote spot to do the job?" asked Cathy.

"It's a good possibility," shrugged Vivian. "I'm not sure that she'd do it along the strip. There are too many cars, people and resorts. Even at this hour things are still alive as you can see."

"Yeah, so what would she do?" asked Cathy. "Couldn't very well just take him back to his condo and politely ask to be invited in to be shot."

"Chances are very good that he did not know who she was," said Chuck. "After all, he was not a part of the good old boy get togethers that she may have attended over the years. But she must have known what HE looked like. Baker was the leader of the group and likely had a lot of info in his files that she had access to after his death."

"Right…she likely knew who he was but he didn't know her. Otherwise he would certainly have noticed her getting on the airplane-- or spotted her in the airplane--if he did," said Cathy. "On the other hand, he must have been aware of his situation and should have been on the lookout for someone. There had to be communications about the possibility that this was a woman. He most certainly was abreast of their conversations."

"I think the suspicion was a man dressed as a woman," said Chuck. "And he knew that nobody could get through security without being found out."

"Unless the airlines didn't care about cross-dressers," said Cathy.

"The guy wouldn't travel in disguise," said Vivian. "Let's assume he had no clue."

"And Rose Baker did a wonderful job of impersonating an innocent old lady....certainly fooled us," said Chuck. "I doubt if the mystery man suspected anything."

"All she had to do was find out which condo he was staying at, ride off in the cab, then come back later and bonk him," said Vivian.

"Or bonk him right in the cab," said Cathy.

"That's what she'll do," said Chuck. "If she was sitting right behind us on the plane, she surely overheard our conversations. And, consequently, she's going to want to take care of business rather quickly. No time to come back later. Bonk now."

"In fact I think maybe the deed is already done and we're just running around looking for the corpse....as usual," said Cathy.

"Did you tell the locals to call you if they came up with anything on that APB?" asked Chuck.

"Yeah, of course," nodded Vivian with a bit of a sneer, seeming a little annoyed that he would ask.

"Well, that may be our only real hope right now," he shrugged. She nodded.

"By the way, how did she get her gun on the plane?" asked Chuck.

"Checked baggage I assume, but they x-ray that," said Vivian. "Good question."

"Maybe she doesn't have a gun," said Cathy.

"She could just have been lucky and it slipped past security as things sometimes do," said Chuck.

"Security is pretty tight, but she's had that kind of luck so far....if you can refer to it as luck," said Cathy. "Perhaps a little help again from whomever."

"Any more condos?" asked Vivian.

"Uh, yeah, I'm sure there are but none of the big advertised variety from these mags," he said shaking his head as he threw the last magazine onto the floor. They sat in the car without speaking for a few minutes. Then Vivian picked up the mic.

"Maui Central, this is agent Cole with the FBI seeking an update on our APB on the brown cab."

"Maui Central," came a woman's voice. "No reports."

"I'll assume this is being treated as an emergency," she reiterated.

"We have all of our active units on the lookout," came the voice.

"Thank you. Be sure to notify me on this channel if anything comes up," said Vivian.

"Roger that," came the voice.

"Cole out," said Vivian.

"They're not out there on the road," said Chuck. "They've

stopped somewhere. In all likelihood it's all over."

"Let's go back to headquarters and wait, I'm not sure what we can really do out here," said Vivian.

"You're kidding, right?" asked Chuck.

"No, we're not accomplishing anything are we?" she whined.

"We're showing the photo of Rose to condos. That's what we're doing," said Chuck.

"You said there were no more condos," said Vivian.

"There are dozens of condo complexes along here," said Chuck. "You know that, this is your beat. Just not the big names. Small ones. And.....so.....we're going to go door to door until we get some kind of positive response." He held up the fax with Rose's picture with two fingers and waved it. "And we haven't even gone to the other part of the island yet."

"Fine, how about this one," said Vivian pointing to an entrance just ahead and sounding a bit annoyed as she pulled away from the curb in a lurch, then swerved into a drive.

"Good as any," said Chuck, grabbing the armrest to keep from falling over into the seat next to her while glancing back toward Cathy in the back seat who had raised eyebrows and was shrugging her shoulders.

Chapter 20

"**J**ust a little farther," said Rose, pointing ahead at the rapidly narrowing road that was flanked now on both sides by heavy vegetation, with no lights from buildings in sight anywhere.

"You said it was just a short distance beyond....." John complained from the back seat, leaning forward with his hand on Rose's headrest.

"It is, just over this little rise ahead," she assured him. Ralphy glanced at her curiously through wrinkled brow, then looked ahead as he slowed to negotiate the curves, with an occasional swoosh as brush swiped along the side of the car.

"Look, this is not right...." John said nervously from the back seat. Rose had carefully and without notice retrieved and installed the silencer, loaded the magazine and inserted it in the gun inside the suitcase and had it firmly in her hand. She now took it out and held it carefully on top of the suitcase. Ralphy was concentrating on the road and did not notice it.

"OK, driver, up ahead on your left you'll come upon a drive," she said, pointing ahead into the darkness. She had no clue whether such a drive existed, but assumed that there must be some side roads ahead and since the ocean was to their right, there must be a drive to somewhere. Sure enough, just ahead they could see an opening in the trees and brush and Ralphy slowed, then pulled up the narrow, one-lane dirt and gravel drive. A moment later they came to a wide spot next to a small clearing. There were no lights visible in any direction. "Stop here," Rose directed. Ralphy pulled to the side of the road.

"I don't see any...." John began. Then he suddenly looked at Rose, his face ashen, his lip taught. He swallowed as his mind raced, having now made the obvious connection that he so naively hadn't even considered before. He retreated back into the corner of the back seat as he made out the gun that Rose had lifted and was pointing at his forehead. Ralphy now saw it too and began to reach for the door handle.

"Stay!" Rose cautioned, not wavering in her aim at John's forehead. Ralphy held up both hands halfway and scrunched as close to his door as humanly possible. "You are in no danger driver. You will live. I have no reason to harm you now. My mission is nearly complete and it doesn't really matter if I'm caught. I'll have done what I set out to do and it'll be over."

"But none of it was my idea," John said in nearly a whine.

"I know that," said Rose. "Yet in some ways, you were the most important of all."

"I was just doing what I was paid to do..... none of it was my idea...."

"I know that," Rose repeated. "But you delivered the message as no one else apparently could. You were as good at what you did as anyone has ever been. You obviously worked persuasive magic on minds that were admittedly twisted and blind with anger.

"I didn't really do anything...." he pleaded.

"You did plenty," Rose corrected.

"I didn't supply weapons. I didn't supply information on how they would do what they did or transport anyone to the right place. I didn't pay them one thin dime. I didn't....."

"But you led them in such a perfect and convincing way that they followed through with what may well have only been a fantasy for them," she interrupted.

"They probably would have done what they did without any encouragement from me or anyone else. These people were largely loners who had minds and distortions of reality all their own. I couldn't create that kind of...."

"But you intervened at just the right time with just the right words..... or whatever you did," she interrupted again.

"It was just words," he said as if to convince her that was all he did.

"I suspect more, but what, I don't know. How could it matter now, John? How could it matter if you tell the truth to someone after all these years. No one else will ever know. These will be your last moments."

"No, please...." he pleaded as the reality of his imminent death began to sink in. "Please, I'll give you anything. I'll tell you anything if you just let me go..."

"No, John, I won't let you go. It will all end here tonight. Here on this tropical paradise, on a back road within minutes of the safety and comfort of your posh condominium."

"Look, I'll make you a rich woman...."

"Riches can never begin to compare with the sweet smell of retribution."

"Retribution? But why? Surely you couldn't have taken all of this personally? These were just political figures that....."

"Just political figures? No, John, they were more than just political figures. These were men who would change history, who would have made so much difference in the world. Their lives were cut short in the very prime of their productive thoughts. Just as they were giving so much to us."

"You're way too wrapped up in the gooey political rhetoric.... these were just men with views that clashed with the views of the mainstream. The solid and secure path of conservatism. The only path that leads to stability and a safe and secure world."

"You were one of them," Rose laughed with a nod. "I guess I already knew that."

"No, I wasn't one of them," said John weakly and not in a pleading voice. "I wasn't just a soft wag sitting around in a stuffy club room ranting about the enemy. I was out there on the front lines doing something about it."

"So you did do more than just talk to these lunatics."

"Sometimes yes. Hypnosis once. Something akin to hypnosis a second time. In most cases just very clever pep talks and how easy it would be for them afterward. How famous they would be. How much better they would feel having rid the world of such dangerous men. Even suggestions of how I, or my sponsors, would see to it that they were cared for."

"But you never gave anyone names, not even your own."

"And I was always in disguise. Sometimes very clever disguises I might add."

"And who could ever trace anything to you or the Baker's Dozen."

"Is that what he called them…Baker's Dozen?"

"Did you know Judd?"

"Not really….only talked with him on the phone. He would pass on information and instructions as well as money…."

"He did have your picture by the way."

"I know, that was foolish of me, but once we thought that we might have to meet."

"How did they manage to do your money by the way?"

"There are dozens of clever tricks. The most common was for me to act as a consultant in a wide variety of capacities, working for any one of them at any given time under an alias, of course. Rarely was I ever paid for the same type of job twice."

"You never met them."

"I never met one of them, or even saw one of them in person. They wanted it that way."

"Surely though, deep in your thoughts, you must have feared this day."

"It never occurred to me that I would be caught… no," he said.

"You thought you would get away with it."

"Yes, of course. The man I replaced years ago had gotten away with it. And unless I was careless and allowed myself to be traced to one of the assassins, I had really nothing to fear. I had constructed elaborate excuses if I ever was somehow traced to any of them."

"The man you replaced? Yes, I guess this thing went on for decades."

"It did."

"You were a loner, with no close friends or family to ask questions."

"Just a dingy girlfriend who believed anything I told her. She never questioned any of it as long as she could buy anything she wanted whenever she wanted."

"Why didn't you bring her here with you?"

"I don't know why... this was somehow different.... I've never felt hunted or threatened before... this was the first time I was ever in any danger of being found out."

"That was a good decision. Although I'd have spared her since you're the last and I don't care if I'm caught."

"So who killed your brother? You? Did you kill your own brother?"

"No, not really. We quarreled and he fell onto a fireplace hearth."

"So that's how it started?"

"That's how it started."

"What made you think that a little old woman could just go around the country and kill off a dozen prominent men?"

"Actually, it was the perfect disguise, and the arrogance of these men was their own downfall. They refused to cooperate with authorities, thinking that their secret society was more important than the safety of its members. They dragged their feet right to the very end. Instead of fleeing to some other place, like you, they just put on an extra security guard or two and they proved relatively easy to walk past."

236

"Apparently."

"Even you. You didn't bring a bodyguard. You weren't even attentive enough to notice it was an elderly woman who got into the cab with you until it was too late."

"Despite the possibility, I still assumed it must be a man... perhaps a man dressed like an older woman...but nonetheless a man....it's so unexpected, so unlikely....."

"I didn't have an opportunity to chat with all of the others. That much I regret. However with a few of them I was able to at least let them know why, and that I knew, and that this was the pay back."

"I think you should let me go," said John calmly. "We could do a book. TV special. Even a movie. The subject matter is a goldmine. Think of all the people who would have an opportunity to learn the truth about history and to rewrite history if you will. There would be a chance to state your position. To once and for all, for all mankind........"

Chapter 21

"Well, we've knocked on a lot of doors and haven't even gotten around to the Kaanapali," said Vivian in an irritating tone as they sat in the car in the drive of a resort.

"Check with the local fuzz once again," said Cathy.

"I just did that ten minutes ago, remember," said Vivian shaking her head angrily.

"I'm going to get out here and walk around," said Chuck. "Somehow, I just can't get the feel for this place riding around in a car."

"I could stretch my legs too," said Cathy.

"Right....and riding around in a car with a cranky little blonde ain't doing it," said Chuck, pointing a finger at Vivian whose eyes were now as big as saucers, her hands gripping the wheel so tightly they were white. Chuck swung open the door and stepped out. Cathy instinctively opened her door and put one leg out as Vivian slammed it in gear and floored it, bringing a cloud of smoke from the spinning tires. The tire slippage gave Cathy time to leap out and slam the door as the white Ford fishtailed down the road, then disappeared into the night, leaving Chuck and Cathy staring after it. They looked at each other and began to laugh.

"Fucking little ill tempered bitch," said Chuck.

"Unbecoming of a federal agent," said Cathy, sounding official.

"Unbecoming of a pit bull," said Chuck, with a snort as he turned and walked down a dead end street toward the ocean. Cathy followed and, in the moonlight, they could see a paved walkway along the shore.

"Perfect," said Cathy as she caught up with Chuck.

"Yeah, a walk in the moonlight," he chuckled.

"I'm sure the deed is done by now, don't you think?"

"As certain as I am that the sun will rise tomorrow," he said without breaking stride.

"I wonder if the cabby got it too?"

"No, this was the last one. No reason for collateral damage now."

"Collateral damage. That's a polite term."

"You know, if Rose had not inflicted so damned much collateral damage, I think I could forgive her for all of the other killings."

"Forgive her? What do you mean?"

"I mean, these clowns deserved to eventually be punished for what they did. You know they would never in a million years be brought to justice and that her little one-woman imitation of Sherman's march through Georgia was the only way they would ever be made to pay."

"What do you mean forgive her?.... you mean let her go?"

"If the opportunity arose, you never know what happens in the field."

"But the collateral damage."

"Yeah, the collateral damage."

"I know, I've actually harbored the same thoughts believe it or not."

"Really? That's hard for me to believe. Me? Yes. Slob. Rule bender par excellance. You, Ms. law enforcement agent of the year. You? No."

"This is such a special case....like nothing we've ever seen or heard of before."

"Yeah, I guess," said Chuck

"So you think she's going to just turn herself in now that it's over."

"Assuming it's over, I really don't know."

"What would you do if you were her right now?"

"I was just trying to imagine that, and I don't know," he replied. "Sense of relief that it was over. Probably sense of accomplishment mixed with the realization of what I'd just done. Maybe a bit of reality setting in. Maybe just exhaustion. Maybe I'd just find a place to lay low for a while before I tried to think of doing anything."

"She lives in Cleveland. Her home is there. Art studio I understand from the summary sheet attached to the photo. A social life, I presume. Would she return there?"

"I don't know," he said. "But somehow, something is still missing or just not quite right about the whole affair."

"What do you mean, not quite right."

"There were a lot a coincidences that helped her. Too many for just plain luck. Too many perfect decisions. As if she had help. The latest was how she was able to smuggle a gun onto a plane which I'm sure she did."

"And you know, I wonder if she really knew she was getting help."

"I wonder too," he nodded.

"Who though?.... not those other guys."

"You mean the CIA? No, I doubt that seriously."

"Liberal action group of some kind?" she asked.

"Possibly, but that kind of group wouldn't be so professional and not likely to be prone to mob-like violence. The help she's had was from folks who know how to do this stuff."

"They could hire professional help....the liberal extremists that is."

"True, they could. But whoever 'they' are, they obviously had the inside information that she did. So they were able to follow her around and help her out at just the right moments."

"Facilitating her actions," she said.

"Perplexing isn't it?"

"What about the families of some of the people assassinated over the years who continue to believe in these conspiracies and wanted to do something about it? Could they be involved?"

"That's a possibility, but again without inside information, how could they follow this macabre tragedy? But?" he queried.

"But?"

"But, I don't know but what.....I guess but it's more organized than just a bunch of hired PIs. This kind of help has to be networked somehow. Almost like they had people there already in every place where she happened to be."

"Like the CIA."

"Nah, they're not going to get themselves involved in anything like this.... and certainly not to the extent of the commitment that they would have had to have made. Nor would they have the secret inside information. Nor do the collaterals. Not them."

"You're right," she nodded. "A foreign power? No. That doesn't make sense either, unless assassination targets were wider spread than we've imagined."

"Nothing at all comes to mind."

"If they're as widespread as it seems, surely they'd be noticed by the agency or the other agency."

"Not necessarily. Not if they operate in the open as a completely different kind of group, but have a secretive side that nobody knows about, not even most of the membership."

"Hmmm," she sighed. "Yeah. I see what you mean. But who?"

"Don't have a clue."

A horn beeped off to their side as they walked. They looked up momentarily and continued their walk. The beep continued, this time more insistent. They stopped and strained to see up into the parking lot where the horn came from. It had stopped now so they continued on their walk. A moment later a shrill voice broke the soft rumble of gentle waves along the shore.

"We've got action!" came the unmistakable voice of Vivian through the darkness. They immediately broke into a run across the lawn and through the landscaping toward the voice. Ahead, Vivian was standing at the edge of the pavement to the lot.

"What's up?" yelled Chuck as they approached.

"Found the car and one John Doe, dead."

"Any ID?" asked Cathy.

"No, just got the report. Male. Caucasian. Late fifties. In a car abandoned in the jungle off the end of the strip toward the point ....on a side road."

"I guess that's it then," said Cathy. "The last one."

"Let's get there right away," said Chuck pointing to Vivian's car.

"What's the rush now?" asked Vivian. "The locals will be able to wrap this thing up for us."

"Let's get there to the scene," Chuck insisted, walking to the car and opening the passenger door.

"So you've a thought about this?" asked Cathy, climbing into the back seat as Vivian fumbled for her keys outside.

"Maybe.... the car shouldn't be abandoned," said Chuck. "Something's not right."

"Why shouldn't the car be abandoned?" asked Vivian as she got in and started the car.

"Where's the driver? Why wasn't the body just dumped and then Rose drives off? What did she do, walk from an abandoned car in the middle of the night out in the jungle? To where? Something doesn't sound right here."

"He's right," said Cathy. "Even if this is her last hit, it doesn't fit her M.O. We need to take a closer look at this.... and hope that the locals haven't screwed up the crime scene."

"I can't imagine they would," said Vivian as they sped down the road. Fifteen minutes later, they could see red and blue lights at the entrance to a narrow side road ahead with a police officer standing in the middle, with a flashlight, holding up his hand toward them as they approached.

"FBI," said Vivian, waving her badge and ID out the window as she pulled up. He pointed up the narrow drive and they wound their way to an assemblage of vehicles, including a medical van, another police car and a panel truck. Off to the side was the beige Chevy cab with passenger side doors open and a collection of uniformed people milling about.

"Where's the victim?" asked Chuck who had gotten out of the car even before it had come to a stop.

"Who might you be?" asked a uniformed man with a red cross on his sleeve.

"FBI," he replied, sticking his ID in his coat pocket with the badge hanging out on display.

"The victim is in the van ready to go to the morgue," said the man, pointing.

"Do you have an ID on the victim?" asked Chuck, who had quickly pawed his way past two officers to the open rear doors of the panel truck. He was addressing a stocky woman with black hair and Hawaiian features who appeared to be in her late forties.

"Ralph Jenkins," said the woman, pointing to the lump under the sheet.

"The cab driver?" exclaimed Vivian as she elbowed her way through.

"He's been IDed?" asked Chuck just as Cathy arrived.

"Cab license....driver's license.... this was his cab," she shrugged.

"Shit!" scoffed Chuck, rushing forward to pull back the sheet.

"Now what?" exclaimed Cathy, moving up beside Chuck to

look. She saw an ashen face with half dried blood covering his clothing and splotches here and there on his face.

"Are you sure…somebody didn't plant ID on him?" asked Vivian, giving the coroner a confused look.

"No, it's him, I've seen him around. It's Ralphy all right. Nice guy. Kind of a loner but never gave anyone any trouble. Too bad."

"The cab driver," Chuck repeated, looking at Cathy. "Definitely, NOT Rose. Something went wrong. Terribly wrong. Number thirteen must have gotten the gun somehow. But….. is there any evidence of blood or other shots fired?" He looked at the coroner who just shrugged and pointed at the two officers who were off to the side talking. Chuck ran to them pointing to his badge as he arrived.

"We know, you're the FBI," said one of the officers somewhat sarcastically before Chuck could speak.

"Was there any evidence of other shots fired or blood or anything resembling a struggle?" he asked pointing down the drive.

"Not really, except about a million nickels scattered around and in this gravel and we haven't noticed any footprints."

"How could you notice footprints, you've got an army of people walking haphazardly over everything," snapped Cathy as she arrived.

"Look, we've got things…."

"You've pretty much fucked things up," said Vivian, in that raspy, annoying voice that had finally driven Chuck over the edge earlier.

"Look, you have no…."

"Bull fucking shit!" shouted Vivian, stepping up in front of the six foot four two hundred fifty pound officer and looking up at him from her five foot one, one-hundred pound frame. "This is a federal fucking case and we just took over this site.... now get your lame asses away from the evidence before it's all fucking gone." The man backed up while looking at his partner who just shrugged and then stepped back with him.

"We need to check in with.....," his partner began.

"You do that bucko," said Vivian. "In the meantime, instruct all of these people to keep the fuck away from the car and not to touch a single piece of anything, anywhere." One officer hesitated then walked back to his car. The other looked at her for a moment then looked around before speaking.

"OK, listen up!" he shouted in a deep booming voice after studying her for a moment. "This crime scene is in the process of being transferred to the FBI. Any evidence that you've gathered, bag it and document it. Otherwise discontinue your investigation until we get confirmation from headquarters."

"Thank you," said Vivian, turning to Chuck. "What's your theory?"

"Uh.... well," he hesitated, momentarily taken aback by her quick and decisive actions of which he approved. He smiled.

"The two of them are on foot," he began. "He likely has the gun. Following her. She's almost seventy. He may be younger. Somehow though, I suspect that he's at a disadvantage. I would never for a second underestimate Rose Baker knowing the history of this episode. So, what's my theory? Well... he thinks he's hunting her down. In fact, she's hunting him down."

"But he has the gun and, if he's the real action man in Baker's

246

Dozen, he may have more than a little bit of experience using one."

"Doesn't matter," said Chuck. "I've investigated a few homicides in my day. Seen a lot of violent crime. Gang hits. Serial killings. A lot of shit. This woman is as clever as they come and completely ruthless. If I were mystery guy number thirteen, I'd be afraid. I'd be very afraid."

"You know, somehow I suspect that he is just that," said Vivian with a smirk. "Afraid. Even though he apparently has the gun and is hunting her, I suspect that he is, in fact, afraid. He's witnessed her march across the country toward him and he ran here to Maui when he knew his number was coming up. Yes, he's clever. But I suspect that deep down inside, he's also afraid, and he's afraid of Rose Baker."

"Yeah," said Chuck, staring off into the undergrowth. "So would I be afraid."

Chapter 22

Rose was running as fast as she could down the dirt road, almost stumbling several times. She knew she could not outrun him, yet she had heard him fall as he came out of the car, hitting hard and then cursing loudly. And the steps behind her were not regular. It was as if he were limping. Then the whiz past her head. He had fired at her as she ran, but not nearly as fast as she had as a younger woman. She was not fast at all, she reasoned, as she struggled, stiff legged. It was almost a fast shuffle. She would laugh but it was not funny. It was deadly serious. He had her gun. He took it when the driver had foolishly grabbed its barrel and Rose had instinctively pulled the trigger, shooting him in the throat. The blood had squirted out in her face as he lurched back, and before she could react, John's hand was on hers and they struggled. The gun came loose and skidded out the door and onto the ground. She had scurried out of the car and groped for it in the dark as John rattled the door handle trying to get out. He finally climbed over the seat to go out the front door as she gave up the search and began to run down the road, but only to discover how difficult it was for her to run fast. It had been too many years. Her memory was of a much earlier time when she could glide effortlessly along. Now she could sense the impending danger. Her limitations. The inevitability of being caught by someone who now had her gun. She lumbered onward, the shuffling limp from John behind her and an occasional zing, sometimes close, sometimes off to the side where it would rip through some leafy bush. Now the highway. She had to decide.... across the road into the brush or up the road back toward the resorts. There were lights of a car to her right toward the resorts. Far in the distance. She ran toward them. Now somewhat faster on the smooth pavement as her Keds no longer stubbed on the gravel and rock of the side road. Another zing, this one pinging off the pavement ahead of her. The car lights ahead seemed to be stationary as she ran toward them. The shuffling behind her was getting closer. She did not know how close, but she knew he would eventually catch her. But could she reach the lights first? If she did, what would she do? She could now see that the lights were moving slowly toward her and she could hear the hum of the motor. Behind her the shuffling ceased. John had apparently stopped. She was now there beside the car where it had stopped. A large white sedan. The back door swung open.

"Get in Rose," came a deep voice from the dark interior. She obeyed instinctively. Exhausted to the point of trembling knees, she collapsed in the back seat.

"Clance?" she asked after having thought about the familiar voice.

249

"We cannot interfere directly, Rose," came the voice. "We can only assist."

"It is you isn't it, Clance?" she repeated as she peered intently into the dark, just making out the distinctive features of the black man in the overcoat on Euclid Ave in Cleveland. The man who had gotten her the gun and the car. Now he was here. Maybe he was other places along her journey, and others with him. But who was he? Who were they? Why could they only assist. Somehow she didn't care right now. Somehow she even understood, even though she wasn't at all sure what she understood. Just that someone was there to help her. Help her do what had to be done. What authorities could not do.

The car moved forward, lights clicking up to high beam. Ahead a figure stood in the center of the road. He now aimed the gun at the windshield and fired. The bullet made a dull thunk as it flattened against the impenetrable screen, leaving only a small gray smudge where it hit. Another shot. Another smudge. Then a click....no more shells. John looked at the gun momentarily before flinging it at them. It bounced off the hood, then the windshield and onto the road beside the car. Rose reached into her pocket for a fistful of bullets and quickly and calmly got out of the car and picked up the gun. The door was still open as she removed the clip and quickly slipped shells into it. John was now backing up in the glare of the headlights, unable to see what was going on. The clip clinked back into place and Rose walked forward toward him. He had heard the distinctive sound of the clip going in and could now see her. He looked one way, then another, finally stepping backward and losing his balance, falling into the ditch in a heap. Rose continued forward, now standing on the roadside looking down at him in the indirect glare of the car's lights. He looked one way, then another and started to get up, then finally just put up his hands and leaned back against the bank. Rose's profile was outlined clearly against the bright background.

"Who are they?" he asked calmly, in almost a conversational tone.

"I have no idea," she replied truthfully.

"I knew that someone was behind this, I knew it couldn't be just you alone," he lamented.

"Doesn't really matter now, does it?" she replied

"No, it doesn't."

"The others, the dozen angry men with the hateful minds..... they could never in a million years have pulled off what they wanted to do by themselves could they?" asked Rose.

"Them? No. They were just blowhards. But they had money. And they bought me."

"But you were different than just your average hired help."

"Yes."

"You believed the rhetoric."

"It wasn't rhetoric now was it? It was action. It was results."

"And now it all ends."

"The offer of the book and movie rights is still open," he half smiled. It was his last. A purple dot appeared just above the bridge of his nose. His eyes opened wide and then he went limp. Behind her, Rose heard a car door shut and the car backed up into a drive, turned around and sped away into the night. She stood silently on the side of the road still shaking from having run to near exhaustion. Tired, sore, but satisfied. She turned

251

and walked slowly back up the road toward the resorts until the faint lights of a hotel along the waterfront appeared. A parking lot was just ahead behind the hotel. In the back of the mostly empty lot she could see the colorful paint of a cab. It was empty. She walked up to it and ducked her head in the open window. On the seat was a clipboard with a set of keys. She smiled and looked back toward the road, thinking of the white limo and Clance. Then shook her head and got in. The key worked and she drove away.

Chapter 23

"There's no suitcase," said Chuck, surveying the empty car. "There's just the scattered pile of nickels. I'll bet she used the nickels to hide the gun or parts of the gun to get by security. Though, I have no idea why they wouldn't look through it, or spot something. Security breach. Another piece of luck. Or perhaps some kind of help....again..."

"Correct," said Cathy. "I think it had to be help."

"She could not have taken her suitcase with her so she had to come back here in a car," said Chuck.

"A car?" asked Vivian.

"Well," mused Chuck scratching his chin then placing his hand around his neck in contemplation. "She had to come back here to get it.... and this is a remote area."

"It's better than a half mile to the nearest resort and there are no other houses around here," said Vivian. "And she's not likely to be crouching out in the bushes somewhere. So coming back in a car makes the most sense. But where would she get a car?"

"Don't know but I'm sure she's safe and warm somewhere," said Chuck. "And I see no way out of assuming that she's had help of some kind. Not necessarily direct help, but some kind of assistance like what we were discussing earlier."

"I must have missed that discussion," said Vivian with a shrug.

"All along she's seemed to have it too easy," said Chuck in explanation. "Like someone was almost running interference for her. Despite her cleverness and daring style, she's managed to do things almost too smoothly and getting away too easily. She was doing the job too quickly and effortlessly. It was as if someone was watching and then giving her just a little bit of assistance. Not that much, mind you, but a little."

"Like somehow appearing tonight as she's being chased and somehow getting the tables turned?" asked Vivian.

"Yeah, something like that," said Chuck.

"And then, she what, hotwires a car or something and drives back here?" asked Cathy.

"Or comes back with her helpers?" asked Vivian.

"No, not with the helpers. I suspect they're watching and assisting, but are keeping entirely clear of any direct involvement."

"Then how would they turn the tables on number thirteen as you suggest?" asked Vivian.

"I don't know. Maybe just by them showing up, number thirteen gets spooked and makes a mistake. I don't know."

"Of course, all of this is speculation," said Cathy. "Maybe Rose did shoot the cabby...."

"No, that much I'm certain of. She wouldn't shoot the cabby

254

unless she had also shot number thirteen in the process. There was no need to shoot the cabby in the first place because this was the last score."

"Unless she wanted to retire safely," said Vivian.

"No, I think Chuck is right on this one," said Cathy. "She wouldn't shoot the cabby unless he somehow got in the way and it doesn't look that way. Besides, it looks like a messy hit, not the neat between the eyes shots she's famous for. This one was bloody. Someone else did it."

"Or it was an accident," said Chuck.

"You mean like he grabbed for her gun and it went off," said Cathy.

"Then number thirteen grabbed for the gun and there was a struggle..."

"Right, that could have been.....," Chuck began.

"What's this?" asked Vivian who had been leaning into the driver's door poking around with a flashlight.

"What?" asked Chuck crowding in.

"A shoe," she replied, taking out a handkerchief and lifting the shoe out from between the seats.

"It looks like he must have caught his ankle between the seat and the emergency brake which is a bit rugged to say the least...... looks like he injured himself..... maybe twisted an ankle, certainly lacerated it by the look of the bloodstains."

"Indications on the dirt here too," said Cathy, crouching beside the car and pointing to a dark stain on the dirt. "One bare foot...gravel, rocks, ouch..."

"So he had only one shoe and an injured ankle. That explains why she was able to get away. It doesn't explain what happened next though."

"Twenty-two shell casing," said Chuck from down the road a bit where he had wandered with his flashlight, combing the surface.

"He was firing at her with her gun."

"Get a team together and let's follow Hansel and Gretel's trail," said Chuck.

"Twenty-two casings? That's like looking for needles in a haystack," said Vivian.

"Not if you know what you're looking for," said Chuck. "They should reflect enough light at night to spot. May even be better than looking for them in the daytime."

"Sergeant," said Vivian to the police officer, pointing at him as she walked up.

"We need a detail of a few of your men with flashlights to go down this road and try to find twenty-two caliber shell casings," she instructed. He looked at her for a moment, then nodded and waved two of his officers over.

"Take flashlights and scan this road for twenty-two caliber shell casings," he directed.

"Just keep following them," Vivian directed as they nodded and turned to follow Chuck who was already well down the road. A few minutes later, they were on the main highway. One officer went left out toward the end of the road. The other officer and Chuck went right, back toward the resort. A moment later Chuck spotted a shell and the other officer turned around and followed them. In a few minutes Chuck was standing over two empty casings.

"Eight, counting the bullet in the cabby," he said. Something off to his left caught his eye. It was a ninth casing.

"Seems out of place," said Chuck.

"What do you mean?" asked Cathy.

"Clear off on the shoulder," said Chuck. "Something happened here."

"Like what?" asked the officer.

"Don't know… let's check the ditch," said Chuck, taking a few steps forward to where the empty casing lie, then pointing the light down and sweeping it to one side, then the other, finally settling onto the corpse of John Averil.

"Ohhhh," said the officer turning away momentarily as the glassy stare reflected back at him.

"Yeah, ohhh," said Chuck. "Number thirteen," he nodded. "Better get back to your car and get on the horn."

"There's the Sarge now," said the officer pointing at the approaching lights and running toward them, hands raised. Behind it was Vivian's white sedan. Both cars rocked to a halt, lights still on as both the Sergeant and Vivian burst out and ran around to where Chuck was standing, still pointing the flashlight onto the corpse.

"Well, that will likely end the siege," said Vivian, standing next to Chuck, shaking her head. "We came in on this in time to have stopped the one in LA and this one, but she went through us like we were invisible."

"She had help, so we don't need to beat ourselves up over this thing," said Chuck.

"Yeah, but how much help? Certainly not enough to have impeded any of our agents from doing their job if they had had an opportunity."

"I agree with that. But she got some pretty timely help here. What kind of help, I can't really tell. He seems to have fired the last two shots in the clip at something from back in the center of the road. Perhaps at a car. I don't see any broken glass. Then, perhaps he threw the gun. Don't know. Rose, of course, had more shells in her pocket and she picked up the gun and whang."

"You got all of that from this?" asked Vivian. "What if he just ran out of ammo and threw the gun at her and she did what you said?"

"The two shots are together in the road, suggesting that he stopped to fire at something. I'm guessing it was a car. Possibly a car with bulletproof glass. Again, don't know. And they— whoever 'they' are-- had let Rose inside, or she would have been hit. He wouldn't have thrown the gun at her if he had missed her. He'd have tried to strangle her or hit her with the gun not throw it at her. But if she were in a car, it all makes sense."

"Oh," said Vivian, nodding and studying Chuck's face as he stared off into the night in deep thought.

"Let's get this guy's real name," said Chuck, pointing at the corpse.

"Officer," said Vivian, gesturing to one of the police officers. He made a grimace, then slowly descended into the ditch and began searching through John's clothing.

"Passport," said the officer. "David Ross". A moment later he pulled a wallet out of John's back pocket. "John Averill."

"John Averill," said Chuck. "The passport is a fake."

"How can you fake a passport with the system we have in place?" asked Vivian with a shrug. "Plus, if nobody really knows who he is, why use false identification?"

"He's had decades to develop false identities, especially living internationally," he replied. "He brings false papers with him just in case. It's John Averill. Let's get that information to the agency."

"I'll take care of that," said Cathy taking her cell phone from her pocket.

"So where is she now?" asked Vivian.

"Found a car somewhere down the road," said Chuck shrugging.

"Why not ride away in the car that stopped to help her?"

"Because whoever it is doesn't do that sort of thing. They assist, then disappear. They are very careful not to get involved any further. They're like guardians but never get too close. They did their thing, then left. She walked away and found a car."

"But where? There's no place to go along here except back up toward the resorts."

"I don't know. Where's the first resort you come to if you walk back up this road?" asked Chuck, walking to Vivian's car and opening the passenger door. She followed and got in.

"Let's find out," she said as they sped away. A half mile down the road on the left, they saw the facade of a hotel with a lighted parking lot in the back. Vivian pulled in and stopped about halfway.

"What now?" she asked.

Chuck looked around, then got out and rested his chin and hands on the open door, staring ahead. At length, he walked toward the end of the nearly empty parking lot, Vivian following slowly in the car. He kneeled down and touched the grass in the planting strip at the end of the lot, then reached down and pulled

259

a small flattened plant upright. By now Vivian was out of the car and standing over him.

"A car was parked here recently," he stated, now standing up.

"What was a car doing parked at the end of the parking lot on the planting strip?" she asked, then looked around. "The lot's practically empty."

"Exactly," said Chuck. "The impressions are fresh, like only a few hours old so the lot couldn't have been full when the car was parked here."

"Left for her?"

"Mmmm maybe," said Chuck. "Or someone who works in the hotel, maybe even a cab off duty," he mumbled in a faraway voice.

"If someone left it, how would they know where....," Vivian began.

"Get the locals on the box and have them get some lab people up here pronto. Then have them find someone in the hotel and ask if anyone here parked a cab outside. That could be a clue worth following up on, even though she's had a lot of lead time to get away, ditch the cab, whatever."

"I'll get on it." Said Vivian, then went quickly to the car and made several calls on the radio, returning a few minutes later as Chuck was now standing in the middle of the lot. He was staring out over the palms at the ocean that glistened in the pale moonlight that was now peeking through the clouds.

"Where do you think she'll go?" asked Vivian. "We've got the airport pretty well covered so she won't get off the island."

"You're kidding, right?" laughed Chuck.

"How would she?"

"If I wanted to get off this island, I could do it," said Chuck. "Steal a boat if nothing else."

"She's a seventy year old woman," Vivian whined.

"Even though she's had some assistance at times, she's pretty much outmaneuvered everyone, walking right through us like we're amateurs, getting away from number thirteen in a one on one confrontation, and you think that being seventy has been an impediment..... at all? Plus she's had some ghostly help...."

"It just seems...."

"I know, but now I'm not sure that she thinks this thing is over.....I think she's now curious about those who helped her..... the ghosts."

"So you think we ought to get a helicopter up there and watch for boats?"

"No, quite honestly, I don't know what we would look for. A boat is just a thought. In reality, I'm more interested in where she might be heading than trying to catch her as she leaves, since I don't think we can."

"Well, I think we can. We have the best equipment and personnel and the modern methods of detection that make it very likely that we'll catch her."

"Right," he said, trying to sound polite but sounding more sarcastic than polite. "I need to think about where she might go next. And right now, I haven't a clue. But like I said, I think that she isn't finished with this adventure of hers." At that moment, a squad car pulled into the lot and stopped behind Vivian's car. An officer and Cathy got out. Cathy came over and stood in front of Chuck. They stared at each other for a moment.

"What about a wife or girlfriend of one of those she killed?"

asked Cathy, anticipating Chuck's thoughts about where she might be. He seemed momentarily surprised at the question, then smiled in recognition.

"Don't think so," he said, shaking his head slowly.

"Perhaps she's going to want to tie up loose ends…as in: who are those guys."

"My thoughts exactly," he nodded.

"Puerto Vallarta?"

"Right."

"But she would have no way to get there," said Vivian, almost laughing. They both looked at her then back at each other.

"We're catching the next plane to LAX, then a connection to Puerto Vallarta," said Cathy. Chuck nodded and pointed at Vivian's car.

"There's nothing out of Maui until morning," Vivian shrugged. "And besides, she hasn't gotten off Maui yet and she won't."

"So we can't get a plane to LAX until tomorrow?" asked Chuck, as if Vivian had said nothing.

"If you really want to, even though you will have no reason, we can heliport you to Honolulu and I'm sure you can catch something going that way," said Vivian shaking her head as she climbed behind the wheel. The other two climbed in and Vivian wound her way out around the squad car and squealed off down the highway, talking on the radio as she drove.

Chapter 24

"Excuse me, senor," said Rose, walking up to the window of a van and addressing the driver.

"Yes, may I help you senora," said the man inside, bowing his head with an ear-to-ear smile.

"Which are the condominiums?" she asked. The man turned and pointed out the passenger side of his van.

"Facing the marina there," he smiled. "The main entry to the resort is around through there facing the ocean," he pointed out the front window in the other direction.

"I'm interested in the condos not the other part….are you familiar with the condo units?" she asked.

"Si," he nodded.

"Are there penthouses?"

"Si."

"Is there an attractive blonde lady who lives in one of them?" she asked, assuming that John would stay in only the best but having no idea if he actually did.

"Uh, si," he nodded, becoming somewhat more serious. "Do you know her and Mr. Averill?"

Wow, he used his own name thought Rose, a bit surprised that he would. She nodded to the man.

"Yes, John has been away on business for almost two months, and I was down here and just wanted to surprise her. John and I don't get along very well. In fact we had a falling out so to speak. I'm her cousin from Los Angeles."

"Ah, si, he has not been around. I know. But she has had company. Visitors. Parties."

"Yes, she likes to party," Rose laughed, knowing in all probability what the company really was.

"Is there a way I can go up there from here?"

"Gess, but you have to go to the…."

"No, no, I don't want her called before I come up, I want it to be a total surprise. Just walk in on her. You know. So, you see, I'll need to go directly up there."

"It is a private entry. Privado. Only owners," he cautioned, wagging his finger.

She reached into her bag, fished around for a moment, then pulled out two crisp 100 dollar bills and held them up to him.

"It means a great deal to me to be able to surprise her….uh, what is your name?"

"Eduardo," he nodded, looking longingly at the money but not saying anything.

"Eduardo, I'll make it three of these if you'll do just one simple thing: take me up to her door, ring the bell, and tell her that you need to check something."

"Senora, I cannot….I could lose…."

"OK an even five," she smiled. "5,000 pesos."

"Uh…. well the television cable has been a problem…." he began, still cautiously, but now intently watching the additional bills being added.

"And then I leave right away?" he confirmed.

"Right away," she assured him. "The second the door is unlocked… then vamanos."

With that he got out of the van and pointed to an unmarked door in an alleyway and they made their way to it. He typed in some numbers on a keypad and the door clicked open. They walked into a pleasant little area with marble floors. There was an elevator door at one end marked 'for the private use of penthouse residents only' and the same message repeated in Spanish below it. Eduardo pointed to the sign and raised his eyebrows, then pushed the button. A moment later they were on a landing overlooking the alleyway and walking toward one of several widely spaced doors. Eduardo walked ahead and pointed to the last door. Rose stopped just before they arrived and stood as close to the wall as she could, then pointed to Eduardo. He pushed the button.

"Yes? Who's there?" came a lilting voice from behind the large carved door after what seemed a long time.

"Eduardo," he said as his eyes glanced quickly at Rose who was now leaning against the wall holding the five bills and nodding at him with a smile.

"I didn't call for maintenance," the voice said, sounding somewhat strained.

"The TV cable is not right," he said, shrugging to her in front

265

of the peep hole.

"John isn't home now and I'm not really supposed to let anyone in," she pleaded, almost as if she were asking him not to press the question.

"It's right next to the door by you in the big gray box…and I'll only be a minute," he begged.

"Only a minute?" she confirmed. "Well…."

"Maybe less," he shrugged with a smile, the five bills clearly in his peripheral vision.

"OK, less than a minute…" she said as one lock then another clicked and the door opened a crack. While she was unlocking the door and wasn't yet able to see past the crack, Rose handed the bills to Eduardo and pushed him on his way down the landing, then whipped out her gun and had it in the woman's face at the same time that she shoved the door open, knocking the woman back against the hallway wall.

"Oh my …..god…" the slender blonde said in a fading voice as she pushed back against the wall, the gun virtually touching her nose. Rose closed the door behind her, not wavering in her aim.

"John won't be coming home as I'm sure you already know," Rose stated in a steady, almost sarcastic voice. The woman didn't flinch but stood silently and watched her, a strange calm seeming to come over her, even a faint smile crept onto her lips.

"So, you're Rose," she nodded finally after a moment, her voice suddenly changing from weak and whining to firm and confident.

"And I guess you're not who everyone thought you were…. especially John," said Rose, nodding with a grin.

"Hmpphh," the woman sputtered contemptuously as if the gun were just a toy and didn't matter. "So I guess you've figured all of this out."

"Not completely," said Rose. "Actually, not everything until this very moment. But much of it became clear to me once I figured out the roles of the various players. I concluded that John could not have been the sole source of all the havoc. That he could not have done it alone. That perhaps, just perhaps, this shadow group that seemed to escort me around the country, helping me at just the right times and then disappearing.....that this group was somehow implicated in ways that I had never imagined. As I reflected back on it, I initially, and naively I might add, assumed it was a liberal group cheerleading me on. Then, as the true nature of the operation unfolded at the very end, I became convinced that not only were they not a liberal cheerleading group, they were, in fact, the very heart of the entire conspiracy. Not just John's helpers but John's group. His board of directors. Baker's dozen were just the money and the hot air. I assumed that John was just a contact man for the group. A middle man if you will. But he was far too generous in his self praise to actually be the big cheese. You and your gang are the big cheese. And you yourself play a central role."

"So that's why you came here?" the woman almost laughed, shaking her head. "To take me out?"

"Of course," she said in a matter of fact tone. "But I'm curious....I'm a woman...I have intuitions about people....but John... didn't John suspect that you were one of the core group's members? Or worse perhaps among its leaders?"

"John was very clever. He was a genius, really, and ruthless.

But he was a fool. No, he never suspected me to be anything other than his 'dumb blonde' through these many years."

"So you were right there with him to make sure that he toed the mark."

"I didn't actually have to do much, he was pretty committed and very careful, but don't doubt for a second that if he'd fucked up and had been found to be connected to any of these things, I would have let him fry."

"Or fried him yourself. For the survival of the cause."

"For the survival of the cause," she nodded with a devious grin.

"So where are they?" asked Rose, looking past her.

"They would never be....." the woman began.

"Uh, uh, uh, uh….let's go see who your guests are, shall we?" said Rose, waving the gun toward the living area.

"You don't want to....." she began again.

"Yes, I do want to. I just have the feeling that this is a grand reunion," Rose said. She put both hands on the gun and pointed directly at the woman's temple. The woman sobered, hesitated a moment, then slowly turned and began walking down a long hallway toward the living area, Rose close behind. The suite was gigantic. The entry foyer of the penthouse was elevated several steps above the main entertainment area which formed a semi-circle looking out through an expanse of glass onto a majestic view of the marina and the lagoon. They entered onto a landing with a rail and steps down to the main living area. Seated along a thirty foot wide semi-circular sofa upholstered in dark green leather sat what looked like a dozen or so people. Rose scanned the group who were now all turned toward them. Clancy, she

268

recognized. There was the man from Winter Park who drove her away from the crime scene at MGM. The man who helped her escape Vail. The woman on the bus from Kellogg. Another from one of the restaurants she ate at. And another man she had seen in the limousine on Maui.

"Well, well," said Rose, surveying the group. "Join them, won't you," she motioned for the woman to go down and sit with the rest of the group. The woman hesitated a moment, then slowly walked down the steps and toward the sofa. Rose remained on the landing studying the faces, recognizing others she had run into along the way, including the man with the laptop in the hallway in New York.

"Thirteen of us," said the woman anticipating Rose's question, then sitting down on the end of the sofa. "Maybe you'd like to join us down here?" she motioned.

"No, I'll stand thank you," said Rose, her gaze wandering from face to face. Mostly men. Three women. All at least in their fifties or sixties. There were a couple of them maybe younger. All younger than Baker's Dozen, she mused. They were like a shadow group. The real group, actually, she thought. But younger, that much was confusing. They used her brother's group to generate money and made them think that they were really behind the whole thing, but all the while they were just pawns in the end. John Averill was the 'middle man'. And he knew that there was more to the movement than Baker's dozen but thought that he played a much bigger role than he actually did. The Dozen knew about this group but also believed that they themselves were the ones in charge, not this group.

"What are you going to do now Rose?" asked Clance, putting

his drink on the coffee table and turning in his seat to face her. "Only eight shots in there," he chuckled, looking around and waving his hand over the group.

"Sixteen," she corrected. "I picked up another clip at a pawn shop in Vegas," she lied. "I filled it before I came up here."

"Surely you don't think you would be able to kill us all, you'd never....."

"How many of you do you think I'd be able to take out before you stopped me?" she asked, looking first at Clance, then at the blonde woman.

"We'd be on you before you could get off two shots," said a man sitting next to Clance, someone she did not know or hadn't seen before. "And from that distance you're not that good of a shot."

"Really.....I think I've done fairly well so far as a marksman.... so let's see, if I only get to take out two or three of you, which shall it be?" she contemplated, sounding almost flippant.

"You can't be serious," said the blonde woman. "You think we're totally unarmed or that we came here without protection?"

"Actually, yes, I do think you're unarmed, and have no muscle backing you up," Rose answered immediately and with a degree of certainty in her voice.

"By the way, Rose, what is your position on gun control?" asked Clance to a few snickers from the group.

"They should be outlawed," said Rose, surprised by such a casual question and hesitating a second before answering.

"Really," said the blonde woman smiling and then looking at the others.

"Yes, I'd have the government go door to door and confiscate every gun in the country," she shot back.

"We don't have guns, never have," said the blonde woman.

"You can kill without guns," said Rose.

"We don't kill," said Clance.

"Does a General kill with a gun?" asked Rose. "Does a Congressman who declares war kill with a gun? Does a dictator from a rogue country kill with a gun? Does the talk show host who whips up his audience with ideological dogma kill with a gun? Who actually kills with a gun? The hapless teenagers who have guns slapped in their hands and are ordered out onto the battlefield. The professional soldiers who are doing their hired jobs. The computer game expert controlling a drone. And deranged political zealots who think they are promoting some obscure cause. That's who."

"If the cause is just," said Clance.

"What cause justifies the inhumanity of killing," said Rose.

"Look what you have just done, Rose," said Henry. "How many have you killed already? Are you keeping tabs? What about your cause? Is your cause just?"

"I have to live with what I've done," said Rose. "I had to try to correct an uncorrectable wrong."

"How many more corrections will there be?" asked the blonde.

"Maybe this little correction will end it," she replied, waving the gun.

"But you can never take us all out so you can never complete your corrections," said Clance.

"I'll go out trying," said Rose.

"But Rose, you've already killed a bunch of old men who

actually thought they were responsible for having promoted the cause," Said the blonde. "In effect they were innocent....they were just pawns in the larger movement....they did nothing."

"Intent," Rose countered. "Intent. They THOUGHT they did what they did. And so they were just as guilty as you or the hapless dupes who carried out your sick objectives."

"So you really thought that we are here without bodyguards?" said Clance with a snicker, raising his eyebrows.

"Why would you?" asked Rose shrugging. "In your own words-- none of you has ever carried, nor used, firearms. None of you has ever dirtied your hands. It's not your way. No, you're unarmed and unprotected. And you really didn't believe that I'd actually get here, and if I did get here that I could never get in."

"But we were supporting your efforts, Rose, and surely you must have appreciated us, especially after our timely interference on Maui when you would certainly have been killed by John," said Clance.

"I thank you for that," said Rose nodding.

"However, you are right, we really didn't think that you would come down here after you had completed your mission."

"But of course the mission wasn't really completed was it?" she sighed. "As it turned out I started eliminating from the wrong end. I just didn't know there was another end. I was as naïve as my Brother and his cronies blowing hot air in their clubhouse."

"And you did such a wonderful job of eliminating that other end," said Clance.

"I'm curious, why did you help me and not try to stop me? After all, these were your supporters, your front, that I was knocking off."

"Giving you a 22 caliber pistol was actually designed for you to fail since that certainly is not a weapon of choice for an assassin....it would be the last weapon that a professional would use. But to everyone's surprise you were successful, so we just went with it."

"Went with it? Why?"

"We decided it was time to change strategies, Rose," Clance continued. "You see, we've managed to develop our own financial resources over the years and no longer needed your brother's group of 'cronies' as you call them. So you were just tidying up possible leaks that might have sprung as these men grew old, feeble and sentimental. You see, a few of them were getting careless in their correspondence. That's actually how you even found out about your brother's activities. Isn't that right?"

"Yes, it IS how I found out," she nodded. "So then I was just 'tidying up' for you?"

"Well, let's just say once you surprised everyone with your successes we decided rather quickly to just assist you to do your job rather than try to stop you. Loose lips could have affected the entire movement."

"And for a while I thought it was the good guys helping me."

"You mean your weak-kneed, bleeding-heart liberal comrades? Hah! Not likely," said the blonde.

"But now it's over for at least some of you, isn't it?" said Rose, surveying the group carefully from her position at the rail plotting in her mind who she might aim at first.

"This is a useless exercise Rose," said Clance. "There are thirteen of us here and countless others that you could never know about in places you could never find. And you have a puny 22 pistol and none of us are at point blank range. We'll scatter immediately and you'll end up shooting all your rounds and maybe wounding a few of us. That's the reality. And we'd get you and then just go about our business. Now why don't you just put that little pea shooter away and we'll let you walk out of here, having done a good deed for us?"

"Sorry, but I can't do that," said Rose, as she thought about what he'd just said and knew that it would be virtually impossible to kill them all. Plus, what if they really did have a vast network of others out there. What good would wiping out a few of them matter?

"Ah, Miss Baker, we do in fact meet again," came a voice from her left in the shadow of the far corner. She kept the gun aimed in the direction of the group and moved her gaze slowly toward the voice. Stepping out into the light at the far end of the room was a familiar face.

"Vincent?" she asked with a half smile.

"Small world, huh, Rose," he said, the black assault rifle cradled in his arm now slowly pointing in her direction. "How'd you get here from Hawaii by the way?" he asked. "It took nearly a month and a half. I was beginning to doubt whether you would make it. Nobody here but me thought you would."

"But you thought I would?"

"Yes, I knew how determined and dedicated you were."

"So, what took so long?"

"Private sailboat to San Francisco. A little time there to recover. Then a long drive down."

"But now you're here, and I've got this…uh…eliminator," he wiggled his weapon. "And you've got that little thing….." he

274

gestured with his finger.

"And you thought we would be here unprotected," said Clance, snickering, looking first at Rose, then at Vincent standing now at the end of the sofa where he had moved, still pointing the rifle at Rose.

"Mexican standoff?" said Rose somewhat flippantly with a strange calm that had now suddenly come over her as she stared into Vincent's eyes. "Or…who knows," she smiled with a nod.

Chapter 25

"I still think she has to be hiding out on the Islands," said Vivian.

"She's long gone," said Chuck, shaking his head confidently.

"Not by air," Vivian said with an equal air of confidence.

"Maybe not, but she's gone."

"If she goes by some type of boat, it'll take a lot longer to get to Mexico," said Cathy. "So if we go to PV by air, we could be there days, even weeks, before she gets there."

"True," said Chuck. "But our agents were never able to pinpoint the residence of number thirteen there so we have some work to do. We could use the time to figure out where it is and be there when she arrives."

"I think you're wasting both yours and the agencies' time and money," said Vivian. "That's how I'll file my report."

"Fine, you do that, and if you find her here, which I doubt very seriously, just give us a shout. We'll be in PV," said Chuck.

With that he and Cathy turned and started down the hall to the waiting airliner.

*****

With the assistance of the Mexican government, Chuck and Cathy were finally able to locate the penthouse condo in Paradise Village, about five miles north of the city. A John Averill had a penthouse condo there. The agency had been looking only in Puerto Vallarta proper, not the outlying areas. A bit of a screwup according to Chuck since many of the upscale condos were in peripheral areas.

They spent the next month on stakeout, finding no suspicious activity even though Averill's blonde wife seemed to entertain guests frequently and her rooftop patio was often filled with festive decorations, music and merriment. After they had been there over five weeks, they received a call from headquarters ordering them to return to their home station in Washington.

"Son of a bitch," said Chuck, mulling over the situation after he had hung up the phone.

"I know, it's been a nice vacation here in paradise," said Cathy. "My tan is better than it's ever been."

"Right," Chuck mumbled, trying to think of his next move.

"Guess she either stayed in Hawaii and melted into the wallpaper, or if she did get off the Islands, she did the same thing someplace else."

"If she went by sailboat it would take three weeks or more just to make it back to the mainland."

"Vivian says that they monitored departures of private boats, though".

"You can't monitor them all," Chuck replied. "A lot of them travel on their own schedule and are difficult or impossible to track. They slip in and out without checking with anyone. You can't zoom every boat out there. Plus if you do the passage in a sailboat to the West coast the preferred route is to sail directly north five hundred miles to pick up the Westerlies before turning east. A departure north out of Kaui might not appear suspicious."

"The agency would know that."

"I wouldn't count on it."

"And you didn't point it out to them."

"I know. It didn't really occur to me at the time."

"Really?"

"Really."

"I'm beginning to think that you want Rose to get away."

"Maybe…well….yes, I guess in a way I do. After this she'll never kill anyone again. It was just this one mission for her. But in the end I guess I'm still an agent and I would still have a job to do if we do catch up with her."

"I know, and so am I even though I have that same feeling about her. So, what do we do now? Go back to DC?"

"Not me, I'm taking vacation time," said Chuck, looking at Cathy for a reaction.

"Yeah, I could have guessed that and you're going to spend it here in Paradise Village."

"Except I'll have to pay for my room."

"Of course Jack will say no."

"Who cares? Besides, I don't think he'd do that after all that's gone down on this case."

"What would you say if I decided to take some vacation time here with you?"

"Wow....yeah....I'd like the company....especially...," he said after hesitating a moment to look her in the eyes and smile. "Especially, your company," he added softly.

They stood looking at each other, barely a foot away, then Cathy slowly drifted closer and Chuck leaned down and touched her lips with his fingers, then, when she raised her face he kissed her. Gently.

"I've been attracted to you for a long time," he whispered almost into her mouth.

"I guess I can't really say the same," she whispered back. "But on this assignment, I've become strangely attracted to you. Almost as if you were waiting there all the time behind your filthy smoking habit and cuss words."

"I am an uncouth son of a bitch," he admitted softly.

"A bad boy," she replied, moving forward and planting her lips on his. He wrapped her in his arms and kissed her with a passion that both had held in as they maintained their professional roles during the case. Now they were off duty. He kicked the door to her room closed with his foot and they made their way quickly to the bed, discarding clothing as they advanced.

"You can't smoke now," she said quietly into his ear after she kissed it.

"You mean in the room?" he clarified, holding the cigarette

pack that he had just retrieved from the night stand.

"Ever," she confirmed.

"Ever?" he asked submissively after looking at her to confirm her resolve, then carefully placing the pack back on the stand..

"So you'll quit?"

"I'll try," he mumbled.

"You can't quit cold turkey, can you?"

"I think that I could."

"We'll see, tough guy. By the way, did you ever date....or uh....go with a woman who smoked."

"No, hell no."

"No? Why not, they wouldn't care if you smoked."

"Yeah, but if they did smoke they'd be dumb as opossums. Any woman who smokes has shit for brains."

"But it's OK for you to smoke."

"I already know how stupid it is."

"And they don't?"

"Most of them....actually....no."

"So you've never dated a smoker?"

"Never."

"You're something else," she laughed, leaning her head on his chest.

They had been on vacation now for over a week in a suite with a peek-a-boo view off the deck of the entry to the penthouse where number thirteen's girlfriend stayed. Chuck had kept a casual watch on the comings and goings to the unit and, and, as he sat in the lounge sipping a lemonade, he sat upright, then scrambled to his feet causing the lounge to skid backward with a loud scraping sound. Cathy came out quickly through the sliding screen having heard the racket.

"Are you all right?" she asked, seeing him pinned to the railing, groping for the compact binoculars he always carried in his bag. He put them to his eyes.

"That's her with the Mexican guy who does maintenance," he said excitedly, pointing.

"How long does it take to get from here to the unit?"

"A long time. It took me almost ten minutes when I did a dry run a few weeks ago. And I did it as fast as I could. There are no direct routes."

"Plus, you know, we're not officially on duty so we don't have any authorized privileges anymore."

"That doesn't mean shit," he said, running back into the room and digging through his bag, finally retrieving his service pistol. He checked the clip, reached in the bag to retrieve another clip and stuffed it into his cutoffs. By now Cathy had done the same and was hurriedly lacing up her tennis shoes. Chuck slipped into his flip flops, then ran to the door, Cathy right behind, one shoe not tied. Before they reached the elevators, the flip flops were behind him in the hallway and Chuck was barefoot, pistol in hand. As he reached the elevator, he stuffed the pistol into the small of his back and pulled his T-shirt over it.

"Let's take the stairway."

"Five floors, you're right, might be quicker," Cathy agreed, already having jammed open the door to the stairs and was now halfway through.

After winding their way out into the lobby, across the lobby, out onto the access road and interior circulation sidewalks, then across to another building and in through that lobby, they confronted a doorman who held up his hand when they burst in.

"FBI!" said Chuck, not having brought his wallet and dressed in blue jean cutoffs and a T-shirt. He looked back at Cathy who grimaced and shrugged to signal she hadn't brought ID either.

"Credentials, por favor," said the man, holding out his hand.

"Look, I don't have time for this shit. Something big is going down right now up in the penthouse," he said, shoving his way past the man who quickly recovered and finally tackled Chuck before he reached the stairwell. Cathy grabbed the man and tried to pull him off but was soon herself grabbed by two other men who heard the ruckus and had rushed out from an interior office. The five of them wrestled on the floor with Chuck's gun coming loose and clanking across the marble floor to the wide-eyed shock of the men, one of whom grabbed it and turned it on him.

"Let us talk with someone in charge!" shouted Cathy. "We're here with the permission of the federales."

"That is over!" said a man who had just come out of the office. "I was informed that the FBI surveillance was over a week ago. You two are on vacation. You're not on duty. And this is my jurisdiction."

"But conditions have changed," Chuck pleaded. "We need to...."

"I'm head of security here and nothing will happen without

my say so," he snapped.

"Look, the woman we were looking for came back and your people should have recognized her since you were given her photo," said Cathy.

"Nobody came through here," the first man countered.

"Well, right now she's up at the penthouse," said Chuck, pointing up.

"That's not possible," said the first man.

"She's up there and whatever happens is on your head," said Chuck first pointing at the first man, then redirecting his finger to the man who identified himself as head of security.

"To appease you, I'll call for armed security to come here and we'll go up to check it out."

"It's likely already too late," Chuck shrugged with a smile, then walked over and just sat down on a bench.

"We'll see," said the head of security, taking out his cell phone and dialing a number. He spoke quickly in Spanish, then added 'rapido' and folded the phone. "We'll wait."

"Why not?" said Chuck as Cathy now came over and sat beside him, taking out her pistol and handing it to one of the surprised men. Ten minutes later, two men, one with a shotgun and the other with a sidearm, walked casually into the lobby and over to where they were congregated.

"Let's go up and see," said the head of security.

"It's been, let's see, about twenty six minutes since I first spotted her at the door upstairs," said Chuck, looking at his watch. "Twenty eight by the time we get up there. Let's say a half hour."

"We'll handle it from here," said the head of security.

"It's all yours," said Cathy, looking at Chuck who just shook his head.

A few minutes later they were all gathered in front of the door to the penthouse. The head of security first pushed the doorbell, then when nobody answered, he knocked. He knocked louder. There was still no response. After a few minutes, he ordered one of the men to go down and get the key. It was another ten minutes before he finally returned, telling them that he had to go over to the main office to get it since it was a penthouse and was not readily available to staff. He put the key in the lock and opened the door, letting it swing open.

"Is anyone home?" he shouted as they all stood in a group listening for a reply. There was none.

"Let's just go in and see what the damage is," said Chuck, shrugging at him impatiently as he pushed his way past and into the vestibule, then to the landing above the living room. Cathy was right behind and the others trailed.

"Jesus holy Christ!" said Chuck loudly as he surveyed the scene. "How in the fuck!" he babbled.

Behind him came cries of horror and several of the men turned away and covered their eyes as they moaned in horror.

The scene was hideous. Thirteen bodies were strewn around the room with spatters of blood and pools of blood everywhere. Some had been shot in the head. Others had multiple wounds to their bodies. It was clear that a 22 caliber pistol could not have wreaked such damage.

"Seal off the complex," said Chuck to the security chief who was entirely overcome by the enormity of the disaster and was just standing there in shock.

"Si," he replied in a hollow voice, pulling out his cell phone which he promptly dropped and had to retrieve from below in the living room. He dropped it again, and it had blood on it as he picked it up. Finally, he clicked it open and dialed a number then launched into a loud and fast outpouring of Spanish as he walked toward the entrance to get away from the scene.

"Is there a back way out?" asked Cathy, trying to peer down the hallway on the other side of the scene.

"Si," said one of the men who had now regained his senses. "Private elevator."

"You're looking for a lady about seventy years old, and an accomplice, of which I cannot give you a description, because I don't know who he or she is, but there definitely was an accomplice. It looks like he opened up from close range," he said, walking down past a body and retrieving a spent shell off the floor.

"Probably an AK47 or similar from the shells and damage done at impact," he confirmed. The rest are 22 caliber."

"They've had over a half hour head start," said Cathy. "Maybe a little longer."

"That's way too long," said Chuck. "I should have checked with security a week ago. It was stupid to assume that the deal we had before was still good."

"We were.....busy...." said Cathy.

"No, I fucked up."

"I was just as responsible for remembering as you," she said.

"Doesn't matter now, I guess. I just wonder where the hell she is and if she's with her accomplice, whoever the fuck he or she is."

Chapter 26

Rose leaned back in the bow of the dinghy as Vincent carefully wound his way out of the Paradise Village marina and across toward another marina on the other side of the lagoon.

"I thought you would never get here," he said, which were the first words spoken by either of them since the shooting started.

"It was a long trip down."

"So glad you made it."

"Thanks for what you did back there."

"No, thank you. I've wanted to do this for a long time and was hoping that you would come down and help facilitate it. I'm sure I would never initiate something like this myself. I'd almost given up that you'd get here at all."

"You were waiting for me?"

"OK, yes, I might have been able to pull it off by myself but I needed the distraction you would create and, as it turns out, the assistance. Without you it wouldn't have gone off as it did."

"And vice versa," she nodded, craning her head back to try to see where they were going.

"So how do you fit in?" she asked. "Why were you here?"

"I'm one of the hired secretives whose primary mission was to keep an eye on your brother's group. Help out where needed. Clance contacted me in Atlanta to see if I could assist you. He also invited me here to Vallarta. Thought I might enjoy the vacation, plus he thought they might need some protection. Actually, I saw it as an opportunity to do what we just did and for which I've been preparing. I'll show you shortly."

"Secretives? So there was one like you watching each of them?"

"That's right. Well, I suspect a lot more like me out there. In fact the lady you killed on Lopez Island with Rex?....she was one of us even though Rex thought she was his lover."

"I wondered who she was. She seemed too young to be his wife."

"And Judd? Someone watched him?"

"Yes, there was one there too, although my cousin Clance liked to do a lot of the watching himself in Cleveland."

"Clance helped watch my brother Judd?"

"Right, since Judd had become the ringleader of the group, he took a more personal interest in monitoring his activities."

"So what was Clance's role in this group we just.....?.."

"Head of overall security."

"And the other PIs like you?"

"You mean are they committed to the cause?"

"Well....to some extent I guess....mostly....obviously not ALL of us....it's more of a job than an obsession as it is for those

287

we just knocked off."

"So who were they....the ones we just eliminated?

"As far as I know they were the brains, the core, the board of directors if you will. Without them the organization may no longer exist for all intents and purposes. At least I don't think so. But operatives like me never really knew how deep the order went. There could be more. I just don't know."

"You don't know?"

"One is never sure with a society like this, but I've been doing this for about five years ever since my father passed. Enough time to figure things out. These are all that I know about. Of course you never know."

"Who recruited you?"

"Clance. He's a distant cousin."

"But you were clearly never ideologically committed."

"No. They assumed I was. I went along with the rhetoric. I needed the job. Plus I'm sure that many of those who did what I did weren't philosophical extremists. They may have been sympathetic to the cause, but have less incentive or commitment to do anything beyond what they do .....especially without leadership. Hopefully we've put a dent in that."

"And the 'cause'?"

"I didn't really know what the cause was, at first, and it took a few years to finally figure it out. But once I figured it out, I was definitely non-plussed but was in too deep to just walk away. They would have offed me had I said or did anything."

"Kind of trapped."

"Definitely trapped."

"So what now?"

"I don't think that we have further work to do if that's what you were thinking. As I said, one never knows for sure, but I think it's over."

"I'm quite tired of this whole thing right now and am not up to more of what we just did," said Rose.

"I can imagine."

"I want to call it a day so to speak."

"Yeah."

"By the way, where are we…..?"

"Nuevo Vallarta Marina," said Vincent, anticipating her question.

"And then?"

"I bought a boat off the wall and have been getting it ready to sail."

"Off the wall?"

"A derelict that was impounded by the marina for nonpayment and put on what is known as 'the wall' over near the Port Captain's office. I found the absentee owner and bought it from him for peanuts, then paid the outstanding debt."

"And is it sailable?"

"Yeah, pretty much. It's older but quite seaworthy and sound. I had new rigging installed by the locals and the engine reworked too."

"And your thoughts for what to do from here?"

"Making for open water."

"Where?"

"Not sure, but I've been laying in a lot of stores so we could be off shore for a long time."

"I just made the passage from Hawaii to San Francisco so I've been practicing."

"How many days off shore?"

"Almost a month."

"I think we can match that," he laughed, twisting back a little on the throttle as they neared a row of boats tied to a six foot high wall.

"Doesn't much matter to me," Rose smiled as they pulled up alongside a white and black boat, and she reached for the rail. "I'm going to have to live with what I've done for the rest of my day. Whether I get caught now makes little difference, really."

"I guess I feel about the same," said Vincent, cutting the engine and handing Rose a line to tie the boat. "I've done something that violates my basic values, yet it was something I felt had to be done even if it meant living with the nightmares forever."

"Overall, though, given a choice, I guess I'd rather just be left alone and not have to deal with all of the attention should I give myself up and be arrested," she said as Vincent helped her get her foot on the ladder that hung over the side and she started up.

"I'm with you on that," he said as he tied off the dinghy and motioned for her to go down into the open companionway. "That's why I got this boat just to get away and be alone. But if I get caught, I get caught."

"Shouldn't they have plenty of opportunity to block or at least monitor departures from here?" she asked, dropping into a seat in the salon and sinking back.

"This is Mexico. A lot goes on down here and there are a lot of gringos wandering around the resorts, coming and going. They can't monitor all of that activity even though they try.

There are a dozen large resorts here in the Nuevo area. There are thousands of tourists, including boaters, constantly coming and going at nearly all hours."

"But not a seventy year old woman whose photo they have."

"True, but they're not looking for a young black man on his own boat which is known around here. I've been seen fixing it up over the past month or so and people around here know me. Plus I've already checked out with the port captain giving them a bogus destination. Besides, nobody saw us come down the owner's elevator, and we didn't run into anyone on our way to the dinghy. Furthermore, the cruisers are constantly going back and forth across the lagoon between the marinas in dinghies, so that wasn't out of the ordinary."

"It would be miraculous indeed if we sailed out of here unnoticed."

"I plan on it."

"So when do we leave?"

"It's just now getting dark. Let's wait until about eleven, eleven thirty, then ease on out of here. Again, it's not unusual for cruising sailors to do that. That way it's not as if we ran immediately from the area as they might have expected us to do."

"How about midnight?"

"Sure."

The marina was perfectly still as they started the motor, untied the dock lines, and slowly and quietly started motoring out through the entrance channel that passed directly in front of the Paradise Village Resort. A boardwalk lined the entrance channel, but at midnight it was empty except for one couple sitting on a rock about halfway out. As they passed, the couple waved and Rose raised her hand slightly in return. The man took out a pack of cigarettes, looked at the woman next to him, threw the pack into the channel, then looked back at Rose and saluted. The woman next to him gave Rose a little wave with her fingers, then both got up, turned and walked back toward the hotel.